Ripples In The Silk

Stephanie M Turner

Ripples In The Silk

Stephanie M Turner

Sasmjadahoha Publishing

Published by Sasmjadahoha Publishing

ISBN 978-0-9929881-1-1

Sasmjadahoha Publishing
Email: books@sasmjadahohapublishing.com
Tel: (+44) 7546856165
www.sasmjadahohapublishing.com

To my husband Stephen, and my children Jason, Damon, Holly and Harriet, for their support, encouragement and inspiration..

CONTENTS

Part One.

All about The Dress.

CHAPTER 1.

Caroline stood in the centre of the Bridal Boutique's dressing room. Mirrors reflected her image on three sides, allowing her to see the dresses from every angle. She was now twisting and turning the fourth dress she had tried on. She lifted the hem and swayed, pressing her lips together, frowning. The Boutique assistant stood to one side, a blank expression on her face. So far she had made no comment on any of the dresses, simply helping Caroline in and out of each one.

Derby, Caroline's close friend sat patiently on a chic pink and blue sofa, bobbing her baby girl Melody on her knee. On a small antique side table stood a bottle of Moet and two half filled glasses. Derby had allowed herself to sip slowly one glass, Caroline was already on her third.

"One of the perks to shopping for a wedding gown."

Caroline had stated when they first arrived at the Bridal Boutique. Derby wasn't so sure, but kept silent. She knew how important Caroline's wedding day was to her, and if drinking champagne whilst choosing her gown helped, then she would happily go along with it. Besides, one day in the not too distant future, she might be doing the same thing. That is if David would hurry up and sign the divorce papers.

"Earth to Derby."

Derby glanced up quickly.

"Sorry Caroline. I was miles away."

Caroline lifted the dress high, plodded over to her friend and plonked down on the sofa next to her. She reached for her glass of champagne at the same time Melody launched herself onto her lap, making both women laugh. The assistant took a tiny step forward, a look of alarm crossing her face, expecting the wine to spill onto the dress. Caroline managed to catch Melody and hold the glass high at the same time. The assistant let out an audible sigh of relief and went back to standing still, her hands clasped in front of her.

"Phew! This is exhausting."

Caroline exclaimed. Derby giggled.

"More so with half a bottle of champagne inside you."

Caroline grinned.

"Yeah, but totally necessary. So what do you think of this one?"

She asked, plucking at the dress. Derby shrugged.

"Hmm, too frilly."

Caroline sighed, and nodded in agreement. She drained her glass, passed Melody back to Derby and bounced to her feet.

"Next one then."

The assistant leapt into action like a mannequin given life. She deftly unbuttoned the dress and helped Caroline step out of it. Turning, she re-hung the dress, and in a flash had the next one ready for Caroline to try on. Once again Caroline turned this way and that, and the assistant went back to her sentry position.

"I like that one."

Derby said. Melody pointed and squealed.

"Looks like Melody does too."

"You sure?"

Caroline asked, uncertainty in her voice.

"Caroline, what do you think? You're the one who is going to be wearing it."

"I know, but…oh fuck, I just don't know."

"Caroline! The baby."

Derby exclaimed covering Melody's ears, even though it was too late.

"Oh Derby, I'm so sorry."

Caroline crumpled to the floor in a heap. Derby quickly went to her friend and kneeled next to her, Melody again pouncing on Caroline. A sharp hiss came from the assistant. Derby looked at her over her shoulder and gave her a withering look. The assistant pursed her lips, and refrained from making the cutting remark her expression suggested she wanted to make.

Caroline put her hands over her face and a tiny sob escaped. Derby leaned into her friend and hugged her, Melody trying to pry Caroline's fingers apart.

"Caroline, come on. It's ok. We can have a break, get some lunch and look again. There's no rush, you have six months until the day."

The assistant, suddenly realising she could be losing a sale, came to life. She poured a glass of water from a jug and stooped down, holding it out to Caroline. In a soothing voice she said.

"Your friend's right dear. Why don't you take a break, and I will get some more of our gowns ready for you to try."

Caroline gave a little giggle. The woman sounded like she was in her sixties the way she spoke, yet she couldn't be more than mid-twenties.

Wiping her eyes with one hand and downing the water with the other, Caroline shifted onto her knees. Derby took Melody and stood up, and the assistant, fearing the dress would get torn, quickly helped Caroline stand.

"Right then, food, I'm starving."

Caroline announced. She lifted the hem of the dress and headed for the door. Derby laughed as the assistant rushed forward to stop her.

"Umm…you can't go out in that."

She said, pointing at the dress. Caroline looked down and burst out laughing.

"Whoops, nearly forgot, sorry."

CHAPTER 2.

Once Caroline was back in her normal clothes, the two women made their way to a café they both liked. Settled at a table by the window, they ordered their lunches. Caroline had pondered over having a glass of wine with her food, but Derby reminded her that it might not be a good idea on top of the champagne.

"Besides, there's still some left in the bottle."
Caroline exclaimed. Derby shook her head, but did it with a smile.

"You're incorrigible girl."
Derby told her and Caroline laughed, replying.

"Ok Mrs sensible. I'm forty seven, well nearly anyway, not twelve."

"Well one of us has to be grown up."
Derby responded. Caroline's face turned serious.

"I've done the whole sensible, be an adult stuff."
Derby placed her hand over her friend's.

"You know Caroline, you've only ever told me that Charles left you and didn't want anything to do with the boys. What happened?"

Caroline leaned back in her chair and gazed out of the window. It was hot out and the street was busy. Exeter in June was buzzing. Not at all like London. There when it got hot, you couldn't breathe, here at least fresh air came in from the sea and up the estuary. She sighed.

"It's all very sordid."

She said. Derby huffed.

"Like I don't know anything about that."

Caroline gave her friend a tiny smile.

"Hmm you got me there. A forced marriage, no sex and a husband who turns out to be gay." She nodded towards Melody. "Now, a hunk of a man and a beautiful little girl. There's hope for me yet…well…not the baby…too old for that and I got me boys."

She said the last part with a Devon twang and Derby laughed, Melody joining in with her mother.

The waitress brought a tray over with a pot of tea and two cups, smiled and told them their food would be out shortly. The women thanked her and Caroline poured their drinks. Derby busied herself, taking sealed tubs from a large brightly coloured change bag, opening them and spooning food into an eagerly awaiting Melody.

"You're so good at that."

Caroline told her. Derby laughed.

"Tons of practice. All those babies and toddlers at the nursery. Still it's different with my own."

Caroline nodded.

"How's Angela handling the management side of things."

"Very well, she's a natural. Sharing the job is brilliant."

Angela was Derby's first real friend after she realised there was a life for her. She was also her senior nursery nurse at the nursery Derby had managed for many years. When Derby met Geoff, her life changed drastically, and even more so when she had her bundle of joy Melody.

Having missed out on being a mother for so many years, Derby decided to take part time hours, so Angela was promoted to joint manager. It meant Derby could work two days a week, have Melody with her at the nursery and Angela covered the rest of the week. It worked perfectly.

Their lunch arrived and for a few minutes they ate in silence. Then Derby lowered her fork.

"So, back to your sordidness."

She said. Caroline took a deep breath and let it out slowly.

"I met Charles at uni. He was everything a girl could want. Tall, thick brown hair, big baby blue eyes, wide and well very, very sexy. I was quite surprised he noticed me at all. I mean, I wasn't a dog or anything, but I wouldn't say I was beautiful. He did though and that shocked me. Told me other girls he'd dated were vain and shallow, that I was smart, could hold up a decent conversation."

She stopped and nibbled on some of her lunch. Her eyes drifted towards the window, and Derby could see memories flittering across her mind. She swallowed and came back to her friend.

"We got on really well. The sex was, totally out of this world and I totally fell in love. Charles said he did too. Anyway, both of us graduated with firsts, and both of us got jobs right away with Randalls, a huge publishing house in London. Charles' job was better than mine, his salary considerably better. Within three months we were married, another two and I was pregnant. Not planned, pill failed. But I couldn't not have the baby. Charles wasn't so eager but didn't argue."

She stopped to nibble more food and sip her tea. Then still chewing went on.

"Anyway, everything was fine at first. Leo came along and Charles was the proud father of a boy to carry on the family name. His parents didn't really like me, the marriage, but they treated me with respect and they doted on Leo. I was happy.

Charles' salary increased rapidly, as did his position in the company. He was sailing up the ranks. I went back to work part time, but Charles wasn't keen on me being there. Kept telling me I should be at home looking after Leo. His mother thought the same. She'd had a privileged marriage, lots of money, nannies for Charles and his siblings. She would constantly remind me that Charles' income was more than adequate for me to stay at home. In the end, I didn't get a choice. Fertile little me went and fell pregnant again. I swear I'm just immune to the effects of the pill. So along came Liam and out went my career. I honestly didn't mind. My boys were and still are my heart and my world. It's just, I would have been good at what I did."

Derby held her little Melody close to her breast, the toddler beginning to drift off to sleep. She could fully understand Caroline's feelings for her children. She had never believed she would be a mother, always believing her husband David was infertile, until she discovered he'd had a vasectomy not many years into their marriage. When she found out he was gay, he had come clean and told her, said he couldn't bear the thought of having a child with her. But Geoff had changed all that. So she knew how precious a child was.

Derby, rocking her baby smiled at her friend.

"I know exactly what you mean. I'm very good at my job, but that doesn't stop me being completely devoted to Melody. Only difference, I've had years of being good at my job, now, I treasure every moment with my angel."

Caroline nodded. She pushed aside her plate even though she hadn't finished, and poured more tea. Holding the cup in both hands she continued.

"Liam coming so soon after Leo really did put an end to my career. But I was still so happy, and blissfully ignorant. We had money, a beautiful big house in London, the in-laws spoiled the boys rotten and…well…what more could I want? A faithful f…sorry, damned husband, that's what."

"Oh."

Was all Derby could say. Caroline clunked her cup into the saucer, tea sloshing over the sides. Her eyes had gone dark and hard.

"Yep, perfect Charles, doting father, was screwing his perfect little assistant. She was rising up through the ranks too, but not high enough for him to be worried. Just enough for her to be interesting. Someone he could talk to and discuss current issues with. Who could hang off his arm at book launches and events, talk smart talk with colleagues. Not like the wife at home, who had nothing to say, except tell him when one of his sons' said or did something new.

Who had no time to make herself look pretty, or dress up. Who always looked drained and tired, who had 'let herself go to seed'." Derby frowned. "Yes those were his exact words. The night I decided to surprise him at the office. I got a babysitter, Leo was four and Liam three. I had my hair and nails done at an expensive salon. Donned a new chic dress and heels." Derby reached for Caroline's hand, knowing where the story was going. But Caroline was ready to let it all out. She lowered her voice to a near whisper.

"I walked into the outer office and at first thought he wasn't there. Then I heard a giggle. I pushed open his main office door and I just froze. They hadn't seen me then. He had a huge leather sofa in his office. He was naked, she was wearing a maid's outfit. He was ready, cock fully erect, his hands up the skirt of the dress, that's why she was giggling.

Then I watched as she climbed onto him and he took her. I stepped into the office, but they were both so far into it they didn't hear me. She rode him like a bucking bronco. We had never had sex like that. I mean at uni, we had a damn good time, and even when we got married. Charles is a big boy and he knew just how to make me come. But I could see with her he was different. He was…I can't really explain it…but his face…glowing, he loved her. That's what hurt the most. Sex is sex. An affair maybe I could've handled, I don't know, but I knew if he loved me and would have come back to me, maybe. But I knew it wasn't me he loved. I was just the mother of his children, nothing more."

Tears trickled silently from her eyes and she swiped at them with her hands. She was angry, Derby could see. After all the years she was still angry with Charles. Derby could understand. She still felt anger towards David, but she knew it was nothing like what her friend felt. Derby knew she hadn't ever really loved her husband, nor he her. Geoff had shown her what it was like to love and be loved, Caroline had believed that's what she'd had, and Charles had failed her.

Caroline sat up straighter and huffed out a sigh. She dabbed at her face with her napkin and gave Derby a wan smile.

"They still didn't know I was there and I couldn't move. I was sort of dazed and could only stand and watch the whole thing. They both had their eyes closed and when he came, well I've never seen that look on his face with me. It was…was…um…ecstasy, and the sound he made. With me he would sort of go 'Humph.' With her he hummed with pleasure, that's the only way I can describe it."

Derby held her hand out and Caroline took it.

"Go on, tell me the rest."

She urged gently. Caroline chewed on the corner of her lip and took another deep breath.

"Charles swung his feet over the sofa, she still straddled him. As he lifted his head from her shoulder he opened his eyes. That's when he saw me. He looked right at me and said. 'Oh. Well now you know so I won't have to tell you.' She looked round when he spoke and gave me a self-satisfied grin. I stood there. Inside I was screaming and crying. I wanted to claw his face, slice off his cock and tear her fucking head from her shoulders, but I was frozen."

This time, Derby didn't admonish Caroline for her bad language. Melody was sound asleep, and though their was a grittiness in Caroline's voice, she kept it low. Derby waited knowing more was still to come.

"Then to add insult to injury, Charles drew her to him, close, like he was protecting her. As he splayed his left hand across her back, I saw his ring finger had no wedding band on. He had taken it off. Not so she wouldn't know he was married, she did. The fucking bitch had spoken to me politely, brought coffee when I'd been to the office, rare as that was. No, it was because when he was with her shagging her fucking brains out, HE didn't want to be reminded that he was married."

Derby sighed, feeling her friend's pain even after all the years that had passed. There was nothing she could say to help her, and half wished she hadn't asked, dredging up bad history. But to know her friend, she needed to know what had happened.

"And the rest."

Derby encouraged. Caroline drained the pot, turning her nose up when she tasted cold tea.

"I turned without saying a damned word and went home. Inside I was like ice. Nothing would come out, no tears, anger, nothing. Not then anyway. At home I waited up for him, but he didn't come home. I barely slept and tried to keep up a front for the boys in the morning. It was so bloody hard, smiling and playing with my babies when I was falling apart inside.

Anyway, Charles came home for dinner. He sat with the boys but ignored me completely. When Leo and Liam were in bed, he sat on the chair opposite me and announced he was getting a divorce. I was still numb. Until he said he was taking the boys, that they would have a nanny until they were old enough for boarding school. That he loved Elaine so much, but she wasn't ready to be a stay at home mum.

My blood boiled. I wanted to knock his smug look from his face, but I knew if I reacted like that he would get the court on his side. So, I did the hardest thing I could ever have done, stayed calm. I simply said to him, 'You get your divorce, but hell will freeze over before you take my boys.'"

A grin broke out on Caroline's face as she took herself back to that night. Derby wondered why, but Caroline soon told her.

"You should have seen his face. He didn't think I would stand up to him. I'd always been meek little Caroline, doing everything he and his parents wanted. But a mother's need to protect her kids, no one can get in the way of that. Well he sort of started spluttering and stuttering and I just burst out laughing. He didn't like that. He took a swing at me." Derby gasped, she had no idea that had happened.

"Yep, planted one right on my face, caught my left cheek and eye. That's all I needed. No one was going to hit me and get away with it. I ran upstairs and grabbed the phone, dialled nine, nine, nine. He followed and tried to grab it, but it had already connected. He was yelling at me to hang up and I was screaming, the operator heard it all. He shoved me to the floor and walloped me again. This time I put my hands up and he smacked into my wrist cracking a bone. Then I heard sirens. Charles sped off downstairs and opened the door, tried to make out it was all a mistake. They found me and arrested him."

Caroline lifted her hand and beckoned the waitress over. She asked for a fresh pot of tea and two slices of hot chocolate fudge cake with chocolate sauce and clotted cream. Derby tried to protest but Caroline wouldn't have it.

"I need chocolate. So you do too."

Derby giggled and let her friend have her way. A little bit of cake wouldn't hurt, and Caroline had been keeping to a strict healthy eating only diet. She didn't have the heart to talk her out of a little chocolate treat.

"So that's how come I got sole custody of the boys. Charles' parents didn't want it broadcast, especially in his line of work, there could have been too much media attention. They pretty much sorted the divorce settlement, which was quite hefty financially. Enough for me to bring the boys up on comfortably, so long as I agreed to move away from London and never contact them again. They didn't even want contact with the boys, nor did Charles. So we came here, came home to Exeter, where I was born. He stayed with Elaine, and here we are today."

"Wow, that's some history. Mine is positively boring compared to that."

Derby said. Caroline smiled.

"Well it's been damned hard though. Explaining to the boys why their father and grandparents didn't want them anymore was heartbreaking. Now they despise them as much as I do. Even the uncles and aunt kept away, not that they were very close anyway, but still, a whole family, because their precious Charles couldn't keep his dick in his pants and his fists to himself."

CHAPTER 3.

Caroline finished just as the waitress brought the tea and cake. She grabbed her fork and jabbed it into the, fudge cake, venting some of the deep seated hurt. Derby poured from the pot, afraid Caroline would spill it if she let her do it. Sliding a cup towards her she pressed her lips together, then took a breath.

"So, given all you went through with Charles, why have you let Frank cheat on you over and over, yet now you're planning your wedding to him?"

Caroline scooped a large piece of cake and clotted cream into her mouth. She closed her eyes briefly, relishing the dessert.

"Mmmm, I've abstained for so long to get my figure right for the dress, but this is bliss."

She said. Derby waited, taking a small forkful of her chocolate treat. Caroline swallowed and sighed.

"When I first met Frank, he was already divorced. Tania had found him in bed with his then secretary Alicia. They didn't have any children so

Tania just up and left, filed for divorce the same day. But Frank, being Frank, ditched Alicia and begged Tania to come back to him. Then she was too raw, so went through with the divorce, refused to have anything to do with him.

Then I came along. Met him at a book festival. Even though I was no longer working in publishing, I still enjoyed the industry. He's in the printing business as you know, so…, well, anyway, we clicked. It was like we had known each other for years. Had so much in common. I'd had a couple of relationships since Charles, but I wasn't interested in serious, the boys were still young and they were my life. I didn't mind. I was still a stay at home mum, had enough money to live on from the divorce.

Derby frowned, sure she had missed something. Then it came to her.

"When I first got to know you, and we went out for drinks, you told me you had been with Frank for four years. But you just said the boys were still young, and you weren't working as an estate agent then. So?" She let the question hang, as Caroline's cheeks began to flame.

"I thought I was going to get away with that." She said, then sighed.

"I met Frank when Leo was eleven and Liam ten. Like I said. I still enjoyed all the book tradey stuff. Well I'd gone to the book festival with the boys and Frank saw us when we were eating lunch at an outside café. He came over and asked if we were enjoying the day. The boys, especially Leo, were suspicious of him. Not surprising after their father, and I hadn't brought any men home since Charles. Just a couple of dinner dates, never anyone to meet the boys. Well Frank's smile was charming and alluring. He kept the conversation innocent and brief, so the boys relaxed when they saw their mum wasn't going to be pounced on.

Later, we were listening to a speaker about children's books, and he appeared next to me. Slipped me a little piece of paper without the boys seeing. It made me feel all warm inside knowing he had sensed the boys' uneasiness. The note was simple, his phone number and the words, 'Please call.' So later when Leo and Liam were in bed, I did."

Caroline shrugged and ran her finger around the plate collecting chocolate sauce. She licked her finger, her eyes very much not in the present. Derby waited. With a deep breath, Caroline pulled her finger out and wiped it on her napkin.

"That first night we talked for ages on the phone. I don't know why, he was just easy to talk to, it was um, comfortable. Anyway, he asked me to dinner and I agreed. We met up the next night. I still didn't want the boys to know though.

Over dinner, he told me about his marriage and swore Alicia was the biggest and only mistake he had ever made. And that though he'd thought a lot about wanting to be with Tania, meeting me changed all that. That I was the one thing missing in his life, and he didn't even realise this until he found me."

Caroline paused and ate more of her cake, sipping tea in between bites. Derby had finished hers and was holding her cup in both hands, listening attentively. The café was busy and a little noisy, but to the two women, it was like they were the only patrons, so engrossed in their conversation.

Caroline took her last piece of fudge cake and scraped the cream and chocolate off the plate with her fork. As Derby had found out a long time ago, Caroline was as much a chocoholic as she was. But Caroline had avoided chocolate treats to help Derby get her figure back after Melody had been born, and Derby was returning the favour for Caroline now, so she could be as trim and fit as she wanted for the wedding dress. Today, however, both women viewed the situation as warranting a little something sweet and chocolaty.

"I know it all sounds so corny. 'I've been waiting for you all my life' 'There's been a huge gap that only you can fill.' All that stuff and I should have known better, especially after Charles. But Derby, hell I was lonely. I missed men, sex. I loved my boys, but I was still young, and Frank got my lady juices flowing like a damned broken tap. He…it's…the only word I can think of is charisma."

Derby grinned. She had fallen for Geoff in much the same way. His charm and charisma drawing her like a moth to a lamp. But Geoff was pure gold, he loved her as much as she did him, and their daughter. She would never have to worry that he would cheat. Caroline spotted the glow on her friend's face.

"You're lucky Derby. Geoff is perfect. But, back to your question, well, at first everything for me was perfect. Frank was totally devoted and after a few months I let him meet the boys. Again, Leo was suspicious, Liam thought he was the bees knees. He used to take us all out and about. We did stuff like camping and adventure parks. He taught us all kayaking and sailing, even bought us a boat, not like the one you two have, but it was great. We would go off for the day with a cool box full of goodies, and fish and dive. The boys loved it."

Caroline paused, a hitch in her throat. Derby could see tears glistening in her eyes as she remembered the past. Patting Caroline's hand, Derby urged her on.

"That's how come Liam decided he wanted to be a Marine Biologist. He spent so much time in, on and under the water."

Derby could see the hurt on her friend's face, knew what was coming, but Caroline was ready to spill what she had kept inside for so long.

"Frank cheated. I'm not sure how long it had been going on for, not long I think. He doesn't keep them long. We had been together, a family for three years. We were supposed to meet at lunchtime to Christmas shop. But he was late. So I browsed and waited. When he did arrive, he was all apologetic, had a meeting that ran late. But something wasn't right. He was flustered and acting weird." She shrugged. "Don't know how else to describe it. And when I went to kiss him, I saw a mark on his neck. It was obviously a lovebite, though he said he had cut himself shaving. Not Fucking likely. His eyes were all shifty and I just outed him then and there. He crumbled and admitted it, but pleaded that it was her, Pamela her name was, and yes she was his secretary. Claimed she wouldn't leave him alone and it had only happened once. Of course I knew he was lying. Sounded too much like when he cheated on his wife. I ditched him right then. Went home in bits and had to explain to the boys as best as I could what had happened. Leo was only fourteen, Liam just thirteen. They were devastated."

Caroline sat back in her chair and sighed. Derby could see it had been a very bad time for her and her children. For a brief moment, Derby wondered how she would have reacted, had she found out David had cheated in the early days. Now she knew he had, with men, not women. Back then she was naïve and never dreamed her husband was gay. That, she had only found out about a little under two years ago, but it explained a lot about her lonely marriage.

Caroline sat up quickly.

"Come on, let's get back to the boutique. Finish finding the dress."

Derby gave her a surprised look.

"But, you haven't told me anywhere near the rest."

She complained. Caroline giggled.

"Now I know where Melody gets that face from when she can't get her own way."

Derby opened her mouth to protest, but knowing Caroline was right snapped it closed again. She nodded.

"Can't argue with that one. But you're going to tell me the rest? It'd be cruel to leave me wondering."

"Of course, just not here. Bet that assistant's ears will wag though."

Derby burst out laughing. Caroline was going to finish her tale at the shop. As she gathered her bits and pieces, and navigated the buggy through the café door, she imagined the look on the boutique assistant's face, as Caroline told her the rest, especially as her language could be quite colourful when she was talking about Frank.

CHAPTER 4.

Caroline pushed the door to the Bridal Boutique open and held it for Derby. Melody was just stirring, waking from her nap. The assistant saw the two women and quickly came forward.

"Hello again. I've hung some gowns on the rail that I think might be more like you're looking for."
She was all smiles and Derby thought the break had done her good too.

Settling on the sofa, Derby watched Caroline as she made a bee line for the bottle of champagne. The assistant had placed fresh glasses on the tray and a stopper in the bottle. Caroline quickly removed the stopper and poured the wine into a glass. She held it up to Derby who shook her head as she lifted Melody from the buggy.

"No more for me thanks. But you go ahead."
Derby said. Caroline grinned.

"Oh I intend to."

Caroline took a large mouthful of the champagne and turned towards the assistant.

"I'm all yours."

She said with a little wave of the glass towards the dressing room. The assistant glanced at the wineglass but refrained from making a comment. Caroline took another, smaller mouthful, topped up the glass and then placed it on the tray. She then followed the assistant as she disappeared behind the curtains.

Derby waited patiently, playing a game with Melody. The baby giggled and then squealed as Caroline re-emerged in another glorious gown. She lifted the hem and walked towards the full length mirrors, angled to show all sides of the dress. She pursed her lips and looked at Derby in the mirror.

"What do you think?"

Derby let out a big sigh.

"Honestly Caroline, they're all beautiful."

Caroline took a deep breath and let it out slowly.

"I know, keep going. The right one will jump at me when I see it. Two months, that's how long I lasted."

Derby understood straight away, but the assistant frowned in total confusion.

"I beg your pardon."

She said. Caroline laughed.

"I'm sorry. I've sort of had a chequered history with my fiancé and we were discussing it at lunch."

"You were telling me what happened and why you're marrying the guy now."

Derby cut in. Caroline pressed her lips together and frowned.

"I know, I know. And that's what I was saying."

Derby now looked as perplexed as the assistant. Caroline gathered up the skirt of the dress and sauntered over to the table with the champagne. She lifted the glass and sipped. The assistant watched her closely, but Caroline didn't spill any of the wine.

"I waited two months and then took him back." She stated flatly. Derby nodded, now back on track. The assistant nodded too, seeming to realise that despite not being privy to the rest of the story, she understood what had happened. Caroline stood, lost for a moment in the past. Then with another sip said.

"He came around one evening and begged me to take him back. I shouted and swore and told him I hated him. Told him he had ruined my life and destroyed my boys. He cried and went down on his knees, literally begging my forgiveness. Leo came downstairs and flew at him. He was tall even then, like his father. Thankfully the only thing he did get from his father."

Caroline smiled, the love for her son shining through the pain that Frank had caused. She looked down at the dress and shook her head. The assistant alerted, swung back towards the dressing room and Caroline followed. Derby again waited, holding out another toy to occupy Melody.

Caroline came out of the dressing room in a terry robe. She plonked down next to Derby and held her arms out for Melody. The child dived into her lap and curled her fingers into her hair, giggling. Caroline nuzzled her, making her squeal with laughter.

"I looked through the dresses on the rail and not one took my fancy. Either too frilly or too plain. So she's going to pull out another load. I know I'm a pain

in the arse." She covered Melody's ears before Derby could complain. "But it has to be just right."
Derby nodded in agreement.

"Tell me the rest whilst we're waiting."
Caroline gave a little shrug.

"Leo was furious and wanted to pound Frank. But I didn't want him to, because I didn't want my son getting into trouble. I stopped Leo and made it clear to Frank why I had. He just stayed there on his knees with his head bent telling me to let Leo do it, that he deserved it. God, he was so good at inducing the sympathy. All of the steam went out of Leo. Anger in a teenager dissipates as quickly as it erupts. He stood there, his fists on his hips and looked down at Frank. He said 'You're a pathetic piece of …' She again covered Melody's ears. '…shit. If my mum takes you back, it's her choice, but I won't forget this.' Frank nodded and then looked at me, tears still pouring down his face. Then he said 'Leo, you have every right to protect your mum and one day I hope you can see beyond what I've done. I swear I won't ever hurt her again.'

He actually looked remorseful, and I believed him. I was lonely and miserable without him. That's the worst part. It hurt what he did, but it hurt…" She mimed. "…fucking…" Returning her voice to its normal volume. "…more with him not there, a part of my life."

Derby covered her friend's hand with her own and this time she lifted the wine glass for Caroline. The assistant still hadn't returned, and Derby got a sneaky feeling she was standing just behind the curtain listening. It made her smile, because Caroline was going to tell her story regardless of the audience.

With a little more wine inside her, Caroline continued telling Derby how she had arrived at this day, choosing a wedding gown.

"Well I took him back and for a long time everything was good. Better than before. Leo sort of came around. Liam hadn't been as angry as his brother, and I think it was his influence that helped Leo. We started doing stuff together again. Frank got Liam connected to someone he knew at the aquarium, and so he got to spend quite a lot of time there learning about the marine life. And we had some brilliant holidays. Frank took us to parts of the world that most people don't see. Places where Liam could observe and learn about different marine species. And it got Leo interested in the travel business. Every school break, we would go somewhere, and even some weekends. Nearly two whole years of bliss and family life."

"So when did you become an estate agent?" Derby asked, as that had been how the two women met. Derby, realising her life and marriage was heading nowhere, had decided she needed a place of her own, to find herself. It was Caroline who found that place for her, and the two had been friends since.

Caroline covered her face with her hands and shook her head.

"After he did it again. Like I said, almost two years of bliss. I hadn't long had my thirty ninth birthday and Leo had just turned sixteen. Thank God it wasn't his exam year. Liam was virtually attached to the aquarium, spent all of his spare time there. Anyway, I went to meet him one day. I don't know why because I didn't go there, wanted it to be Liam's place, no parental interference, but I just thought for once it would be nice. Anyway I was sitting in the café waiting for him.

Frank was supposed to be in London that day for some meeting or another. So I was happily tucked away at a corner table waiting for my son. Then I saw Frank walk in. He didn't see me. He went up to the counter and the girl serving, Celia, well, they were just too familiar. So I lifted the menu to hide behind, but watched as well. I saw him. He smiled at her like he smiled at me. He touched her cheek with his fingertips and made her giggle. She was only about twenty.

Frank leaned towards her and said something. She nodded and he left. Liam didn't know I was going to be there, so I got up and went after Frank. I caught up with him just outside and confronted him in the street."

Caroline paused. Her voice had gone hard and Melody scrunched up her little face and whimpered. Derby took her daughter.

"Oh baby, did I scare you?"

Caroline said tenderly. Melody immediately cheered up, snuggling into her mother. Derby sighed, wondering why Caroline had put herself through so much for Frank, after being so strong when her husband had cheated. Caroline could see the question in Derby's eyes and nodded.

"Yep, stupid me. Well, he told me nothing had happened. I didn't believe him. Told him I couldn't trust him. Then Celia came out of the side door. She didn't know who I was, so strolled up to him and linked her arm through his. He went scarlet and then paled.

Caught out again. I just gave him the most evil look I could drag out of me, at the same time my heart was breaking again. This time I stayed dignified and just walked away. I didn't want to have to tell the boys it had happened again, but I had no choice. Liam shocked me. He didn't believe it.

We had an almighty row. He said I would spoil everything for him at the aquarium if I broke up with Frank. Leo was furious with his brother, but he was only fifteen. All he could see was how it would affect him. Leo was great. He didn't fly into a temper again, just cuddled me and let me cry.

Frank came around that evening and tried to give me some bull sh.., sorry, that it was all innocent, Celia was just the daughter of a colleague. I knew he was lying and told him so. But I also told him how Liam had reacted and that took the stuffing out of him. He tried the old 'It just happened, she came onto me.' stuff , but I was having none of it.

I told him I couldn't be with him anymore, but I wasn't going to have things ruined for Liam. Well, the thing with Frank is, he's charismatic, but he's not very strong, in the mind that is. He tried all the 'I'm so sorry Caroline, please forgive me, it meant nothing.' business, but could see it was no use. So he backed down and promised he would make sure nothing changed for Liam at the aquarium. Then as he was leaving he said. 'I won't give up on us Caroline. I will prove myself to you.' Of course I didn't believe it.

Anyway, he kept his word and Liam's time at the aquarium wasn't affected. I was grateful for that and Liam was happy. Leo not so. He could see how unhappy I was and he hated that. I kept as much of my hurt hidden as was possible and a year down the line, I could see a little light at the end of the tunnel. It was during that time I got the job at the estate agent. At first it was to fill my time. The boys were older, didn't need me around so much. Then I began to enjoy it."

The curtain moved and both women looked up as the assistant came towards them. She was brushing her fingertips across her eyes, and Derby got the distinct impression she had shed a few tears on hearing Caroline's history with Frank.

"I…um." She cleared her throat. "I think I've found the right one, dress that is."

Caroline smiled gently at her. It seemed the young woman was more sensitive than she had appeared to be.

"Thank you."

Caroline said, standing. She followed through the curtain and soon emerged in yet another gown. This time though, Caroline's smile made it clear she had found the right dress.

Layers of ivory silk fell to a long train. As she glided in front of the mirror the front folds parted to reveal soft net encrusted with glistening crystals. The bodice shone with the same crystals, and hugged Caroline's trim but curvy figure, showing just enough cleavage to stay demure.

"I love him Derby. I know I can't fully trust him ever, but I don't want to be without him. I'm not strong enough, I'm pathetic, he's under my skin and I can't change that." She took a deep breath "He will be faithful this time."

Her eyes didn't reflect that she fully believed what she was saying. Derby didn't have the heart to contradict her conviction.

"Caroline, I spent forty years being pathetic before I got the strength to change my life. You don't have to explain to me what I know you feel."

Caroline stood staring at her image in the mirror.

"On my fortieth birthday, Frank turned up with a diamond set. Necklace and matching earrings. The boys had arranged a surprise party. Somehow Frank found out. Even though I've never asked and he's never said, I think Liam might have let it slip to him. Well he came, and Leo was furious, but kept quiet, didn't want to cause a ruckus at the party. In front of all the guests, Frank gets down on his knees again and begs forgiveness. Presents me with the diamonds and swears he will never cheat again. That he will spend his days making me happy."

Caroline turned and looked directly at Derby. She lifted the skirt of the dress and a small sob escaped her lips.

"I was so unhappy. I missed him like a part of me was gone. The physical side too. We'd always had great sex."

She paused as the assistant gave a little cough. Caroline looked at the girl and smiled at the blush that was staining her cheeks. Caroline shrugged.

"Sorry if that embarrasses you, but it's the truth. Sex with Frank is awesome."

She stated in a sing song voice. The assistant went scarlet all over and Derby felt a little sorry for her.

"But…he was great at other things too. We always laughed. We had fun whatever we did, even when we were just sitting watching a film. I enjoyed his company as much as I enjoyed his body. So once again

I let him back into my life and…for five years he kept his promise. Remember, when I met you we had just broken up again. His ex-wife and his secretary."

Derby nodded remembering the story. Caroline had found out Frank had cheated yet again, and set up a lunch meeting to ensure Frank, his ex-wife and secretary would all be present. Then she'd outed him again in front of them. Tania knew about Caroline but not the secretary, and the secretary thought she had Frank exclusively.

"Well, as usual he came around begging me to take him back. That time I was sure I wouldn't. I didn't even tell the boys about it then. Both were out of the country anyway. I shut the door in his face determined not to let him come back. But the months went by, and once again loneliness and craving his body made me relent. He kept phoning and emailing and eventually I gave in. We went out for dinner and ended up in bed. It was like coming home after a long journey away. Frank had champagne on ice." Caroline scowled. "He was that sure of himself." Then she smiled. "And he proposed." She crossed her fingers.

"This time, he's kept his word. This time, he's been just mine. When he proposed, I had reservations. I asked the boys and Liam was like, 'Go for it mum.' Leo, well, not so sure, but he supported me, and told me if that's what I wanted he would be happy for me. So here we are, and here's the dress, perfect."

The assistant actually gave a little clap that finally the dress was chosen. Caroline went back behind the curtain and returned in her normal clothes. She sat next to Derby and finished the rest of the champagne.

"Derby you know it's because of you that I started my literacy agency."
Derby gave her a look of pure surprise.

"No I didn't, how, why?"
Caroline giggled.

"After I met you. I was determined not to get back with Frank, and I needed something more than being an estate agent. You inspired me to change my life like you did. So I went back to my career roots and set up the agency. It was really hard to begin with, but…Frank helped. He had connections with publishers and that was really important. Now I have a healthy client list and am loving every bit of it."

The assistant came out and began the process of ordering the dress.

"A few weeks before the day we'll call you for a fitting, length, veil, accessories etcetera. If you can bring your chosen shoes then we'll get it exactly right. Then just before the big day you come back for a final fitting. Any adjustments that are needed can be done then. We'll deliver your dress the day before. Of course, if you want to get your veil and so on elsewhere, that's fine, just bring them with you for the first fitting."
Caroline gave the assistant all her details and with a beaming smile turned to Derby and Melody.

"Well, that's it now. Dress chosen, it's a definite. Now we have to find your bridesmaid dress."
Derby laughed, and secretly crossed her own fingers that Caroline's big day would happen, and would go smoothly.

Part Two.

All About Caroline.

CHAPTER 1.

The Waterside Hotel overlooks the river on Exeter Quay. It isn't a large hotel, only fifteen rooms. But its reputation for quality far exceeds its size. Each of its rooms are individually designed to give the guests outstanding comfort. Decorated to the highest standards, a feature wall covered in designer paper is enhanced with the remaining walls in shades of paint that perfectly balance.

The king size beds have deep mattresses dressed in Egyptian cotton linen. Chic armchairs have plush upholstery, and the remaining furniture is wood and polished to shine. The bathrooms are spacious. Each has a walk in double shower as well as a large whirlpool bath. Thick fluffy bath sheets, terry robes, fresh flowers and hospitality packs ensure the guests more than enjoy their stay.

Caroline stood on the balcony of her room facing the river. She was wrapped in a thick terry robe and held a mug of hot coffee between her hands. The air was crisp and cold, a slight haze of mist hanging over the water. It was still early, only half past seven. The light from the winter sun was gradually bringing colour back to the world. Caroline sipped her coffee, her mind on the day ahead. December first, her wedding day. The day she had waited for almost all of her life. That is her second wedding day. This day she was marrying Frank, who would be faithful to her, so she told herself.

A sound from the river brought her out of her wonderings. She glanced down and saw a sweep rowing boat gliding rapidly through the water. The noise she'd heard was the coxswain directing the crew. For a while she watched the boat as it progressed along the river.

She drew her attention back to the day. Everything was ready. She had chosen the Waterside especially for that reason. Searching for her wedding venue had taken time, but she had been determined that it would be the exact right place. Frank had told her she could have anywhere she wanted, regardless of the cost. She knew it was his way of telling her again that he was sorry for all the past hurt, and that he would never cheat on her again.

The cost was not what Caroline was concerned about. Research had told her the Waterside provided the best wedding package. She had been assigned a wedding planner, who showed her samples from invitations to table decorations. All she had to do was choose and on the day, get herself ready. Even the rooms had been allocated for family and guests involved in the wedding itself, like her sons and Derby and her fiancé Geoff and their daughter.

Caroline sucked in the cold clean air and looked above her. The honeymoon suite was at the top of the hotel and had a large balcony. Frank had told her she wasn't to go in the room before they were married as he had a surprise arranged. Caroline sipped her coffee and smiled to herself. Knowing Frank, the surprise would involve hundreds of roses and copious amount of champagne, but she promised to stay out.

The sun was brighter and the sky crystal clear. She could hear birds tweeting in the trees that edged the river and the day looked set to be perfect. A December wedding had been her choice. Frank had wanted them to get married within a couple of months of proposing, but Caroline wanted to plan it properly. And winter days always seemed to be dry and more beautifully sunny than other times of the year. Yes it was cold, but that didn't matter to Caroline. The wedding ceremony and reception were all indoors, but she did want outdoor photos. The chances of that happening in the winter were higher, so Caroline deemed. It looked like she had been proven right as there wasn't a cloud in the sky. She had also told Frank that if it snowed, that would be alright, as a white winter wonderland was far better than a grey dull damp day. Luckily, it was the sunshine that had won, and the forecast showed no change in that.

Caroline heard a tap on the door to her room. She finished her coffee and padded across thick carpet to open it. Derby stood in the corridor.

"Good morning sweetheart."

Derby said as she entered.

"I've spoken to Frank and he's sending up breakfast."

Caroline's look of surprise had Derby giggling.

"Have you seen him?"

She asked. Derby shook her head.

"Just spoke on the phone. He rang our room and asked me to pass the breakfast message on. Geoff's going to get Melody bathed and fed and keep her occupied whilst we get sorted."

Caroline plonked down into one of the armchairs, still holding her coffee cup. Derby stood behind her and rested her hands on her shoulders.

"You ok?"

She asked gently. Caroline took a deep breath and nodded. A knock at the door indicated room service. Derby opened it and a young man smartly dressed pushed a laden trolley into the room. He held out a cream envelope.

"For Caroline?"

Caroline reached for it, her hand shaking. Derby thanked the young waiter then turned to Caroline who had gone pale.

"What if it's Frank backing out?"

She said, her voice breaking. Derby took both her hands, clamping the envelope between them.

"Caroline, I spoke to him not half an hour ago. I think if he was going to do that he would have told me, not send breakfast up."

Caroline calmed, but with still shaking fingers slit open the envelope. She read silently then handed the note to Derby, a huge smile on her face.

Caroline.

You have my heart.

You have my soul.

You are my life.

You are my whole.

Without your love.
There'd be no light.
Your beauty blinds me.
You shine so bright.

Today we make our vows.
Today will last forever.
Today we will be one.
To part we will never.

Derby read the poem aloud and grinned at her friend. Then she lifted the bottle of champagne from the trolley and began unwrapping the foil.

By mid-morning Caroline's room was bustling. The hair and makeup stylists were there as was the nail technicians. Leo and Liam were in and out frequently, checking on their mother, and everything that was going on downstairs. The wedding planner flitted about keeping a watch on the time, and having snacks and drinks sent up. The florist arrived with Caroline's bouquet and Derby's posie, placing the delicate flowers on a space indicated by the wedding planner.

Caroline sat in one of the armchairs surrounded by people. Everyone seemed to be chattering at the same time and her head was aching. Derby sat next to her in the other chair, one of the nail technicians painting her nails as the other hair stylist twisted and twined her hair. The stylist then held it all together with a beautiful rose patterned comb encrusted with crystals.

Derby glanced at her friend and saw Caroline had her eyes scrunched, creating a frown.

"Can you give me a moment please?"

She said to the women attending her. The nail technician pursed her lips.

"Try not to brush against anything, they're not dry yet."

Derby nodded and stood up.

"Everyone, hi, could we just have a little break. Caroline looks a bit frazzled."

The wedding planned jumped to attention, clapping her hands.

"Ok, can you all please go downstairs to the Parlour. I'll have coffee and pastries sent in. Half hour I think."

She looked towards Derby who nodded in agreement.

When the room was quiet, Derby handed Caroline a glass of water and two paracetamol tablets. Caroline took the medication and smiled gratefully. She emptied the glass of water and leaned back in the chair with a sigh.

"Thanks Derby. I really needed this bit of time. I swear my first wedding wasn't as hectic, and that was big."

"Probably more champagne this time."

Derby said with a giggle. Caroline broke into giggles too.

"You got that right girlie."

She said.

"Have you eaten anything since breakfast?"

Derby enquired. Caroline frowned and shook her head.

"You know, I don't think I have. All this stuff going on around me and to me, I think I forgot."

Derby went over to the side table where a tray of croissants and fruit had been laid. She took a tea-plate and piled it with two croissants, strawberries and blueberries and carried it back to Caroline.

"Just mind your nails. That girl will have my arse if you mess them up."

Caroline burst out laughing, but she took a pastry carefully between her thumb and forefinger and bit into it with relish.

"Mmmm, I didn't realise I was hungry until you mentioned it."

She said as she popped a strawberry into her mouth. Derby patted her shoulder.

Exactly half an hour later the room filled up again, but Caroline was ready. Both hers and Derby's nails were inspected closely and passed with a smile from the girl.

"Wonderful, now the top coat and we're done."

She announced joyfully. Inwardly Derby sighed with relief. But looking at Caroline, she saw that her friend was now relaxed and enjoying the pampering.

Finally it was time for the dresses. The wedding planner helped Derby step into her dress and buttoned it up. Although Derby had been allowed to choose her own dress, she made sure Caroline had a lot of input. It was her wedding and she wanted her friend to have the last say. Caroline had come through. Derby's dress was stunning. In ivory silk georgette, it was simple in style, hugging Derby's figure. Full length and strapless, it had a draped bodice and pleated drape detail at the front skirt.

Then it was Caroline's turn. Again the wedding planner assisted. Caroline stepped into her dress and the planner laced up the back. The folds of silk and net flowed like water, the crystals shimmering with her every movement. Once she had her shoes on the hair stylist stepped forward.

Caroline's hair had been piled high with a few tendrils hanging to soften her face. The stylist lifted the veil, placed it over Caroline's hair and held it in place with a delicate tiara of crystals. She gently teased out the three layers of lace edged net, so that it cascaded down the back of the dress. Finally, Caroline was ready.

"The photographer is outside and would like to take a few shots."

The planner announced. Caroline smiled nervously at Derby and nodded. All at once the room emptied of everyone but Caroline, Derby and the wedding planner. The photographer came in, and for several minutes took photos of Caroline and some with Derby too.

Leo and Liam arrived, cued by the planner by text. Caroline had to bite back tears so as not to spoil her makeup, when they told her how beautiful she looked. Leo was going to lead her down the aisle, so Liam kissed her on the cheek and headed down to the ceremony hall.

"Well mum, this is it."

Leo said to her gently as the photographer backed out snapping his camera. Caroline took a deep breath and let it out slowly. She held Leo's arm with one hand and the shower bouquet of roses and lilies with the other. Derby followed behind clutching her posie of the same flowers. The wedding planner ducked around them and trotted down the stairs. She would meet Caroline at the bottom and oversee her arrival.

The double doors to the hall had been opened wide. Caroline stood just out of view of the guests. She could see the rows of chairs decorated with linen and bows. She could see garlands of fresh flowers, and right at the end of the aisle she could see Frank, his back to her. She let out the breath she hadn't realised she had been holding, and felt Derby's hand gently pat her shoulder in reassurance. Both women were relieved to see Frank waiting.

Caroline stood for a few minutes. She could also see Liam, he was turned towards her smiling. Behind the table where the registrar stood, a large screen faced the gathered guests. The wedding planner had talked them both into having a slide show of photos of her, Frank and the boys. The slide show would begin when the music began, and Caroline commenced her walk down the aisle.

Caroline stepped forward and stopped inside the doorway. Some of the guests realised she had arrived and turned in their seats to watch and admire her. Others began noticing too, and suddenly everyone in the room had their eyes on her. All except one guest. A little knot of fear crept into Caroline's heart. The guest was a woman. She sat on the far side of the room in the back row, and her head was covered in a wide brimmed black mesh hat. Caroline's instincts told her she knew who the woman was, but her mind didn't want to register the fact. She took in a sharp breath that both Leo and Derby heard.

"What is it mum?"

Leo asked.

"I…I'm not sure."

Caroline replied, a tremble in her voice and an ominous feeling in her breast.

Several things happened at once. The music began, Delibes Flower Duet rang out across the hall.

Frank turned and smiled, the screen sprang to life, and the woman turned and looked straight at Caroline, an evil smile spreading across her ruby red lips. Caroline gasped and froze. It was Tania, Frank's very ex-wife. Caroline had no idea what the woman was doing there, she wasn't on the guest list. But a moment later her life was shattered, and her heart was torn apart.

As Caroline stood rooted to the spot, the slide show flashed the first pictures. Innocent shots of her and Frank at their engagement dinner were displayed. Then to Caroline's horror the photos changed, no longer those she had painstakingly chosen with Frank and the wedding planner.

Instead, the photos showed the inside of an opulent room. A beautiful carved four-poster bed surrounded by flowers and champagne was the main focus. But the worst part, was the man and woman on the bed, the covers thrown aside, so every part of them was visible, Tania and Frank. From what seemed a great distance, Caroline heard voices. Exclamations of "Oh my God." And "Turn it off." And over them all, Frank bellowing. "What the hell?"

None of the voices registered, only what Caroline could see on the screen. The photos kept flipping, one after another. Frank on top of Tania, both very obviously naked, and very obviously engaged in sex. Close ups of Frank's face as the still shots showed Tania's legs wrapped around his waist. Tania's face enjoying every second, and then ones with her eyes wide open, looking directly at the camera and smiling, a smile that was aimed directly at Caroline.

Frozen though she was, Caroline felt the tug of both Leo and Derby's hands as they tried to pull her away from the door. But she couldn't move. She could only stare at the screen, watching the photos replay over and again. Then her eyes registered movement from two angles. Tania was getting to her feet and heading in her direction and Frank was stepping into the aisle, also heading her way.

Frank didn't get far. Liam leapt in front of him, pulled back his fist and rammed it straight into Frank's face. Frank staggered and fell backwards. Leo fled towards his brother and grabbed his shoulders, pulling him back so the kick he aimed at Frank missed. Liam was struggling, but Leo was bigger and held him fast.

"I should let him go and pound the living shit out of you, you bastard."

Leo yelled at Frank whose nose was pouring with blood, staining the front of his white shirt and cream linen suit. Liam was trying to free himself and bellowing at Frank at the same time. The wedding planner and registrar tried to intervene, but backed away quickly when it became obvious they wouldn't get through to the two boys.

Tania had finally made her way to Caroline and tried to get in front of her. Caroline was still too shocked to react, but Derby was furious. She grabbed Tania by the arm and pulled her into the corridor.

"You evil vindictive bitch. Get out of here before I have security throw you out."

Tania grinned, not in the least bit remorseful at what she had done. She shook Derby off, and swung back to Caroline.

"It was so easy. He was easy. Now you know what it feels like."

Caroline's mouth opened but no sound would come out. Then she felt the first flush of anger penetrate deep down that spurred her into action. She drew back her hand and slapped Tania hard across the cheek. Tania's head rocked, her bright red lipstick smeared where Caroline's palm had connected. Caroline wiped her hand across the front of Tania's dress and leaned towards her. Derby was so proud of her friend in that moment, for the look on her face had Tania stepping back, a flicker of fear in her eyes. Caroline pointed a perfectly manicured painted finger.

"I have never done anything to you. I didn't even know Frank when you divorced him. You're the one who couldn't let him go. Well now he's all yours. I hope he does to you what he's just done to me."

With that she flung the bouquet at Tania, picked up the skirt of her wedding gown and strode from the hall outside into the gardens. Derby stared at Tania for a second then followed her friend. She found Caroline sitting on a bench in a circular grassy area surrounded by shrubs. Caroline was rubbing her palm. Derby sat next to her.

"Fucking hurts like a bitch. But it was worth it." She ground out.

CHAPTER 2.

Derby put her arm around Caroline's shoulder and let her friend lean into her. Caroline sat still rubbing her palm, dry eyed. Derby knew the shock would seep into her soul soon, and the tears would come in a torrent. But for now the two women remained silent.

From over her shoulder Derby heard a noise. She glanced back and her Geoff stood a little way off holding their daughter Melody. He approached quietly and leaned down to Derby.

"I've had the DVR and screen shut down."

He whispered. But it was Caroline who answered him.

"Thank you Geoff."

Geoff stood up straight and nodded. Derby could see in the darkness of his eyes that he would like to continue doing to Frank what Liam had started. But she knew Geoff very well, and he wouldn't go down that route.

Melody held her arms out to her mother and Derby took her onto her lap. Caroline smiled at the little girl and twiddled her hair around her fingers. Melody giggled.

"Do you want me to take her back to our room?"
Geoff asked.

"Can you leave…"
Caroline began, but stopped when she saw Frank coming towards her, Leo and Liam close at his heels. Derby and Geoff followed her gaze and Derby quickly handed Melody back to her father. Geoff had no intention of allowing his child to witness what was going to be a very verbal, and possibly physical confrontation. So he quickly gave Derby a kiss and said.

"I'll take Melody to Alison, then I'll be straight back."

Frank reached Caroline's side in seconds. Leo still had a hand on Liam's arm, struggling to hold him back. Caroline stood up and so did Derby.

"Caroline…"
Frank said, his hands outstretched in a warding off pose.

"Caroline what?"
Caroline shouted.

Before Frank could say another word, her pent up anger erupted.

"Caroline I'm sorry. Caroline it meant nothing. Caroline it's you I love. You don't' know the fucking meaning of love. You just know about fucking. She told me, Tania did. You were easy. Did you fucking know about the camera?"
Frank opened his mouth to speak, but Caroline cut across him.

"Don't say a fucking word. I'm not done!"

Both Leo and Liam edged closer. Liam seemed to have gained control of himself at his mother's outburst, and stopped straining against his brother. The boys waited for their mother to continue.

"That was the fucking honeymoon suite, wasn't it?"

She yelled. Frank's mouth opened and closed like a fish gasping for air. He was sure he wasn't supposed to actually answer, and it would have been comedic had it not been so heartbreaking.

"You…you're just a weak minded fucking…um…uh…spineless, waffling bastard who's ruled by his fucking penis."

The wedding planner jogged up to the group, her hand covering her mouth in astonishment at Caroline's verbal attack of Frank. She opened her mouth to speak, but also closed it quickly when she saw the thunder in Caroline's eyes. Derby stepped towards her and took her elbow, turning her away from Caroline, at the same moment Geoff returned. He grinned when he saw his fiancée's don't mess with me pose. In a low voice she said.

"Best let her have this one. I know it's probably upsetting some of the people back there, but I know Caroline. She will sound off and nothing will stop her until she gets it out. Most of them are guests anyway and those who aren't…well I think they might sympathise with her."

The wedding planner looked like she was about to argue. So Derby dropped her voice even lower.

"Don't. You might want to think about how those photos got changed on the DVR. I mean, someone had to have access to it, and I don't think it was the woman in the pictures. For that matter, the camera in the room was hidden too, so someone must have let her in to plant it."

The wedding planner gasped, and in a hushed tone replied.

"Oh my God, Oh Jesus, this could ruin us. If other wedding parties get wind of this they might cancel, and we have bookings right through until August next year. Look, try and calm her down a bit, but I get you, she has every right. I'm going back in now to sort things out in there. And I am going to find out who the culprit is on my staff. Believe me, they will not be working here when I do, and they will not get a reference either."

The wedding planner stepped over to Caroline, put out her hand as if to pat her arm, but pulled it back when Caroline glared at her. She shook her head and backed away. As soon as she was several steps away, she turned and marched back towards the doors to the hotel.

Frank stood with his hands hanging limply at his side. Leo and Liam flanked their mother, guarding her like two snarling beasts from hell. Despite her pain, Caroline felt warmth spread through her heart from her sons. With a last very deep breath she flung at Frank.

"We're done Frank. This time for good. Fuck off and don't ever, ever come near us again. The boys don't need anything from you anymore, and neither do I. My agency is strong, so am I, and I'm completely independent. You on the other hand need someone to hang off your arm. Well it's no longer me. Go and run after Tania, or…whoever your next fuck partner is, 'cos

I'm betting she's not the only one." Frank's eyes shifted and Caroline knew she was right.

"Hmmm…secretary, assistant, or some other poor sap taken in by your charm? You know what, I don't give a fuck who she or they are. You go and screw yourself and them."

She held a hand out to each of her sons.

"Leo, Liam. Can you please escort me back inside. I'm going to speak to our guests. Even though they all saw what happened, it's only right I tell them personally the wedding is off…for good."

The three turned away from Frank. Geoff put his arm around Derby and smiled at her proudly. Then Caroline briefly looked back over her shoulder at Frank.

"The only thing you need to be here for now is to pay the bill."

Geoff burst out laughing and Caroline gave him a brief but wan smile, however, Frank still didn't move.

Once inside, Caroline straightened her shoulders and lifted her head high. With an arm linked through each of her sons' and Derby and Geoff bringing up the rear, she marched into the reception room. The wedding planner had ushered all the guests in and had made them comfortable with drinks and food. They were all standing in little groups.

Murmurs of conversation could be heard. As Caroline entered, these slowly began to cease and the room quietened. Alison, made her way over to Derby and handed her Melody. The baby nestled into her mother's neck and Geoff drew his family close.

Caroline stood for a moment watching her guests warily watching her. There were not as many on Frank's side as there were on hers, and for this she was grateful. Some of Frank's friends fidgeted nervously, worried she might verbally attack them, expecting them to have known. But Caroline wasn't gunning for anyone. All she wanted to do was say her piece and get out of the room.

One woman whom Caroline knew to be a colleague of Frank's, wouldn't meet her eyes. She stood close to a tall handsome man in his fifties, her hand clutching his arm. Caroline's suspicions arose, and once again her temper flared. She was sure this was one of the other women that Frank had been unable to deny.

The woman realised Caroline had guessed, and whispered something to the man. She then tugged his arm and tried to pull him towards the door at the back of the room. But instead, he pulled her towards Caroline. The woman lowered her head as they approached. The man reached for Caroline's hands and took both in his. The woman had let go of his arm and seemed to be trying to hide behind him.

"Caroline, I'm so sorry. Please don't think for one moment that I, we, knew about this."

Caroline looked into his face and saw sincerity.

"I don't think we've actually met. Your Edward?"

The man nodded.

"Yes, I am. I play golf with Frank. This is my wife Renee."

Caroline glanced at the woman. She was biting the corner of her lip and kept flicking her eyes up and down nervously.

Caroline took a deep breath. She had no beef with the man in front of her, and didn't want to intentionally hurt him. But she was also not in the mood to give anyone mercy, especially Renee, who was duping her husband, and he seemed such a nice man.

"Edward, I'm sorry to have to tell you this, but Renee does know."

Edward swung around to his wife just as she gasped. He frowned questioningly. She took a step back shaking her head.

"In fact, I'm pretty damn certain she's had or is having Frank too."

Caroline stated.

Renee brought her hands up to cover the heat that flooded her cheeks. She backed away and swept her eyes around the room. Amongst the murmurs and gasps of the other guests Caroline matched Renee's steps, pointing a finger at her.

"What the fuck is wrong with you women. You have husbands who obviously care, or boyfriends or whatever. Even if you're single, why Frank?"

Several other female guests put their heads down, some with partners, and Caroline knew she had just flushed out Frank's harem.

Renee turned and fled from the room, Edward close behind her. Caroline could see the paleness of his face and felt sorry for him, but decided it was better that he knew. As she cast her eyes around, she saw several couples, anger on the faces of the men, engaged in furious exchanges of words. And for the first time since the day had gone so horribly wrong, Caroline felt like laughing.

"Hey, everyone!"

She yelled out. A sudden silence replaced the chatter, including the arguing couples.

"Eat, drink and be merry. It's all on Frank anyway."
With that she lifted the hem of her dress and marched from the hall.

Caroline fled up the stairs to her room. As she stomped through the door, all of her energy and fury left her. She staggered to the bed and collapsed in a heap, tears flooding onto the pillow she clutched in her hands. Black smears of mascara stained the pure white linen, but she didn't care. Every bone in her body shook, and every muscle ached, as the tears released the pent up tension she had held onto.

Derby quietly entered the room and padded over to her friend. She slid the satin shoes from Caroline's feet and released the veil from her hair. Gently she pulled out the pins holding the style in place, and pushed Caroline's waist length red blonde hair away from her tears.

"What am I going to do Derby?"
Caroline mumbled, the pillow muffling her words. Derby dabbed at her friend's face with a soft tissue.

"What you always do, minus one thing."
Derby replied. Caroline shifted, looking up at Derby, a frown on her make-up smudged face.

"Huh?"
The sound coming out nasally.

"You're going to get on with your life. Keep building your agency, have fun with your sons. But no Frank. I forbid you to go anywhere near him ever again. Well, maybe except once, to knock his teeth out, but that's it."
Caroline gave her a weak smile and sighed.

"I know. And don't worry, I won't be going back."
Derby frowned sternly.

"I mean it Caroline. He will not change, no matter what he says. I bet he's already planning his next move to entice you back. Believe me girl, I'll kick your arse if you so much as have a glass of water with him."

Caroline managed a tiny giggle. It was so rare to hear Derby swear, even mildly, that her words had a huge impact. She dragged herself to a sitting position and crossed her legs underneath the folds of wedding dress. She grabbed a handful of tissues from the box Derby held and scrubbed at her face.

"You need wipes to get that off. You'll make your face sore."
Derby reprimanded her softly. Caroline shrugged. Then she changed the subject.

"I want to see the honeymoon suite."
Derby looked alarmed.

"You sure that's a good idea. It will upset you more."

Caroline unfolded herself and stood up. She swept into the bathroom and Derby heard running water. Caroline emerged drinking a glass of water and wiping her face with a make-up remover wipe.

"No it's not a good idea, I know it's going to hurt. But I have to see it."

Derby got the idea that for Caroline it would be some sort of closure. If she actually saw the place where Frank had last been unfaithful, she could move on. Physically seeing the bed would seal the reality of it where the photos could not. All she could do was be by her side, and hold her when the tears would undoubtedly flow again.

Still in their wedding gowns, both women stood in front of the elevator that would take them up to the honeymoon suite. The corridor was quiet and Derby wondered what was going on downstairs. She expected that Leo, with Geoff's help would be tending to the guests. Her main worry was what Liam would do. She hoped he wouldn't go searching for Frank, and had asked Geoff to keep an eye on him when she had followed Caroline.

The elevator arrived and thankfully it was empty. Two floors up they stepped out. The honeymoon suite had a set of double doors with ornate handles. Caroline stopped, and for a few seconds simply held the handles without turning them. Then she took a deep breath, slowly exhaled and opened the doors.

The scent of roses invaded her nostrils as she stepped over the threshold. It was exactly as she expected. Vases of white, red and yellow roses adorned the room. She could see the balcony through the long French windows, the river sparkling in the winter sun. On a small table in front of the sofa was an ice bucket. It held a bottle of champagne and two gold rimmed flutes.

The door to the bedroom was open and Caroline hesitated. Then lifting her dress she marched purposely forward. The bed was exactly like the photos. Four posts with elaborate carvings stood guard at each corner, supporting a canopy of rich mahogany. Silk and brocade curtains hung from the posts and at the back of the bed and trimmed the canopy.

Caroline froze in front of the bed. It was perfectly made, not a wrinkle or crease in the linen. On one of the bedside tables was a basket of fruit and a beautifully wrapped box. Caroline inched forward and lifted the gift. It was small and light. She ripped off the paper and found a velvet jewel box underneath. Lifting the lid she moaned. Nestled inside was a bracelet. It was silver and had just two beads attached. One had a C carved into it, the other an F. A wedding present from Frank.

Caroline flung the box onto the bed, the bracelet tumbling out. Derby appeared behind her friend.

"Oh!"

She exclaimed. Caroline surged into action. She grabbed the covers from the bed and flung them to the floor. She threw the fruit on top and pounded her fists into the pillows and mattress. Derby stood back and let her vent her anger and hurt.

A noise from the sitting area alerted Derby and she swung around. Frank was coming into the suite. He stopped in the doorway when he saw her. Caroline hadn't yet noticed him, but as she turned, a handful of pillowcase scrunched in her fist, she spotted him. Large spots of fury spread across her cheeks.

Caroline threw the pillow down and hurled herself at Frank. He stood rooted to the spot. Caroline raised her fists and pounded them against his chest screaming at him. He didn't try to stop her, but Derby did. She grabbed Caroline's arms and tugged.

"Caroline, it's not worth it!"

At first Caroline ignored her, then all of her steam disappeared and she let her arms drop to hang loosely at her side.

"Caroline…I…"
Frank began, but Derby held a hand up. He closed his mouth rapidly, but didn't move. Derby could see blood on his cheeks where Caroline had dragged her freshly manicured nails across his skin, gouging deep marks.

"Get out Frank! You've done enough. Don't even try to get around her."
Derby growled. Frank still didn't move.

"I want to hear Caroline tell me that herself."
He snapped back. Caroline raised her head, anger in her eyes.

"I already did you prick."
She said, her voice low and threatening. Then staring him straight in the face she said.

"Derby, will you please fetch Geoff to remove this piece of worthless shit from my sight."

Frank paled. He knew Geoff was big and though very gentle, he was very strong. He had also been a marine, so there was no doubt he would be able to get rid of Frank with minimal effort, and Derby knew without harming him, something Frank was obviously not aware of. The threat of Geoff had him spinning around and all but running from the suite.

Again Caroline's spurt of anger dissipated and she crumpled to the floor. Derby knelt next to her and held her as more tears gushed from her eyes.

"Sh sh…"
She soothed. Caroline sobbed and her body shook so hard Derby was afraid she would break something. But she stayed and held her and let her cry.

Gradually the tears abated and Caroline's breathing began to steady. She rested against Derby for some time. Then she pulled herself up onto her knees.

"Come on. We're done here. Let's get out of these dresses, get my boys and your Geoff and Melody, and leave this lot to whoever the fuck wants to sort it all out."

Derby smiled at Caroline's ability to switch from a mess, to a strong determined woman in one breath. She stood up and helped Caroline to her feet. They left the suite as it was and strode out of the room.

At Caroline's request, Derby rang Geoff's mobile and asked him to bring Leo and Liam to meet them in the gardens. She also asked him to quietly let Alison know that none of them would be coming back inside. Geoff agreed and took the boys to one side explaining. Then carrying Melody, he, Leo and Liam left the wedding guests and strolled outside.

Caroline wrapped her arms around both her sons and Derby leaned into Geoff. Both women were exhausted.

"Where do you want to go?"

Geoff asked Caroline.

"Home. No actually, can we go back to your house please?"

Geoff nodded.

"Have you two got everything?"

"Everything I need."

Caroline replied indicating with her hand the small suitcase nearby. Derby nodded too.

"I've got all our stuff too. We're ready to leave."

Leo hugged his mother.

"Everything's going to be alright. Liam and me will look after you."

"I. Liam and I."

Caroline corrected him. Leo laughed heartily.

"Hmm, I can see you're on the mend already mum."

Caroline patted his arm and then linked with both her sons. She stepped forward with a little skip and the boys marched with her. Geoff passed Melody to Derby and lifted their luggage. They too walked away from the wedding that didn't happen.

CHAPTER 3.

Caroline slumped down on the soft sofa in Derby and Geoff's lounge. It was warm and cosy, despite the size of the old Victorian room. Geoff had lit the open fire, and it was giving off a shimmering soothing glow in the now descending darkness outside.

Geoff and Derby were in the kitchen making tea, and Liam and Leo were both sitting at the table, arms folded and looking miserable. They hadn't wanted to leave their mother alone, but she had begged some alone time, just for a few minutes. So reluctantly they had let Derby lead them from the lounge, to where they now sat feeling helpless.

"Give her some space. I won't try and persuade you that she'll be alright. She won't, not for a long time anyway."

Derby said to the boys, placing a mug of steaming tea in front of each. Leo leaned back and wrapped his hands around the mug.

"Thing is Derby, I'm sort of angry with her too."
Liam looked up at his brother sharply.

"This is not her fault!"
He said, too loudly. Geoff stepped forward and laid a hand on his. Liam glanced up furiously, but saw no threat in the big man by his side.

"Sh Liam. Your mother does not need to hear you two fighting. I think what your brother is saying, is that your mum let Frank manipulate her for years."
Liam opened his mouth to protest, but Geoff cut across him.

"That doesn't make this her fault lad. Just that she fell for his charms over and over. Wanted to believe that he would finally be faithful."

Some of the steam went out of Liam and his shoulders slumped. He grabbed his mug and held it the same way as Leo. He flicked his eyes towards his brother.

"Remember Liam, once you wouldn't accept that Frank had cheated on mum. He's got something, for the love of God, I don't know what, but something that has women falling at his feet. That's what I meant about being angry with her too. I just wish she…she, oh I don't know. I just hate that she's hurting so much."
Leo said to Liam.

"Can I have some of that tea please?"
They all jumped as though caught out, as Caroline stood in the doorway watching them. Derby recovered first.

"I was going to bring it through, but since you're here, let's all sit at the table. I've got homemade chocolate biscuits."

She said with a wicked smile to Caroline.

Caroline slid into a chair between her sons. She patted each of their hands and smiled, but it didn't reach her eyes. She was in far too much pain. Derby put a mug in front of her, and Geoff reached for a tin of biscuits. Caroline had the lid off barely before he had put the tin down. Melody, who had been leaning into her mother, sat up straight as she saw the biscuits. Caroline grinned, and handed the baby half a triple chocolate cookie, and watched as the tiny child took a bite.

"Just like her mother."

Geoff said lovingly, and Caroline folded.

She hunched her shoulders and covered her face with her hands, tears pouring through her fingers. She cried silently, her body shaking with the sobs. Leo and Liam looked on helplessly. There was no comfort they could give. Geoff took Melody from Derby so she could go to her friend. Leo gave up his chair for her, sure she could do more for his mother than he or his brother could. Geoff indicated to the boys, and the three men and the baby left the kitchen.

Caroline leaned into Derby and just cried. Derby knew words couldn't help. Her friend was grieving. She knew she was suffering pain of extreme loss, as though a death had occurred. As though reading her mind, Caroline mumbled in a nasally voice.

"You know, it's like he died, but worse, because he's not dead, he's just with someone else. Whether it's Tania or another woman, she gets to see him smile, feel his arms about her. She has his kisses and oh…he will be making love to her. He's so good at that. Every touch is in exactly the right place. His fingers are like

feathers and he just knows how to set me on fire. She'll hear him say words of love and…well…just everyday words, chat. She eats with him, cooks for him. He buys her wine and helps her choose clothes. All the things we did together, and stuff I thought we'd be doing until one of us actually does die. But not anymore. He's gone, but not gone, do you know what I mean?"
Derby nodded, knowing words were not necessary.

"He's still walking around. It's like being haunted by a ghost. I can see him, hear him but I can't touch him. Oh Jesus, Derby, what am I going to do?"

Derby stood up and pulled a box of tissues from a cupboard. She grabbed a handful and dabbed at Caroline's face, the same as she would to Melody, gently and lovingly. Caroline pulled out a handful herself and pressed them to her eyes, which were now swollen and red.

"Fuck it. I can't breathe now. I'm all stuffed up from crying."
Derby again stood and opened the freezer. She took a handful of ice cubes and wrapped them in a tea towel. She then held the cloth against Caroline's forehead.

"This might help unblock your sinuses."

Caroline leaned into the cool towel and sighed. Her head was aching and her eyes were sore. The ice began to relieve some of the physical pain, and she wished she could wrap her heart in it too, freeze her emotions. But nothing could undo what Frank had done to her.

"Fuck Head Frank does it again."
She muttered. Derby had to smile to herself. That was the name she had given to Frank when the two women

first went out for drinks, and Caroline imparted to Derby some of her life history.

"I've been really stupid Derby. Look at the years I've wasted."

Derby gave her friend a little shake.

"No. I will not accept that Caroline. Do not put this on yourself. I felt sorry for myself, let my life go on and on with nothing. You have had many happy times with Frank. You trusted him and he betrayed you, but those years have not been wasted. Yes he's a complete prick, but think what you and the boys have achieved. Ok, you all might have gone down the same route without him, but I don't think so. What you and Leo and Liam are today are partly because of Frank."

Caroline screwed up her face.

"I'm not defending him in anyway."

Derby stated.

"Not about his infidelity anyway. But you cannot deny that for most of the years you have spent with him, your life and that of your sons has been good."

Caroline's face relaxed and she slouched in her chair. She knew Derby was right. She knew how well her boys had turned out, and that a lot of it was down to Frank as a father figure. Their own father hadn't wanted to know his sons at all, had no part in their upbringing, but Frank had made her family complete for large parts of the time. Yes the boys would hate him now, but he had given a great deal of himself to their welfare.

"I know. And I know in his own way he loves me and the boys. Trouble is he can't resist every other woman who bats her eyelashes at him. But I am done Derby, I'm not going to let him charm his way back in this time. It's not fair on me or the boys. I have to get on with my life now. In fact, I'm going back to work on Monday."

"Really, isn't that a bit soon? Why don't you take a little break?"

Derby asked. Caroline sat up straight and jiggled her shoulders, releasing some of the tension.

"What else am I going to do? I sure as hell am not going on the honeymoon he booked for us."

She gazed across the kitchen.

"But that would be nice. Three weeks in the Seychelles, mmm, sunshine, cocktails, soft sand and…"

Her voice trailed away and tears again shimmered on the ends of her lashes. She bit her lip.

"And no sex. No I won't be going there, tempting as it is. He's probably already changing the name on my ticket to Tania anyway."

She growled.

"Nope, reckon going back to work will be best. Even though I left an automated email reply, and a note on the website, I bet I still have a couple of hundred submissions waiting, so might as well get to it. Help keep my mind off Frank."

"Well at least stay here over the weekend. The forecast says the same weather for tomorrow, cold but sunny, so Geoff could get the barbeque out."

Caroline laughed.

"You're the only person I know who barbeques in the middle of winter, in this country anyway."

Derby shrugged.

"It's fun. I'll bundle Melody in her snowsuit and boots, and Geoff and I will be wrapped up in woolies."

She waggled her eyebrows.

"And hot chocolate with Baileys, followed by homemade hot fudge cake."

Caroline's face smiled genuinely for the first time since the failed wedding. She licked her lips and Derby grinned.

"You've got me girl. Burgers and sausages maybe, fudge cake yes, but hot chocolate with Baileys added, that's a definite oh yeah."

Geoff peeked his head around the kitchen door and was relieved to see the two women smiling. Caroline at least looked more composed, but he knew inside she was still coming apart. Derby looked up and saw her fiancé. She gave him a tiny nod and he retreated, returning with Caroline's sons. The boys strode over to their mother and she reached up. They both took a hand and held it firm.

"I'm ok. I've cried buckets and will probably dehydrate myself crying more. But I am ok. I won't lie to you that it's going to be easy for me, but I will get through, and don't worry, I will not be letting Frank back in."

Both boys let out breaths on long sighs. It hurt Caroline that her children were hurt too, and that more than anything strengthened her resolve to move on with life empty of Frank.

"I'm going to stay here for the weekend, Geoff's barbequing tomorrow."

She giggled at the astonished look on Leo and Liam's faces, and the surprised look on Geoff's.

"I am?"

Geoff said and Derby patted his arm nodding.

"Barbeque in December?"

The boys said together and Caroline chuckled.

"Derby likes barbeque any time of the year. Any weather for that matter."
Geoff told them, winking at Derby behind their backs and making her blush. The first time she had a barbeque with Geoff, they had ended up making love in the middle of the garden in a raging storm.

"I like being outdoors."
Derby stated, justifying herself.
The whole discussion of the upcoming barbeque lightened the mood.

"Can we come then?"
Liam asked excitedly, sounding more like a fourteen year old than his twenty three years. Leo mock punched his brother.

"Your stomach rules again."
He taunted. Liam closed his fists and took up a boxing stance, doing air punches.

"Come on then bro."
The boys fooled around for a bit and Caroline sighed. They would be alright.

CHAPTER 4.

After spending the evening in front of a roaring fire with Derby, Geoff and her boys, the day finally caught up with Caroline. She nursed a very large measure of malt whisky in her hands, and felt her eyelids drooping. Liam was chatting animatedly with Geoff about boats and Leo was telling Derby about a new holiday resort he was looking into. Derby spotted the glass begin to slip from Caroline's fingers and managed to rescue it before it spilt.

"Come on, let's get you upstairs."

Tucking Caroline into bed was like settling Melody. She looked fragile and exhausted. Derby pulled the duvet up under her friend's chin and kissed her forehead.

"Rest sweetie. Have a lie in."

"I'll try."

Caroline whispered and Derby suspected her friend would spend most of the night awake, reliving the day and grieving over the lost wedding night.

Caroline was lost in a dream of Frank. His arms were around her, his fingers caressing her softest centre. Her body was stirring in all the right places. He whispered how much he loved her and kissed the ring on her finger. She pressed her body against him, her pelvis tilting to meet his fingers as they plunged deeply. Her breathing increased as she began to peak. Then he was gone. She was left burning as she turned her head and saw him next to her. Tania was in his arms and the two were writhing, their bodies entwined, laughter on their lips as they stared at her.

She came awake with a start, the dream vivid as her eyes snapped open. Darkness surrounded her and loneliness enveloped her. She threw off the duvet and slipped from the bed. She wiped at her eyes and felt wetness, tears that had begun to drop during the final part of the dream. Without turning on any lights, she reached for her dressing gown and wrapped herself in its warm folds. She padded to the window and carefully drew back the curtains.

The room she was in looked out over the front of the house. The night was clear, the sky full of twinkling stars and a soft silver glow from a half moon. The trees and shrubs surrounding the property were white with frost. It was a beautiful sight and so very different from her own home.

When she had first met Derby, she had lived in a small detached house at the end of a cul-de-sac. Not long after, and influenced by Derby's determination to change her life, she had sold it and bought a town house at the marina close to the city. It was new and modern and luxurious, and she loved it. But Geoff and Derby's huge Victorian house had so much character and love within its walls, Caroline felt soothed just looking out of the window.

She shivered, partly from the cold, and partly from the remnants of the dream. She leaned her forehead against the cool glass and imagined fingers of frost touching her, freezing her pain. The cold was good, numbing. She wished it could stay that way. She missed Frank more than she would admit to anyone, to herself even. But she had been weak in the past, gone back so many times. Not anymore.

Caroline had no idea what the time was. She guessed it must be very late as the old house was silent. For a tiny moment she shivered, not from the cold but from fear. The silence was eerie, as though she were the only person left in the world. There was nothing but trees and shrubs outside the window. No cars drove past the gates. No other homes could be seen, hidden by the living boundary of the old house. Beautiful as the stark night was, she was gripped by an irrational terror of aloneness.

Grabbing the collar of her dressing gown, Caroline turned from the window. Panic had settled over her heart, shortening her breaths. She stepped over to the bed and picked up her phone. She pressed a button and the screen lit up, the glow settling her nerves. Her phone, modern and active brought her panic under control, and relief flooded her veins, sending warmth to her extremities.

She lifted the phone and her pulse quickened. There were twenty five missed calls and voicemails, and a hundred messages. She had switched her phone to silent as soon as they had left the hotel, and hadn't looked at it since. She guessed some of the calls might be from friends checking on her, but believed most of them, and the messages would be from Frank.

She didn't want to open any of the messages or voicemails, but her fingers were already pressing buttons. Torturing herself she listened to the voicemails. As she supposed, some were from friends asking how she was. Stupid question, she thought, angrily, then waited on bated breath to hear Frank's voice.

Each of his messages were given in a desperate voice, pleading and begging her to call him, to forgive him, he loved her. She listened to each one, her face scrunched in agony, her heart pounding from the sound of his well known loving voice. She then went on to read the texts. Again a few were messages offering support and sympathy, but most were from Frank. At first they consisted of the same content as the voicemails. Then they just kept repeating over and over. *Don't leave me Caroline. Call me or text.* All ending in a series of kisses.

Caroline finished reading and flung the phone onto the bed. She stood trembling, not with cold or fear, but anger. How dare he try and pretend he loved her. How dare he make out what he did with Tania didn't mean anything. Her shoulders slumped, the anger disappearing as fast as it had come. She plonked down on the bed and picked up her phone again. Slowly and deliberately she deleted each and everyone of Frank's voicemails and messages.

As she clicked onto one message, ready to throw it into her phone's trash can, she realised it was a message she had missed, and it wasn't from Frank. It had an unknown number. Curiosity had her reading it, replaced quickly by fury. The message was from Tania.

So you get your own way again you fucking bitch. Now he won't speak to me. I hope you rot in hell. You ruined my life once and now you've done it again. He was mine, always mine, you took him from me and I took him back. But all your sobbing made him go running back to you. One thing though, when he was fucking me, he told me I was better than you have ever been, that he missed me most when he was screwing you, saw my face when he looked at you, and had to bite his tongue to stop from calling my name. He will come back to me again.

Tania.

Caroline couldn't move. Fury had her rooted to the spot. She was numb. She didn't really believe Tania's words. Even in her anger at Frank, she couldn't believe he would say those things. But what if he had duped her so much. She shook her head. She wouldn't accept that he could be so callous. Tania was twisted. She had been long divorced from Frank before Caroline even met him. And if she was determined to be used by him over and over again, then let her get on with it.

For the first time since waking, she looked at the time. It was a few minutes after five. She grinned to herself. Then began to tap a message.

Tania

Thank you so much for your message, it was very enlightening. He's all yours. You're welcome to him. I won't degrade myself by assassinating your sexual prowess, I'm sure you're a real Goddess between the sheets. Just one tiny thing though. Frank always used to tell me how deflated he would become when you took your clothes off, so he always tried to keep the lights off.

Best of luck.

Caroline.

She sent the message hoping it would wake the woman up. Then she hugged her phone to her breast and giggled silently. As childish as she felt the message had been, she also felt like she had taken back a little control of her life. She laid the phone on the bedside table and slipped back under the cosy duvet. Her toes were cold, but the soft feather bedding soon sent warmth to them. She huddled down, but couldn't return to sleep. She heard a slight vibration from the table, and knew a new message had come in. She reached for her phone, opened the message and grinned. It was from Tania. The woman obviously couldn't think of a suitable reply and had simply sent a fuck you emoticon, instead of words.

Caroline laid her phone back down and snuggled deeper under the duvet. The grin stayed on her face. She might be suffering from a broken heart, and in pain at the loss of a planned future. But she had a little satisfaction, knowing she had got right under the skin of the woman who had contributed heavily to her life's destruction.

Caroline didn't get any more proper sleep. She dozed in and out, snug and warm as the winter dawn began to break. She heard a sound at the door and opened her eyes as a thread of light appeared.

"I'm awake."

She whispered. Derby pushed the door open fully and came in, perching on the side of the bed.

"Did you get any sleep?"

She asked. Caroline nodded.

"Until around five. Then a dream woke me."

She went on to describe the nightmare to Derby, and also the messages on her phone.

"Evil bitch."

Derby said in a hushed but harsh tone. Caroline shrugged.

"I agree, but she's not right in the head. I mean, I've lost something I thought was going to last a lifetime. She's just delusional and…well…fucking crazy."

Caroline said in her usual blunt way. Derby huffed out a laugh.

"Geoff's downstairs. He's got the fires going and he's making hot drinks. What would you like?"

Caroline swung her feet over the side of the bed. She still had her dressing gown on.

"I'm coming down. I don't want to be on my own."

Derby nodded and led the way from the room.

"The boys are still sleeping."

She said to Caroline as they both padded down the stairs. Caroline nodded.

"They'll both sleep for England unless you wake them."

"I peeked in before I did you, and they're flat out."

Derby replied.

"I'll give them a nudge later. I expect they're exhausted too. Do them good to stay away from the world for a bit longer."

Derby knew her friend wished that's what she could do as well, but didn't voice her opinion.

Geoff was in the kitchen feeding Melody a bowl of toddler porridge. The baby was giggling, enjoying a game only she knew, as she turned her head from side to side, getting most of the breakfast around her mouth. Geoff looked up as the women entered.

"Coffee and tea in pots. Made both."
He announced as he deftly inserted a spoonful of oats into Melody's tiny mouth. Derby planted a kiss on her fiancé's head and one on her daughter's.

"Thank you darling. Having fun?"
Geoff grinned, nodding.

"Today, she's discovered how to put the spoon in my hair rather than her mouth."

"Lovely."
Derby replied, holding up both pots to Caroline who indicated the coffee.

"There's warm croissants in the oven too."
Geoff told them.

"Mmmm, perfect for a Sunday morning."
Caroline said, taking a steaming mug from Derby.

Caroline sat at the table and munched warm buttered croissants, watching Derby as she cleaned her baby's face and lifted her from the high chair. For a moment a little stab went through her heart, as she remembered doing the same with her boys. But that was a long time ago. They were grown up now, but they still needed her just as much as Melody needed her parents.

Derby had told Geoff about the messages from Frank and Tania. She could see he was seething, and knew him well enough to know he could keep it in. One thing Geoff never did, was show any anger when his daughter was present. But his words conveyed what he was feeling.

"Think maybe I should get both of them down the gym, and put them in the ring with some of my more experienced fighters."
Caroline laughed.

"I'd pay to see that."
She said. Geoff grinned.

"Hmm, maybe adding the boxing to the gym was a good move. I had my doubts, but perhaps we could advertise."
He held up his hands as though displaying a banner.

"Revengercise. Put your lying cheating partner in the ring and watch them get pounded. Great workout for the broken heart."
Caroline burst into laughter as did Derby. Melody giggled along with the adults, totally unaware of what they were laughing at.

"Frank would go on his knees in seconds, begging for mercy. But Tania. I can see her going a few solid rounds before she broke."
Caroline told them, her smile becoming haunted. Derby noticing the change in her friend looked at the clock.

"The time's flown. Shall we get the boys up?"
She asked. Caroline shook her head.

"No let them sleep a bit longer. I'm alright, I promise. If it's ok can I go and get bathed, look a bit more together when they do get up?"

"Of course you can. I've already laid out towels for you. Take your time."
Derby said. Caroline's face lit up.

"Oh I intend to. That tub of yours is huge."

By mid-day the frost had given way to bright but very cold sunshine. A few patches of white lingered in the more shaded areas of the spacious back garden of the old Victorian house. Caroline sat next to Derby on a patio chair bundled up in winter woolies and gloves. True to her word, Derby had made rich hot chocolate, laced with Baileys and topped with thick whipped cream. They each held a large mug in their gloved hands. Melody was half crawling and half walking in front of them, picking up and discarding toys, then moving on to another and repeating the process.

Geoff stood over an old fashioned charcoal barbeque, preferring the flavours it gave to the meat, to a more modern gas one. Leo was standing chatting with him and Liam was wondering around the huge garden. Even though his interests were mainly in marine biology, he loved land nature almost as much, and despite the fact that the trees were bare of leaves, and much of the shrubs were winter resting, he found a lot to occupy him.

The smell of barbeque meat wafted across to the women, and as Liam appeared from off the pathway in the trees, to him too. Caroline smiled wistfully.

"The smell of food always brought him out from wherever he was adventuring. Except the water of course."

Her cheeks were glowing red, both from the cold air and from the very large slug of Baileys Derby had put in her drink.

"Geoff's barbeque could entice from a hundred miles away."

Derby replied. Caroline looked at her friend.

"You have a very good man there. I'm so glad you two found each other. You really are soul mates."

Derby glanced back a her fiancé and nodded in agreement.

"Set a date yet?"
Caroline quizzed.

"Not an exact date, but in about a year. We thought it would be nice for Melody to be properly mobile."
Derby replied a little hesitantly. Caroline leaned forward and patted her knee.

"It's ok to talk about it Derby. I'm fragile, but not so much that I'll break every time a wedding is mentioned. I want to see you married to Geoff, want to be a part of the planning and celebrations. And, you never know, I might even have a plus one to bring by then. I'm not going to sit around moping about Frank. He's my past. No I'm looking to my future and I'm going to make it a damn good one."

"Here, here!"
Yelled Liam through a mouthful of burger and bun, making Caroline throw her head back and laugh.

The weather forecast had warned of fresh ice as soon as the light began to fade. So Geoff piled Caroline, Leo and Liam into his four by four before darkness descended. Kissing Derby and Melody goodbye he set off through the gates and down the road towards Caroline's home. Derby stood and waved until his lights disappeared around the bend, and hugging Melody, took her daughter back into the warmth of the house. She was worried about Caroline, but knew her friend would cope. It would take time, but time was the greatest healer.

CHAPTER 5.

As soon as Caroline and her boys stepped over the threshold of the town house, she dived for her bedroom. She stopped inside the doorway and took a deep breath. On Frank's side of the bed was the book he had last been reading, a photo of her inside the pages, acting as a book mark. His slippers were just tucked underneath the bed, not neatly, but as he'd taken them off. His dressing gown hung from a hook on the wall.

In the ensuite bathroom, Frank's razor stood on the shelf above the double basins. Various other male toiletries took up shelf space in the cabinet on the wall, and navy towels hung alongside pale blue striped ones on the heated rail. Caroline had purposefully chosen those colours, navy for Frank, hard and masculine, pale blue stripes for her, soft and feminine.

With a little sob that she bit back, Caroline grabbed the navy towels and yanked them from the rail. She dumped them on the floor and threw on top the razor and the rest of Frank's bathroom bits. She swung back to the bedroom and grabbed the slippers. She opened the doors to the double built in wardrobe, and snatched all of his clothes from their hangers.

Soon a pile of shirts, pants, trousers and suits joined the pile of things in the bathroom. She heard a noise behind her and swung around. Leo and Liam stood in the bedroom doorway. Leo held a roll of black bin liners. Caroline reached out a hand and Leo gave her the roll. She tore a bin liner off, grabbed at the pile and stuffed a bundle into the bag. Before long, everything of Frank's was tied up in bin bags.

"I'll take them down for you."

Leo offered, but Caroline shook her head.

"You can help, there's too many for one trip, but I want to throw them into the bins myself. Rubbish to feed rubbish."

She said as she lifted a bag in each hand.

Caroline felt intense satisfaction in disposing of Frank's items. She didn't care if he was angry that she hadn't returned them. It was his own fault. Getting every reminder of him out of her house was the important thing. She didn't want his stuff hanging around for him to collect, and she had no intention of going near his place to deliver them. So the bins were the only alternative. As the last bag was dropped into one of the large communal bins, Caroline brushed her hands together, finality in her action.

Leo and Liam stayed at their mother's house for the night, and when Monday morning broke, the three spent a pleasant but unusual breakfast together. The boys departed to their respective jobs and Caroline got herself ready for her own. She didn't bother with any makeup, and donned casual jeans and jumper. As she was supposed to be on honeymoon, she wouldn't be seeing anyone or answering any calls in her office, so dressing for the office wasn't a priority.

With a deep sigh, Caroline unlocked the door to her literary agency. Both outer and inner offices were quiet. Adele, her assistant had agreed to take three weeks of her holiday at the same time as Caroline. Especially since Caroline shut the office the Christmas and New Year's weeks, thereby giving the girl five weeks off with pay. Caroline was glad. The peace was nice, and she just wasn't ready for a bombardment of questions.

With a pot of coffee bubbling and hissing, Caroline sat at her desk and booted up her computer. She opened her emails and sure enough had one hundred and fifty submissions waiting. She sighed. No matter how many messages she left on her website, telling prospective clients not to submit during the dates she was supposed to be away, there were always those who ignored the messages and sent in their work. If she had have been away, it would have annoyed her. Finding them on her return, she would have pushed the pile to the back. But since the honeymoon had been cancelled, she might as well look at them and get them out of the way.

With a mug of steaming coffee by her side, Caroline began to read each email, synopsis and sample chapters. A couple warranted further thought, so she flagged them and moved them to a separate folder. About half way through, she came across a submission from an author named Jude Lore. Caroline stuck her tongue in her cheek and rolled her eyes.

"Please, do you think I'd fall for that one, putting a play on the actor's name."

She said out loud to herself. She glanced at the title of the novel and giggled, *Lost In Lust.*

"Ok, let's see what this guy has to say."

She again said to the empty office. She shrugged, thinking she had nowhere else to be, and began reading the email. It was very short, and usually she would discard something so lacking, but for some unknown reason she was intrigued. Jude Lore had written.

Dear Miss Caroline.

I am Jude. I am thirty years old and I am me. That is all there is to say. My novel, *Lost In Lust* will speak for me. Read it and decide.

Yours

Jude Lore.

Caroline cracked up. It was obvious to her that the man was writing under a pseudonym, and didn't have a clue about how a submission should be presented. She stood up and refilled her mug, sipping the beverage as she looked out of the wide window and down at the boats bobbing on the water. She had chosen her office at the same time as her house, and it too overlooked the marina, and was only a few steps from her front door.

With resolve, Caroline turned from the window and sat back at her desk. She opened the attachment containing the synopsis and blinked twice at what she was looking at. There were no words, just a sketch of a man and woman, naked and entwined on a bed of rose petals. The picture had the same title as the novel.

Caroline shook her head and decided she had gone far enough with Jude Lore's submission. She opened a standard rejection letter template, added the writer's name and her own signature, and was about to press send when she hesitated. She had no idea what was making her pause. The whole submission was poor and bordering on the ridiculous, but she didn't have the heart to reject it.

Closing the rejection email, Caroline instead clicked on the sample chapters. She smiled to herself. At least there were words this time. Quickly and skilfully she read the first three chapters of *Lost In Lust*. It didn't take her long to conclude that she should have sent the rejection letter. Apart from the very bad writing, the story was weak and the leading character had no character.

With a big sigh Caroline leaned back in her chair and closed her eyes. For a moment she regretted coming into the office. It seemed futile and depressing. Her mind drifted away from everything, the silence of the office enveloping her. She took some deep breaths and wished she was far away. For a few seconds her mind allowed her yearning, and the pain in her heart eased, coated in a protective layer. But it didn't last. All too soon she felt the twist and squeeze of betrayal penetrate the protection, and the hurt flooded back in.

Caroline opened her eyes and angrily stood up. She leaned on her desk and was about to shut down her computer. But Jude Lore's synopsis was still an open document on her screen. The picture, which she had barely taken note of before, was actually a very well sketched drawing. She wondered if Jude Lore had done it himself.

Still standing, Caroline let her eyes wander over the details. The man was wiry, but his muscles were well defined. He had long floppy hair and a beatific expression on his face. He was very realistic in comparison to the woman. She was merely a sketch with very few clear features. Caroline studied the picture, and concluded the artist had drawn a real person in the man, but the woman could be anyone or no one.

Caroline decided that Jude Lore had indeed done the sketch himself. She thought that his writing skills were awful, but his artistic ones were very good. So purely on a whim, and certainly not because she believed his novel could ever be published, she opened a new email.

Caroline wrote Jude Lore a brief letter thanking him for his submission. She didn't criticise or comment in any way about his work. Instead she simply asked him to come to her office for a meeting as soon as possible, preferably within the next two days. She sent the email without further contemplation and then shut the computer down. She felt exhausted. Not so much physically but mentally.

Caroline locked her office and stepped out into cold sunshine. This side of the marina was bathed in it, whereas on the opposite side, she could see shadow, and little patches of frost in the most shaded corners. She pulled her coat close around her neck and sucked in the chilled air. Then she set off at a brisk pace, past the boats and past her home.

Caroline walked for two hours with no purpose or destination, along the path that ran alongside the river. Further into countryside the temperature dropped, and the surrounding fields were white with frost. She plodded on, her breath coming out in puffs of white vapour, barely noticing the beauty of the scenery around her. The path was quiet. Most people were either at work, or not brave enough to venture out on such a chilled day. Caroline liked it. She saw only one dog walker and a jogger.

Eventually the countryside gave way to a few houses, and Caroline realised she had walked to one of the villages bordering the river. She stopped, and it dawned on her that she was quite worn out and thirsty. She was familiar with the village, and knew there was a small cosy coffee shop in the centre. So she stepped off the path and headed for the café.

The door jingled as she pushed it open. A plump smiling woman greeted her and waved her hand around the interior.

"Sit anywhere you like love."

She said. Caroline unbuttoned her coat and pulled off her gloves, sliding into a chair at a small table near the window. A snowy white cloth dotted with a holly pattern covered the table. A china santa tea light holder sat in the middle, and as Caroline took in her surroundings for the first time, she was shocked to remember Christmas was very close.

In a corner, a fresh green tree was giving off a scent of pine. It was adorned with glittering ornaments and sparkling lights. Glancing up, she saw bells and balls hanging from the beams, and tinsel draped across them. Even the windows were decorated with fake snow sprayed onto stencils.

"It's a bit over the top, I know. It's just my grandchildren love to decorate everything this time of the year."

The woman said, making Caroline jump a little.

"It's beautiful, really Christmassy."
Caroline replied with a smile that didn't reach her eyes.

The woman pressed her lips together and held up a little notepad.

"What can I get you, and are you alright dear?"
She asked. Caroline's breath hitched a tiny bit. The woman was looking at her so kindly and not in a nosey way at all. She breathed deeply.

"Hot chocolate please, with all the trimmings. And no, not really, but I will be…in time."
She hadn't meant to say anything other than order her drink, but the woman looked at her so gently, almost in a motherly way. Even though Caroline suspected she was probably only about ten years older than herself. The woman jotted her order down and nodded as though she knew exactly what Caroline was talking about.

"Be just a minute."
She said and bobbed off towards the counter.

Caroline sat back in the chair and stared out of the window. The sky had clouded over blocking out the sunshine. She wondered if it would snow and hoped it would. The woman appeared by her side, and placed a huge mug of frothy hot chocolate in front of her. Caroline grinned. It definitely had come with all of the trimmings. Grated chocolate was melting on top of a thick layer of whipped cream, not the foamy stuff from a can, but real cream. On the saucer was a flake and several marsh mallows, not the mini ones either.

"I make the hot chocolate myself, not that powdered stuff."
The woman said. Caroline picked up the mug and sipped. It was delicious. Rich and very chocolaty.

"Mmmm, it's wonderful."
Caroline told her, a genuine smile lighting her eyes.

"It won't put right all the wrongs, but it will give a little comfort."
The woman said, then grinned wickedly.

"Well, that's unless you're trying to lose weight or keep trim, 'cos my hot chocolate is most definitely not for those who want to do that. It's a full fat total sweet treat. Wouldn't like to even consider how many calories, probably a whole day's worth. But well, sometimes, it's just the thing that's needed."
Caroline giggled. This woman was cheering her up where nothing else had been able to.

"I'll leave you to it then. Just give me a yell if you need anything else."
She said and trotted back to her counter.

Caroline wrapped both hands around the mug and sipped slowly, delighting in every mouthful. She stared out of the window, her mind only on the chocolate. An old couple waddled past hand in hand and Caroline smiled. They looked cute, and obviously still very much in love with one another. They were also very old, probably in their eighties, Caroline guessed. They strolled out of her view, then she heard the jingle of the door bell. Looking over her shoulder she saw the couple had come into the café.

"Mornin' Edith, Tom. Usual?"
The owner of the coffee shop said. Caroline heard murmurs of acceptance and the light scraping of chairs being pulled out.

"See the Grandkids have been busy again."
Tom's deep gruff voice rang over the shop. The woman laughed. Caroline swung around a little and watched.

"You ok Edith?"
The woman asked. The old lady nodded.

"Buzzing Vera. Got some new pills from the doc for me blood pressure, but it's all good, nothing else going on with the old bod. We're having a get together at the weekend, it's our diamond anniversary, just in the pub, but come along, it'll be fun."

"I'll be there, do you need me to bring anything?"

Caroline's mind drifted away from the conversation and it faded out, as a spike of pain pierced her heart. Her own parents were in their seventies. They lived in Spain, but her dad had been advised against travel due to ill health, so hadn't been able to come over for the wedding. Although she missed them, and would have loved to see them, she was relieved they had not witnessed the betrayal. Leo had rung them and explained what had happened, and promised they would all get out to see them in the new year.

Her mug empty, Caroline sat twirling it in the saucer. Tom, Edith and Vera were still chatting, but Caroline wasn't bothering to follow the conversation. Once again misery had settled over her, and she couldn't push it away. She didn't want to move, but didn't want to stay either. She had no plan. The sky outside was getting darker as clouds thickened.

"It's gonna snow."
She heard Tom say. His words brought her to life and she realised how far from home she had walked. She frowned, worried now about getting back. She wasn't wearing the right footwear for a walk in the snow, and the path along the river got slippery quickly, even with

a little rain. She pulled her phone from her bag, she had no signal.

"Um, excuse me. I haven't got a signal on my mobile. Could I use your phone to call a taxi please?" She asked, interrupting the chat between the three. Vera smiled and was about to agree when Tom piped up.

"You got to go far love?"

"Just back to the marina, that's where I live. I hadn't realised how far I'd walked."
Caroline told him. He raised his eyebrows.

"Blimey, that's a fair few miles. Well a taxi won't come out 'ere for about an hour, and if it snows before that, prob'ly not at all. We can drop you back though in our four by four."

Caroline was about to reject the offer, the words on the tip of her tongue. Then she smiled. Why not take up this couple's kindness? S he didn't want to have to call one of the boys from work, so she nodded instead.

"Thank you, that's so nice of you. Anytime your ready."
Tom nodded and lifted his tea cup.

Snow flakes were falling fast and heavy as Tom turned his big sturdy car into the marina. Caroline sighed wearily as her home became visible in the thickening white outside the window of the car. Tom eased the car to a stop, and Caroline opened the door and hopped down. The ground was slick, but the snow was settling.

"Thank you so much. Please be careful driving back."
She said to the old couple through Tom's open window. Edith looked around her husband and smiled kindly.

"You're welcome love. And don't you be worrying about us. Tom 'ere has bin driving about in worse weather than this for a lot o' years."

Tom grinned and nodded in agreement.

"You get on in. It's gettin' proper cold out now."

Tom told her. Caroline smiled back, and stepped away from the four by four. She lifted a hand and waved as the old man manoeuvred the vehicle in a turn.

"Merry Christmas!"

Tom yelled over the roar of the engine."

"You too!"

Caroline called back. Then she stood and watched the tail lights of the car as they faded into the snowy night.

CHAPTER 6.

Caroline turned and faced her house. Snow blurred the building, making it difficult to find the outline. Now she was here, she didn't want to go inside. It would be warm and comfortable, but it would still be lonely. Glancing over her shoulder, she saw the marina restaurant was open. A large brightly lit Christmas tree and white fairy lights twinkled inside.

Making a decision, she spun around. The paving underfoot was slippery and she slid a little. She gasped in cold air and found herself giggling. Suddenly the restaurant lost its appeal too, and childish delight for the snow took over. She pushed one foot forward flat on the ground, then the other. Holding her arms outstretched she began to shuffle towards the railing overlooking the water. A couple of times she nearly lost her footing, but managed to reset her balance in time.

Reaching the railing, she grabbed on, letting her feet slide backwards and forwards a few times. The snow was falling faster. Huge flakes like saucers sped to the ground in front of her eyes. A lot settled in her hair and on her clothes, and she giggled again. She imagined she would soon look like a living snowman, minus the carrot nose and stone eyes. She heard a noise below and looked down. The boats were bobbing gently on the water, but snow was piling up on the cuddy covers and sticking to the masts. It was a beautiful sight, one she had never seen.

Caroline stood for a time she couldn't measure, absorbed in the falling snow and the swaying boats. Her mind was blank, locking out memories that caused her pain. She didn't feel cold, just numb. Hands on her shoulders had her jumping and squealing.

"Caroline, it's me."

A deep and very familiar voice said behind her. Caroline turned quickly, anger penetrating her deadened sensations. She pressed her lips hard together and her eyes took on a temperature lower than the falling snow.

"Fuck off Frank."

She hissed. Frank took a small step back, dropping his hands to his sides, but still close enough to make her feel trapped.

"Please Caroline…"

"Please what? No don't answer that, I've heard it all before, many, many times."

She snarled. The fury emanating from her finally got through to Frank, for he took a much larger step backwards, giving her space to lift her hand. He closed his eyes flinching, expecting a blow to his face. But Caroline simply pointed at him.

"There is nothing you can say or do this time."

Frank opened his eyes and looked at her. She could see tears glistening on his cheeks. He brought his hands up and swiped at them, and then held them out palms up, in a beseeching manner. Caroline wanted to back away, but she had nowhere to go. The railing was at her back, so instead she lifted her own hands in a warding off gesture. In a flash, Frank covered her hands with his, drawing her close to him.

At first, Caroline resisted, tugging against his hold. Then she gave in and let him pull her into his arms. Immediately she felt warm, the heat of his body coming through his expensive wool coat. She could smell his scent, citrusy and woody, so familiar she could pick him out in a crowd.

He brushed the snow from her hair and rested his head on her hers. She melted. Frank splayed one hand across her back and pulled her closer, pressing her body into his. He threaded his fingers into her wet hair at the nape of her neck, and massaged exactly the right place. He was so good at soothing her, had always known how. He kissed her forehead lightly and slid his hand from her nape to cup her chin. He tilted her head back and she didn't, couldn't resist. He kissed the side of her mouth, teasing, and slowly trailed his lips alongside her neck. She moaned deep in her throat, trying to turn her head so her lips could meet his. Finally, he brought his mouth back to hers and gave her what she craved.

As the kiss deepened, fire began to ignite deep within her. She pressed harder against him, wriggling to get closer. Frank moved his hand away from her back and unbuttoned his coat, wrapping it around her. Now she could feel him, hard and hot. She lifted onto her toes, setting her feet further apart, tilting her pelvis forward. She heard his throaty laugh as she slid up and down his erection, pleasuring herself as well as him.

"God you feel so good."

He murmured into her neck. Caroline took his chin in her hand and dragged his lips back to hers.

She was breathing hard, her body throbbing, deep at her centre as her internal muscles clenched and unclenched. All she could think of was Frank inside her. She didn't care what he'd done. What he was doing now was all that mattered. He was so good at making her feel this way, so practised. Despite his age, Frank was a brilliant lover. He was a big man, and he kept very fit, with a flat stomach and hard muscles, and he was very virile.

Frank clasped her buttocks in both hands and squeezed. He pressed into her and thrust his hips forwards. She writhed against him, desperate for release, and even through their clothes she could feel it building, a fire burning hotter and hotter ready to explode.

The snow kept on falling, the pathway empty except for the two of them, the railing at her back, as Frank leaned into her, thrusting harder and harder. She moaned and ate at his mouth, her tongue flicking his. She could feel the pounding of his heart as his desire began to peak, matching her own. Then she came. She squealed against his kiss, her fingers gripping the lapels of his coat. Her body went rigid and her heart skipped several beats, her mind blank. Pleasure flooded through every nerve ending making her shudder. Frank thrust hard and then his body went stiff and he huffed out a breath.

Caroline's body gradually relaxed, and Frank held her in his arms rubbing his face in her hair. It was as it always was after. Even though this time they hadn't touched one another, it still felt damned good, and exciting. Caroline giggled.

"What?"

Frank whispered.

"Like a couple of teenagers, doing it over the clothes."

She whispered back and heard him chuckle.

"And outside too."

He added. She nodded into his shoulder.

"When we get inside we can take each other's clothes off and start all over again."

Frank said. His words hit her like an icy snowball. She tilted her head back and looked at his face. He had his eyes closed and was smiling.

"Jesus. What the fuck am I doing?"

Caroline hissed. Frank opened his eyes wide and looked down at her.

"What we always do baby. We make up by making love."

Caroline stepped away from him, her hands curled into fists. She was as angry with herself as she was with him. Once again, she had let his charms manipulate her. She had succumbed through misery and loneliness and sex. She stamped one snowy boot, furious that she had let him do it so easily. She hadn't put up anything like a fight.

"No!"

She yelled. Frank put out his hands to calm her, but she sidestepped him.

"God how fucking stupid am I?"

She was shaking, not from the cold that was now seeping into her snow sodden coat, but from rage.

"Caroline, calm…"

"Don't tell me to fucking calm down. I hate myself for what I've just let you do, and I hate you even more for doing it. How dare you come here and pretend everything is just dandy. It is not, never will be. God." She dragged her hands down her face and clasped her wet hair in her fists as though she could tear out her anger. A sharp stab of pain shot through her scalp, and knowing it would do no good to yank her own hair out, she relaxed her grip. She took some deep steadying breaths.

"Go away Frank. It's over."

"No Caroline, I don't believe you. Not after what we've just done. You still love me and I'm not giving up. You're angry You don't mean it."

Caroline felt a scream begin deep within her soul. But she held it back. She didn't want neighbours to come running, thinking she was being murdered. Even though at that point, she thought murdering Frank might actually be quite satisfying. That idea brought a near hysterical giggle. She let it slip out just a tiny bit, then bit it back. She wouldn't lose control now. Taking a deep breath and letting it out very slowly, she turned her head to one side and held her hands up.

"But I do mean it Frank."

She said with a calmness she didn't know she possessed. That gave Frank pause for thought. Caroline always shouted and swore when she was upset. Then he could appease her with soft words, kisses and promises. But this Caroline was different, and a tiny thread of fear stabbed at his heart.

"Caroline, please, you can't mean it."
His voice had taken on a thin whiny tone that Caroline had never heard before. With sudden realisation, she knew she had the upper hand, maybe for the first time since they had met. It gave her strength.

"I do Frank. I absolutely do mean it. It's taken me far too long to realise you won't ever change. Yes I still love you, and will do for a long time. But that will change eventually. What I cannot, and will not do is live another minute with you as part of my life. Go to Tania, or whoever you want to screw, because it won't be me, ever again. We are through. Full stop."

Frank reached out a hand towards her, but she ignored him. She didn't feel better but she did feel liberated. With a determined step in the deepening snow, she turned her back to him and made her way towards her front door. She stamped snow from her boots and stepped inside the warmth of her home. As she closed the door, she saw Frank still standing where she had left him, a dark shape against the whiteness.

CHAPTER 7.

For a moment Caroline just leaned on the closed door. Then she began to peel off her clothes. She was wet through. Naked, she grabbed the pile of soggy garments and plodded towards her utility room. She stuffed them into the washing machine, loaded it with detergent and fabric softener and stabbed the button to start. The action was cathartic. For a moment she watched the machine fill, then mentally shook herself.

In her kitchen she flicked the switch on the kettle and grabbed a mug from the cupboard. She spooned in instant coffee then leaned on the counter waiting for the kettle to boil. As soon as it clicked off, she poured the water over the coffee. Still naked, Caroline carried the mug into her bedroom. Without turning on the light, she padded over to the window that looked out over the boats. The snow seemed to be slowing, but had settled in a thick layer on the ground.

Caroline sipped her coffee and stared at the spot where she and Frank had been. She felt her cheeks begin to flush, embarrassed now at what they had done so visibly. She pressed her forehead to the glass and sighed. Anyone looking out of their windows would have seen the whole thing, despite the snow.

"Just like a couple of horny teenagers."

She mumbled to herself, then laughed. If anyone had watched they had probably enjoyed the show.

As she kept her eyes fixed on the spot by the railings, she imagined herself watching a couple from her window. The thought brought fresh heat between her thighs. She put her half empty mug on the window sill and covered her breasts with her hands. Her nipples were hard. The over the clothes orgasm hadn't been enough. She realised that her anger had simply dulled her desire for a while, that had she given in and let Frank come home with her, they would indeed be in bed, and Frank would be inside her.

She stepped away from the window and bent down to her bedside table. She pulled open the bottom drawer and lifted a velvet bag with a drawstring. Inside she removed her well used, very trusty vibrator. She pressed one switch and the head, shaped like a very large penis hummed. She pressed another switch and it began to rotate. Caroline held the rubber organ with one hand between her breasts and teased herself.

Her free hand slid down her belly and stopped almost of its own volition just above the tiny trimmed bush of hair. Slowly and purposefully Caroline walked her own fingers further until she touched her hard little nub and flicked it. Pleasure spiked deep inside. But she wanted to take her time, wanted to make it last, so she moved her fingers away.

Caroline looked over her shoulder towards the window. She couldn't go outside and do this, but she wanted to. Instead she moved back to the window and looked out into the snow. A couple were huddled together walking carefully along the pathway. Seeing them tipped her over, and leaning one hand on the sill she plunged the vibrator deep inside herself. With its throbbing and rotating action, and her own hand pushing it in and out, she moaned and writhed. Her hips moved against the toy, her mind only on the wonderful feeling of pleasure she was giving herself.

As the fire inside increased so did her movements. She bent her knees and met the vibrator plunge for plunge. She lifted her hand and slapped it against the window, bracing herself. Her breath fogged the glass as she panted. Her internal muscles were clenching and unclenching against the rubber hardness. She felt her orgasm coming and slowed her hips, again wanting to delay her climax.

Then as she pulled the vibrator out a little, her insides went to liquid as her thumb brushed over her most sensitive spot. Her hips thrust hard and she came fast and furious. She screamed out in pure pleasure, her body clamping and shuddering around the shaft of the toy, and as she pulled it back again, the vibrations made her come again.

Breathing hard and fast, Caroline slumped to the floor beneath her window. She sat with her legs splayed inelegantly, the vibrator slipping from her insides and buzzing in her limp hand. She felt satisfied. Closing her eyes, she smiled, an image popping into her head. She saw Frank walking into the room, a look of sheer shock on his face seeing her flopped on the floor. He had never seen her use the vibrator. Didn't know she even had it. Always, she had kept it hidden, and only pleasured herself when completely alone, and always with a locked door. Now she felt free and unfettered, and it felt very good.

Caroline stayed where she was for quite some time. She had switched off her toy and it lay still and quiet next to her. She was warm and comfortable, despite being propped up underneath the window. She dozed a little, tiny dreamless bouts of sleep. Eventually, stiffness in her spine began to irritate, and she rolled to her knees, massaging the small of her back.

Once the ache eased, she stood up and wrapped herself in her satin dressing gown. She had no idea what the time was and didn't really care. Without much thought of anything, she plodded into the lounge. The big modern clock on the wall told her it was only a quarter to six, it seemed much later. Maybe because so much had happened during the short December day, she mused.

A rumble from her tummy gave her a start. She hadn't noticed she was hungry. She frowned, she hadn't eaten all day. All she had had was coffee and hot chocolate.

"Hmm, stupid, stupid woman."

She told herself as she headed for the kitchen. She scrunched her face as she perused the inside of the refrigerator. There wasn't much, as she had expected to be on her honeymoon and hadn't filled it like she usually did. What there was, the boys would have finished up when they checked on the house, but of course, that wasn't needed now either.

Caroline found some cheese, and from the freezer took a microwave jacket potato. She shoved it in the oven and set the timer. Whilst she waited she grated the cheese and opened a bottle of Shiraz. She poured the wine into a large glass and took a gulp. It slid down her throat very nicely, so she took another smaller swallow. Topping up the glass, Caroline carried it and the bottle into the lounge. She put both on the coffee table, and went back to the kitchen just as the microwave pinged.

Caroline ate the whole potato, which she had smothered in butter and cheese. She had spent months watching her diet in readiness for the wedding and honeymoon. Even though she hadn't been overweight in the first place, she had just wanted to be toned. Now she indulged herself, and tomorrow she would worry about healthy eating again.

Despite her intention to down the entire bottle of wine, Caroline resisted and actually only had two glasses. Her empty plate sat on the coffee table, and she sat curled on the sofa cradling the glass in two hands. She had turned on the television, but hadn't watched anything. A jingling came from near the floor. She hadn't remembered bringing her handbag into the lounge, the last time she recalled seeing it was in the hall when she took off her clothes.

Sighing, she reached down and took her phone from the bag. There was a message showing on the screen from Derby. She opened it.

You ok Caroline. Haven't heard from you today and got worried. Boys said you were fine this morning. Please text and just let me know. xxxxx

A wave of guilt passed over her. Derby was her best friend and she hadn't given a thought to her all day. Quickly she tapped a reply.

So sorry sweetie. I'm fine. It's been a strange day. I'll call you tomorrow and tell you all about it. I'm tired but ok. Just chilling and having a glass of wine. Don't worry. I promise I am ok. Xxxx.

She hit send, then leaned back into the soft cosy sofa, exhaustion filling her. Her phone trilled.

Goody good. Get some proper sleep and I'll talk to you tomorrow. Xxxxx

Caroline finished her wine and lowered the glass to the floor. She didn't want to move. She shifted and settled more deeply into the sofa closing her eyes. Gradually her body relaxed, and the sound of the television faded as sleep took over. Strange dreams of snowmen dancing on the path outside her house invaded her sleep, but didn't wake her.

Caroline came awake slowly. Her eyelids flickered open and for a moment she wondered where she was. Blinking, she remembered and stretched her cramped legs. She was very warm. She pulled the front of her robe open and let the air cool her a little. Sitting up she wiggled her toes and let her feet drop to the carpet. She scrunched her toes into the pile and sighed at the pleasant feeling it gave her.

The clock on the wall said half past ten. Caroline was surprised she had slept so long. Stretching her arms wide and above her she felt refreshed. As she shifted, she saw her phone wedged in between the cushions. She pulled it out and habit had her pressing buttons and looking. Her mail icon showed a heavy inbox. She closed the phone not wanting to read any of them tonight. For a moment she tapped her hand against the back of the phone, then unlocked it again. She opened her mail and clicked on work mail. She quickly scanned the inbox, ignoring everything until she found the one she wanted. Jude Lore had replied.

Dear Caroline.

It would be a pleasure to meet you. I can be at your office at ten tomorrow. Please confirm.

Yours

Jude.

Caroline wrote a short reply. She explained the date and time would be perfect for her, but he should check if he could get to her office because of the snow. She pressed send and closed her phone, laying it on the coffee table. Bouncing to her feet, Caroline trotted to the kitchen and pulled a jar of hot chocolate from the cupboard. As a little luxury, she heated milk in a pan, instead of using hot water. It still wouldn't be as rich and creamy as Vera's yummy drink, but it would do.

With the mug in one hand and a plate of chocolate digestives in the other, Caroline returned to the lounge. Tucking both feet underneath her, she balanced the plate on her knee, dunked a biscuit in the hot chocolate and bit into it.

"Mmmm lovely."

She said out loud. She re-dunked and sucked the melting chocolate from the biscuit, giggling as it began to crumble between her fingers.

"Oops. Oh well. No one to see."

She popped the rest of the biscuit into her mouth, and licked chocolate from her fingers. She sipped her drink and then leaned forward retrieving her phone. She opened mail and found a new email from Jude Lore.

Dear Caroline.

I have no problem with the weather. I will be at your office at the aforementioned time. I have directions.

Yours

Jude.

Caroline burst out laughing. Jude Lore certainly had a way with words, even if he couldn't write to save his life.

"Well I assume you're a guy."

Caroline spoke to the phone, then shrugged, knowing she would find out the next day.

With her mind focused on work and her hurt pushed into a locked box at the back of it, Caroline switched off the lights and went to her bedroom. Her vibrator was still on the floor and she left it there. It didn't matter, no one else was going to be in her room.

Before climbing into bed, she looked out of the window. No one was out, and she expected that everyone was tucked up warm and snug. She opened the window a little and breathed in the crisp air. There was barely any sound, the white blanket muting even the clanging from the boats. A few flakes still fell, smaller and softer, floating gently to the ground, settling on the three inches already coating the paving. There were no tracks yet. Caroline drank in the sight, knowing as soon as the sun rose, the virgin snow would be disturbed and churned.

For a while she simply stood savouring the beauty of the night. Clouds still swirled above, occasionally breaking and allowing the odd twinkle of starlight. But from her little knowledge of the weather, it looked to her like more snow was on the way.

She closed the window and slipped out of her robe, slipping under her puffy warm duvet. As she settled under the cover and closed her eyes, she hoped Jude Lore would be able to get through, and their meeting could go ahead.

Caroline dressed carefully for her meeting with Jude Lore. Her usual office attire consisted of navy, black or grey suits and white blouses, but today she wanted something less formal. She wanted to look feminine but professional at the same time. So she donned a deep red pencil skirt, and an off white turtle neck cashmere sweater. She pulled on a pair of wellington boots for the short treck to her office, carrying red low heeled shoes in a bag to change into when she arrived.

The office was warm, the timer having been set so the heating came on earlier. Even though she was supposed to be on holiday, she didn't want to risk any problems caused by weather whilst she was away. She set the coffee pot and booted up her laptop. She sent Jude Lore's submission to the printer and poured herself a cup of coffee whilst she waited. It didn't take long. She lifted the very small pile of paper from the printer tray and tapped it against the desk to line it up.

Sitting down, she sighed. Three chapters in so few pages was not a good sign. She hadn't really noticed when she scanned it on the computer. Now sipping coffee, she quickly and expertly began to read. She was in fits of giggles after the first chapter. The main character spent the whole time in a log cabin, in front of an open fire, on a fur rug, drinking champagne and having sex with a stream of beautiful buxom women. Each description of the experience was the same, each woman virtually identical except for the colour of her hair. Chapter two and three was a repeat, but each with a different setting.

Caroline put the sheets back together and laid the pile in front of her. She folded her hands on top and lowered her head. She sighed. She had no idea what she was thinking of, asking to meet Jude Lore. He or she, couldn't write. So why was she bringing the poor person to her? Jude Lore would be thinking there was a chance of a publishing deal. There was no likelihood of that ever happening.

Feeling frustrated with herself, Caroline stood and paced her office. It was too late to contact Jude now, the meeting was too close. Shaking her head, she poured more coffee and took her cup over to the window. The winter scene was very different from the night before. Early in the morning, someone from the marina's staff had shovelled a lot of the snow from the paths, and salted the cleared areas. There was still deep snow around the edges and in parts of the car park, but it now looked dull and grubby.

She watched a big black Mercedes four by four enter the car park. It glided efficiently over patches of packed snow and into a parking bay. A man in a dark suit hopped from the driver's seat and opened the back door. Curious now, Caroline stared. A tall man stepped out of the car. From the angle of her office she couldn't discern his features, but she had an inkling this might be Jude Lore.

For some reason unknown to her, Caroline suddenly felt nervous. Usually when she was about to meet an author she felt in control and sure of herself. Today was different. She checked her hair and makeup in the mirror hanging behind her desk, and then sat down. She clasped her hands on top of the note pad she had placed next to the sample chapters, and then immediately stood up, her hands behind her back.

A buzzing made her jump until she realised it was the external door phone. She quickly answered.

"Good morning."

She said, a nervous quiver in her voice. A very deep, sexy, and very male voice replied.

"Hello, my name is Jude Lore, I have a meeting with Caroline Shelton."

Caroline cleared her throat and hoped she didn't sound as nervous as she felt.

"Yes, top floor, middle office on the right."

She replied pressing the button to unlock the main entrance.

Caroline waited in Adele's office, and jumped again when a tap came on the outer door. Taking a deep calming breath she reached for the handle and turned. She placed a smile on her lips as she came face to face with Jude Lore. He wasn't at all as she expected, although she thought she hadn't really known what to expect.

He was tall, over six feet and very blonde. At first she thought his hair was dyed, but his skin was so pale she guessed it was probably natural. Not wanting to stare and freak him out, she glanced back over her shoulder and indicated the office with her hand.

"Come in."

She said, stepping back to allow him access. Jude Lore stepped over the threshold and took the hand she held out. He had a firm grip.

“I’m Caroline. My assistant is on holiday, long story, but please come through to my office.”

Caroline heard herself gabbling, but couldn’t seem to stop. He smiled down at her and she felt her insides go to mush.

Caroline’s cheeks began to flush, and to hide it she turned quickly and led the way into her own office. As she reached her desk, she took a breath and believing she had gained some composure, turned to face him. He had stopped near the chair opposite hers. She held out a hand.

“Please sit down.”

Jude Lore smiled again as he lowered himself into the comfortable leather seat she had offered. Caroline sat down and placed her hands on her desk. She closed her eyes briefly, then opened them and looked at him full in the face.

He was still smiling and Caroline felt mesmerised. His smile was alluring, showing perfectly straight gleaming white teeth. Naturally white, she thought. His blonde hair reached his neckline, and was fashionably cut so the front flopped over his face. But it didn’t cover his eyes. They were blue, piercingly blue, sapphire with a ring of diamond bright flecks.

Unable to tear her eyes away she drank in the rest of him. He was young, his email had said thirty. Slender, wide shouldered and wiry, but she could see muscle under the ivory linen suit he wore. His cheekbones were high, almost feminine except for his very masculine square jaw. His skin was so pale against full deep pink lips that Caroline shuddered slightly. Vampirish, she thought. Jude Lore's smile widened and Caroline believed he had actually read her mind. She almost expected to see long fangs emerge. Jude Lore gave a small chuckle, deep and sexy. Caroline gasped, sure he definitely knew what she was thinking.

"So what did you think of my novel?"

Caroline mentally shook herself as his throaty voice penetrated her thoughts and broke the hold he had on her. She swallowed and then cleared her throat in a professional manner.

"First, excuse my manners, it's been a strange few days. Would you like some coffee?"

His smile widened even more, and his eyes seemed to give off their own internal light.

"Tea please, black and unsweetened."

Each word was perfectly pronounced, purely English, but so masculine Caroline felt fire flicker at her centre. She nodded and stood up.

"I have to go through to Adele's office to get it. Make yourself comfortable please."

Caroline leaned against the small table in Adele's office waiting for the kettle to boil. She was shaking a little and had no idea why. The young man in her office was doing something to her that she couldn't control. She had no idea how he was doing it. Charisma didn't even cut it. Frank had plenty of that, but even he couldn't cause this trembling, and wetness she felt between her legs just by looking at her. Again the idea of vampire invaded her thoughts, and a tingle on the back of her neck had her looking over her shoulder. She almost expected him to be there, silent and waiting to sink those glistening teeth into her neck, but the office was empty.

The kettle clicked off, making her jump again. She took some steadying breaths and told herself to grow up and stop being stupid. She made his tea, choosing a delicate cup and saucer instead of a mug. She believed she'd read him right enough that he would appreciate the gesture. She carried the beverage into her office on a small tray, and with every ounce of control, managed to deliver it to him without spillage. He watched her every move, the smile never leaving his lips.

"Thank you."

He said as she retook her place at the desk. He lifted the cup and sipped.

"Mmm that's very nice."

He said. Caroline lifted the sample chapters and tapped them together, even though they were already neat. Jude carefully placed the cup in the saucer and held out a hand palm up. Slender long fingers and neatly clipped pearly nails had Caroline's mouth watering.

"So what did you think?"

He asked again.

Caroline picked up a pen and rapped it against the papers. She pressed her lips together and sat up a little straighter. She was determined to take control of the meeting.

"Well first Mr Lore, you can tell me your real name."

His smile changed to a full grin, transforming his sculpted features into boyish mischievousness. Caroline's internal muscles clenched and her heart began to race.

"How did you know?"
He asked cheekily. Caroline took a deep breath.

"I'm an experienced literary agent. Besides, Jude Lore, a play on Jude Law the actor."
She replied, her professionalism finally breaking through and snapping the hold he seemed to have on her. Jude Lore tilted his head to one side and penetrated her with his eyes. Caroline felt heat radiating through her body. This man isn't human, she thought. His eyes are like fucking lasers. She bit her lower lip, afraid she would say the words out loud. Jude Lore grinned.

"My name is Gregory Taylor-York."
He told her, giving her a look that said the name should mean something to her.

"Am I supposed to know who you are?"
She asked, again reasserting herself. He shrugged and tapped a finger nail on the edge of the saucer.

"Taylor-York, of the York Estate. Second or third, fourth, something anyway cousins to the Queen."
He stated regally. It was Caroline's turn to shrug.

"I'm sorry, I'm not familiar with your name nor your heritage."
She was beginning to regret the meeting. It wasn't going the way it should. Gregory sensed her mood, threw his head back and laughed. A wonderful deep sound that had her nerves tingling.

"Oh do not apologise, please. It's so refreshing to meet someone who does not know my family name. God, mother and grandmother would have you sent to the tower. Well a hundred years ago anyway, but today, they would still feel the same."

Caroline felt herself begin to relax for the first time since she had seen him step out of his car. His words sounded so mature compared to his looks and his smile. It was like being in the room with two people. Giving herself a mental shake, she turned the conversation back to the reason they were here, the novel.

"Ok, Gregory, now that's cleared up, let's get down to business."

She said, reshuffling the papers on her desk. Gregory slid down in his chair a little and lifted one long leg, resting his ankle across his knee. He raised his hands dramatically.

"Let's hear it. And please call me Gregg, Gregory sounds so…English."

Caroline huffed out a chuckle. Everything about him was so English. But she would comply.

"Right Gregg. Well I have to tell you straight. Your novel won't get a publishing deal."

Gregg frowned.

"If that's so, why ask to see me?"

Caroline leaned back in her seat. She rubbed her tongue over her teeth and tapped her pen.

"I was intrigued."

She stated.

Gregory grinned. He dropped his foot to the floor and leaned forward placing his elbows on the desk. His jacket cuffs slid up a little, exposing wrists as pale as his face, covered in almost gold blonde hairs. He clasped his fingers together and gave her his piercing laser stare. Caroline felt herself being drawn forward, as though he was pulling her on an invisible thread.

"What intrigued you?"

His voice had gone lower and husky, oozing sex appeal. Caroline's mouth watered. Involuntarily, the tip of her tongue slipped between her lips and her breasts rose and fell as she took short sharp breaths. His smile widened knowingly.

"So?"

It was barely a whisper, his lips hardly moving. Caroline's gaze was fixed on his mouth, imagining his lips on hers, his tongue flicking hers, then plunging into the wetness between her thighs, sating the throb that was deep inside. Her hand was already reaching across the desk towards his, when she realised what she was doing. Blinking, she brought herself out of the near hypnotic state he had put her under. She bit her lip and sat back, regaining control.

"Um." She coughed. "Well, if I'm honest I don't really know."

She finally managed to say. Gregg simply watched her, waiting. She fiddled with her pen and the papers, then cleared her throat. Her mouth was now dry. She took a sip from her mug and swallowed stone cold coffee, but it helped.

"First I checked out your synopsis. Hmm, what there was of it. You know, a sketch isn't a synopsis. I nearly binned your submission then and there."

Finally Caroline felt composed. Her professionalism took over and she relaxed into her work. Gregg opened his mouth to reply, but now she had her emotions under control, she didn't want to risk them jogging off elsewhere again. So before he could speak she continued.

"I don't actually know what made me read the sample chapters. All I can say is it's been a dreadful

weekend. One I want to put behind me, so I came into work when I shouldn't be here at all."
She was gabbling again, but couldn't stop, and Gregg was silent, still and listening intently.

"You know, you're lucky I even opened your submission. My website expressly stated I wasn't accepting submissions until the new year. Yet you and about a million, well a couple of hundred, still went ahead and sent them anyway."

She sighed deeply, agitated without understanding why. Gregg still sat like an alabaster statue. So still and calm, Caroline thought he had drifted to sleep with his eyes wide open. Or dead, she thought with a jolt. That would really top off the last few days. Then she saw the gentle rise of his chest as he breathed calmly and steadily. He was waiting for more.

"So. Well, sorry. Rant over. Where was I? Oh yes, the synopsis. A brilliant sketch, very detailed."
She blushed a little and a tiny almost imperceptible smile creased his lips. She looked away, embarrassed he'd noticed.

"Um…yes very good. But not a synopsis. You have to write that. I need to know what the novel is about. What the key characters are like."
She paused.

"Do you want another cup of tea?"
She asked.

Gregg leaned back in his chair and stretched his long legs under the desk. He lifted one arm and ruffled his blonde hair at the back of his neck. His white shirt parted where the top button was undone. Soft hair, like on his wrists, peeked out of the V of his shirt.

Caroline's eyes were transfixed on the gap. Gregg let out a long slow breath.

"No thankyou. I want you."

Caroline gasped, unsure she had heard his words correctly.

"Wh…pardon?"

Gregg leaned forward and whispered.

"You heard me."

CHAPTER 8.

Caroline stood up and pushed her chair away from the desk. She was confused, and fear crept up through her like icy tentacles. She looked about her office. She was alone, on the top floor. No one could see her through the window, and the offices had been designed for privacy, so no one from the other businesses would be able to hear her if she screamed. Her eyes flicked to the phone. But she wouldn't get to it fast enough. Her thoughts collided and she tried to organise them. How stupid she'd been to arrange this meeting. No one knew she was here. No one knew he was here. Always meetings took place with Adele in her own office, a safety valve that had never been needed.

In her state of near panic, Caroline didn't see or notice Gregg move from his chair. She flinched when he came to her side and nearly screamed out then. She bit it back wondering if her fear would drive him. In all her years she had read and admonished women who put themselves in dangerous situations. Always prided herself on keeping to rules that kept her safe. And here she was breaking every one of them. She dug her nails into her palms, trying to plan a flight or fight strategy in her mind.

She did cry out when she felt feather like fingers slide across her cheek. Then she bit it back before it became a full blown scream. She went rigid, hoping her stillness would deter him. His fingers were gentle and slowly closed around her jaw, cupping it tenderly.

"Sh, Caroline. I'm not going to hurt you."
His voice was soft and soothing. His thumb massaged her mouth just to the side of her lip. Still she remained tense.

"I promise you Caroline. I will not do anything that you don't want me to do."
His lips were close to her ear, his warm breath fanning her cheek.

"Then let me go."
She said, her voice trembling with fear. He chuckled dangerously.

"I'm doing nothing to stop you."
She looked up into eyes that were now burning with desire. And as suddenly as the fear had come it was gone. But he wasn't. She turned, just a fraction and in that moment her body reacted, tipping her over, filling her with lust, wanting his hands everywhere.

Gregg sensed the change and lifted his other hand cupping her face. He planted his feet firmly, leaving a gap between their bodies. Then, his eyes boring into hers, he lowered his head. She waited, holding her breath for his lips, but he held them just away from her. She couldn't move. Then he gave her what she craved. His mouth covered hers, and as her lips parted he plunged his tongue inside. Caroline melted, her knees going weak. She gripped his hard muscular arms to stop herself from falling and drank in his kiss. As it deepened, it took all of her resolve not to lift her legs and wrap them about him. Gregg still maintained the gap between them and Caroline squirmed to get closer, desperate to press up against his body. She was sure she would feel hardness if she could only make contact, and frustration was mounting inside.

Then he moved away. His lips left hers and she felt bereft. He stroked her hair as tears began to trickle down her cheeks.

"Caroline why are you sad?"

He asked. She lowered her head until her chin practically touched her chest. She was throbbing inside, angry and embarrassed at the same time. She wanted him inside her, wanted him to give her relief. She wanted to come around his hard cock.

"Why did you stop?"

She mumbled, hating herself for asking. She didn't do this, sex with a stranger. Yet that's exactly what she wanted to do, then and right there. Gregg chuckled.

"I haven't stopped, because I haven't even started yet."

Caroline's head snapped up.

"What? Oh God what am I thinking? I can't do this."

She moved away from him. The distance, even though small, breaking his magnetic hold. She stepped over to the window and looked out onto the normality of the day. Inside she was still shaking, her deepest centre aching for release. But she had some modicum of control now.

"I'm sorry. That was so very unprofessional." She murmured. She didn't hear him move, and was shocked when he whispered into her ear.

"Don't be sorry Caroline. Let's sit down and go from there."

Caroline pulled herself away from the window and sat back at her desk. Gregg retook his own seat and settled himself into a relaxed position.

"So, your submission. Like I said, it's weak and has no characterisation…"

"Nothing has changed Caroline."
Gregg cut across her. She sat up angrily. He smiled, that same devilish grin that had her insides burning all over again.

"Then what?"
She snapped. He remained calm, infuriating her more.

"I still want you Caroline."
Caroline picked up her pen and slammed it on top of the papers. She frowned and gave him a look that could freeze water.

"Look I don't…"
Gregg lifted a hand silencing her outburst.

"I didn't know I wanted you until I saw you standing in front of me. I really did come here to talk about my novel. But…as you have given your professional opinion of it, that no longer applies. What does, is my desire for you."
Gregg paused. Caroline wasn't sure if it was for effect, or just to let his words sink in. It did both.

"And?"
She said sarcastically, to which he simply grinned more. Caroline closed her eyes and sighed.

"I'm rich Caroline."

"So?"
She said abruptly.

"I'm very rich. More than I actually know."
He replied with all the patience of a saint.

"Good for you. And I say again, so?"
Disdain dripping from her tongue. Gregg didn't react which made Caroline even madder. Instead he continued as though she hadn't spoke.

"I can buy anything I want, have anything I want…"
He began, but Caroline cut him off furiously.

"Not me you can't!"
Gregg shook his head slowly.

"Caroline, Caroline. That's what I'm saying. I can have anything my heart desires that money can buy. That includes some women, but not you. I want you, but only if you're willing and…ready."

Caroline blushed, her cheeks matching her skirt. She had been ready and he knew it. He smiled at her flush and again she had the feeling he could read her mind. She didn't know what to do. She opened her mouth to speak, still unsure of what she was going to say, but Gregg held up a hand, again silencing her.

"Before you say anything there's something you need to know."
Caroline bit her lip.

"Go on."

"I'm rich and I have personal doctors. I'm also very careful."
He paused and Caroline wondered where his words were going.

"I like sex very much, but I like my health even more. So to start with I have to insist on using a

condom. My doctor will take a full sexual history from you and check you over…"
Caroline's mouth opened in shock, but she couldn't respond. Gregg carried on as though she hadn't moved.

"Once your tests come back clear, we can indulge fully. You will enjoy it, I can guarantee that."

Caroline couldn't believe what she was hearing. She stood up and placed her hands firmly on her desk. Leaning forward slightly she gave him a contemptuous look. She was about to launch into a tirade that would send him from her office with his tail between his legs, and all of his riches shoved up his backside. But as she took in a breath to begin, a thought niggled at the back of her mind. She tried to grasp it. It slipped away, floated and reappeared. Closing her eyes, she grappled with it and finally caught it. As it materialised in the front of her mind, so did realisation.

"Oh God. Oh my God!"
She cried out. Gregg stayed in his seat and shrugged.

"I'm sorry if I've upset you, but that's the way it has to be."

"Go. You have to go. Now!"

Gregg stood up and pushed his chair under the desk neatly. He clasped his hands in front of him.

"Think it over Caroline. I will not give up easily. I can give you pleasures beyond your imagination. I have your card, I will call you tonight. Be ready."
The only indication Caroline had that he had left the office was the quiet click of the door. She opened her eyes and slowly sank into her chair, her knees weak. She felt flutters of fear in her heart. Not from Gregg's

ultimatum, but from the thought that had invaded her being.

Caroline shakily reached for the phone and tapped out a number she knew by heart. She dreaded speaking to Frank, especially after the night before, but she had to know. He answered quickly.

"Caroline, I didn't expect to hear from you."
He said, joy in his voice. Caroline swallowed the lump that was stuck in her throat.

"First of all Frank, I don't want to speak to you, but I have to."

"Ok."

"Just one question really. All those other women you've been fucking behind my back, were you careful, and have you ever had yourself tested?"
She closed her eyes, dreading his response, unsure if he would tell her the truth.

"Caroline it was only Tania."
He replied. She winced. He hadn't been straight with her she knew, she remembered the women at the wedding. In a low furious voice she said.

"Do not fuck with me Frank. I know there have been others. Tell me the fucking truth. You do know about STIs don't you? You're not stupid, you know about HIV. I just want to know the truth."
She waited and heard him sigh.

"Alright Caroline. There's been others. But I swear I used a condom with them. They… they…um…were…young. I didn't want them to get pregnant."
Tears began to seep from her eyes. Tania was her age, and although pregnancy was still possible, she didn't think for one minute he had taken the same precautions

with her. She had no idea how many sexual partners Tania had had, nor if she practiced safe sex. The women at the wedding had been of various ages, and had partners. But since Frank made no mention of them, Caroline knew he wasn't being completely honest with her, wouldn't admit to them if she asked.

"And Tania?"

She asked, her voice trembling. Frank was quiet and she thought he wasn't going to answer.

"Fuck you Frank, answer me you prick!"

She screamed down the phone.

"No all right. No. I didn't use anything with Tania."

He finally replied. Sobbing now she could barely get out her next words.

"I hate you Frank. Not once ever, have you thought about what you might do to me, and to my boys. Now I have to go and get tested and pray to God that I'm ok. Go to hell Frank, Tania's welcome to you."

She slammed the phone down and laid her head on her arms crying uncontrollable. On Saturday, she hadn't thought Frank could hurt her more when she discovered his infidelity again, but today she knew she was wrong.

Caroline had no idea how long she stayed motionless sobbing. Eventually the tears began to subside and she slowly lifted her head. The office looked out of focus, the furniture bleary. She knew it was because of the puffiness and moisture in her eyes. She sniffed, barely able to breathe. She hated crying. It bunged up her sinuses and made her head ache.

Feeling like her head was submerged under water, Caroline dragged herself to her feet. Her nose cleared slightly but her ears still felt muffled. With her shoulders limp she plodded to the window and yanked it open. Icy air rushed at her and she took some deep breaths. It helped a lot. The stuffiness began to ease, and after a few more gulps of coldness, she could breathe clearly again.

If only the winter cold could ease her aching heart too, she thought. She began to shiver, her jumper not thick enough to compete with the temperature. But she didn't move. She watched the boats bob gently on the water, and heard the sliding sound of snow falling from the masts. Across the marina, the shops were busy. Most of them sold specialist products, and people came from all over the county to buy unusual Christmas presents.

That train of thought took her to the gift wrapped in expensive paper and satin bows, buried at the bottom of her suitcase. The present she had bought Frank and should have given him on Christmas morning on a sunny beach. For a moment she imagined the scene. He would unwrap it, a gold identity bracelet with the inscription *From your wife Caroline.* He would kiss her and smile and say how much he loved it. She would wrap her arms around him, and that would lead to sex.

A shiver that shook her, brought her back to reality. She was very cold by now. She tugged the window closed and wrapped her arms around herself, rubbing her shoulders. She slipped out of her heels and reached into the little storage cabinet at the back of her office retrieving her wellies. Soon she was bundled in winter attire. She grabbed her bag, checked her phone was in it and locked up the office. She jabbed the button on the lift and waited.

When it arrived she sighed, thankful it was empty. As she descended, she mulled over what she was going to do. Go home first and get changed, she told herself. The lobby was empty too and that surprised her. The small block of offices was usually very busy. Outside she glanced towards the car park. There were few cars, most of them belonging to employees of the shops and marina. She only recognised one that belonged to a small advertising agency on the middle floor. It seemed most people had stayed at home because of the snow.

As she trod her way carefully to her home, Caroline thought she had locked herself in a bubble since Saturday. Apart from being at Derby's and the walk along the river, she hadn't been anywhere, or really seen anyone. She hadn't bothered with television and hadn't listened to any news. She mentally shook herself. She would rectify that as soon as she was home.

The minute she walked into her home, Caroline yanked off her boots and flicked on the television to a news channel. She stripped out of her clothes as she watched. The headlines were all about the weather. The whole country was covered in snow. Roads were closed, and cars and lorries were stuck in drifts, some as high as eight feet. Rural areas were cut off, and emergency services had been working non-stop to reach the vulnerable. There were power outages across parts of the North, Wales and the South West. Caroline was quite shocked, and for the first time since he had left the office, she thought about Gregg. How had he got here this morning, and was he alright going back?

Caroline collected her clothes and strolled into her bedroom. She returned in jeans and a thick jumper and caught the end of the weather forecast. More heavy snow was expected, and it didn't show any signs of letting up, at least not for the rest of the week. Caroline made herself coffee and sat on the sofa absorbed in the news. There were brief reports on other events, the stock market and some from around the world, but mostly it centred on the extreme weather. According to David Brayn, the meteorologist, it was the worst snowfall in eighty years.

Caroline sipped her drink and for a moment tuned out, thinking back to her childhood. She remembered one winter where the snow had fallen thickly. They had a little dog, not a pedigree, just a small black and white mongrel called Cindy. She was cute and only a puppy at the time. She had bounded out into the fresh snow and leaped at a drift against the wall of the garden. She disappeared. Then as Caroline watched from the warmth of their lounge, her head bobbed up and her black ears peeked out from the drift. Her father had gone outside and lifted Cindy out of the snow. She came excitedly, wagging her tail and trying to lick him all over. Later that day, her whole family had gone into the garden and built snowmen.

Caroline's mind came forward to when her own sons were little. There had been very few snowfalls during those years. On the odd occasions the snow had come, she had spent time with Leo and Liam, throwing snowballs, making snowmen and snow angels. Her small family had laughed and enjoyed those moments. And when they were all wet and cold, they went inside, changed into snug cosy clothes, and cuddled up on the sofa watching DVDs, and drinking hot chocolate.

Caroline smiled at the memories, before she re-focused on the news of the day.

Even though the snow was causing disruption almost everywhere, Caroline wanted to go out. She had already bought Leo and Liam's Christmas presents, and gifts for Derby, Geoff and Melody. A parcel had been mailed to Spain for her parents and another to Richmond, Virginia, for her brother Noah and his family. She missed him. They hadn't seen each other in three years. They emailed and talked on Skype, but Noah couldn't afford to come back to England for a visit. He had managed to fund a trip to Spain to see their parents, and was hoping to come home sometime next year.

Since setting up her literary agency, Caroline hadn't taken time off, in fact the honeymoon was going to be the first real holiday in all that time. Sighing, she told herself that she would make an effort to visit America and Spain, see all of her family. The business was doing well, and though she wasn't rich, she had a healthy bank balance.

That thought brought her back to the day. It was still early, so she decided to go into the city and get a few more presents. A smile broke across her lips. She would also buy a tree and new decorations. Her old artificial one was in the storage unit that came with her house, along with decorations bought years ago. Today, was a new beginning, and a new tree and pretty ornaments and lights would be part of it.

Driving into the city was dicey, but Caroline took her time. Luckily for her it wasn't far and the main road in had been ploughed. It wasn't completely clear, two lanes down to one central one, but it was traversable. Parking was more difficult. All of the outside car parks were covered in deep snow, but the multi-storeys had been salted at the entrances and the lower levels were clear.

The city centre was quiet due to the weather. Most of the pavements had been cleared and gritted, but the side roads and park areas were blanketed. It all looked beautiful, but dangerous. With several shopping bags, Caroline entered a well known chain of coffee shops. She ordered and sat at a window seat. She had already bought her tree and stowed it in the car. In the bags were decorations and lights, and more gifts for Leo and Liam. She wanted to spoil them, they had been hurt too. That train of thought led to the problem of Christmas day. She knew her boys had planned to spend it with friends, but she was supposed to be away. She sighed over her coffee, wondering where she was going to be on Christmas morning.

On her second cup of coffee, Caroline took her phone from her bag. She hadn't bothered looking at it since leaving her office, and she hadn't heard it from the bottom of her handbag. There were three messages. The first was from Derby.

Hi sweetie, how are you today?xxxx

Caroline quickly tapped a reply.

I'm ok. Got some stuff to tell you, will call this evening. Don't worry I haven't changed my mind about Frank.xxxx

She knew she had to add the last bit to the message or Derby would worry and had good reason. She had gone back to Frank so many times, but not any more. The second message was from Frank. She read it with an angry frown.

Darling, please don't let this be the end. I know I've done wrong and I'm sorry. Call me, please, I love you. Xxxx

Caroline deleted that one. The third was from Leo.

Mum, just checking in on you. Liam and me want to be sure you're ok. Do you want us to come round tonight, I'll cook. Love you lots xxxx

Caroline giggled, her heart filling with love for her son. She tapped a reply.

I really am alright but would love you two to come over. You cook? Pizza it is then. Love you so very much and tell Liam the same. See you about seven. Xxxx

Caroline set her phone by her side and finished her drink. If she was honest with herself she was a little disappointed. She had hoped one of the messages would be from Gregg. But he said he would call her tonight. Her heart gave a little skip. She should be furious with him. She should dislike his arrogance and selfishness. Then she realised, Gregg was and had been far more mature about sex than she was.

Not once in all the years had she thought about her own sexual health. In all honesty it had never crossed her mind. Yes she had taken precautions to avoid pregnancy, but even though Frank had cheated so many times, she hadn't ever considered sexually transmitted infections. She had talked to her boys about safe sex, but never once thought about it for herself.

She shuddered, afraid again of the possibilities. She would have to get herself down to one of the clinics and get a full screening. She didn't know anything about them or the process though. She felt a flush of embarrassment creep across her cheeks. A grown woman of forty seven and she was more naïve than a teenager. she didn't know where to begin, didn't even know where any of the clinics were. She didn't even know what they were called to do a search on the internet.

"Are you ok?"

A young assistant asked her as she began clearing the table. Caroline looked at her, puzzled.

"You just look as though something has really bothered you."

The girl said. Caroline gave her a tiny smile, and for a second had the notion of asking her if she knew where she should go. Instead she said.

"Um, I'm fine. Just a few things on my mind. Thanks for asking."

The girl nodded and lifted the tray with the empty cups, spun on her toes and carried on with her job.

Caroline lifted her bags and left the shop. The sky was grey and heavy with clouds. David Brayn had been right. It was going to snow again. The first few flakes were beginning to float down to the ground as Caroline walked into the car park. With deep concentration and care, she drove towards home, the snow falling more thickly every minute. By the time she reached her own parking space at the marina, she could barely see in front of her. She grabbed her bags, and the box with the tree and plodded through fresh snow to her door.

Once inside, she stamped her feet and dumped her purchases on the floor. She took off her coat and hung it up. She pulled her boots off and padded into her lounge with her shopping. She left the presents for the boys in their carrier bags. The decorations she tipped onto the floor, carefully as some were made of glass. She plonked down onto the carpet and began unwrapping the tree.

An hour later the tree was standing in the corner just to the side of the large window overlooking the water. She had chosen it because it was different. Ever since she was a child she'd had a traditional green tree. Sometimes a real fresh pine one, other times an artificial one. Her knew tree was neither.

It was six feet tall and looked like a tree, that is one with branches, no leaves and covered in sparkly snow. With white lights and gleaming baubles, it twinkled and glittered. A silver angel sat on top, her hands clasped in prayer, her wings glistening. Caroline sat on her sofa and just looked. Outside the sky had darkened, night coming early in December. Snow was still falling, in straight lines, no breeze to swirl it around. The room was unlit except for the tree and it felt peaceful and calm.

Her mobile phone tinkled and Caroline smiled. It would be Derby. She had purposely set the ring tone to recognise her friend, and the sound was like Melody laughing.

"Hi."

She said on answering.

"How are you doing?"

Derby replied. Caroline shrugged even though Derby couldn't see her.

"I'm alright. The boys are coming 'round later, Liam's cooking."

There was a pause from Derby and Caroline giggled.

"Yeah, I know, that means chucking a pizza and garlic bread in the oven, but I don't care. Just having them here will be great."

"Good to know. So what have you been doing today?"
Derby replied. Caroline went on to tell her about the day, but for some reason held back all that had happened with Gregg. She only mentioned she had a new client but no details. She did elaborate on her shopping trip and the tree though.

"So you're coming to us for Christmas then?"
Derby said, and Caroline took a breath. Christmas day had given her pause for thought earlier, but Derby actually mentioning it brought it to stark reality. Of course she would spend it with her friends, her sons had plans, but she suddenly felt like she would be intruding.

"Um… I don't really know Derby. I'll be miserable and it won't be fair on your family to inflict that on you…"

"Caroline, shut up. We're your best friends, and I know Geoff will agree with me when I say we refuse to allow you to be on your own. So no arguing, you're coming here for Christmas. And if the boys change their minds and want to come too, well that's even better."

Caroline knew she didn't stand a chance of disagreeing with Derby once she used that tone. Despite having been a mouse for most of her life, Derby had fully come out of herself over the last few years. She was now a force to be reckoned with when her mind was set. Caroline didn't object, she was happy that her friend had finally found her way in the world.

"Ok, I give. Yours it is. I'll check with the boys later."

She sighed, not realising it was loud enough for Derby to hear.

"What's wrong?"

She asked, her voice gentle now. Caroline felt her breath hitch and a tear rolled down her cheek. She swiped at it.

"It's horrible Derby. And I don't know where to go to get it sorted."

"Caroline, you're not making any sense."

Derby said, concerned now. Caroline took a very deep breath and let it out slowly. She then launched into her argument with Frank. She omitted Gregg's part. She heard Derby gasp at the end of the phone.

"My God Caroline. That man needs his balls cut off."

Caroline found herself laughing. She imagined her friend's face, all scrunched up and furious, and definitely not in the presence of Melody. She heard Geoff mumble something in the background and Derby saying, "Yep him." to her fiancé.

"I totally agree Derby, but what do I do?"

Caroline asked.

"Um…do you want me to ask Geoff?"

Caroline felt her cheeks heat. But she also knew Geoff would be sensitive and caring about her situation. She was nodding before she realised Derby couldn't see her.

"Yes please."

She said barely above a whisper.

"Ok. Hold on a mo'."

The line went almost quiet except for a little low murmuring. As she waited patiently, Caroline strolled over to the window and watched the snow falling. It was again coming thick and fast. For a moment she worried her boys wouldn't get over, she worried Derby and Geoff would get snowed in, their house being out in the country, she worried about her health. Just as she thought her worries would take over, Derby came back on the phone.

"Geoff says you can go to a dedicated clinic where they will take a confidential history and do all the tests. I'll text you the address and number to call them. If you want, I'll come with you."

Caroline thanked her friend. She knew Derby would do just that, but the thought of going to such a place had her trembling all over. She didn't even know if she would go, knew she had to do something, but dreaded doing it.

"I'll call them tomorrow and let you know."

Caroline told her before saying night, night and hanging up.

Still in front of the window, the snow forgotten Caroline mulled over her predicament. Her phone chirped and she saw a message from Derby with the details of the clinic. The address was in the city. Caroline wrapped her arms around herself. How could she, a forty seven year old woman go there. It would be full of teenagers and twenty somethings, she was sure. They would all be aware about sexual health and would give her disparaging looks. She could just imagine their heads shaking as if to say, 'She should know better at her age. Look at us we're careful. Grown ups lecture us on safe sex, but don't practice what they preach.'

She battled with her mind. If they, the young ones were at the clinic, maybe they weren't so careful.

Maybe they had been stupid too. They couldn't all be there because of a mistake, or a torn condom. But no matter how she looked at it, the thought of going still brought her terror. Then a new thought invaded. What if she saw someone she knew? Exeter was a big place. Her sons had grown up here. One of their friends could be there.

Caroline crumpled. She had to know if she was ok. But there were so many reasons not to go to the clinic. Maybe Gregg was right. She could see his personal doctor, have all the tests done and no one would know. But that would mean accepting his conditions. Was she really up to what he obviously had in mind.

"Yes you idiot. You got all hot and juicy when he was just sitting opposite you."

She growled out loud. Then her face flushed and she felt a throb between her thighs.

"Caroline, you know what you want, and you know you want him. Fuck, I bet he won't even phone tonight. Bet I've blown it."

She admonished herself, her nails digging in her palms.

CHAPTER 9.

Caroline was curled up on the sofa sipping a glass of red wine when she heard her boys in the hallway. She smiled and stood up to greet them. She padded towards their voices and warmth flooded through her. Her sons were chatting. She overheard Liam bragging about something he had done at the aquarium that had impressed a new girl. Just as she poked her head around the door, she caught Leo throwing a mock thump at his brother's shoulder. Liam saw his mother and put on a face.

"Ouch. Mum, he's punching me again."

He pretended to whine. Leo barked out a laugh and Caroline creased up too.

"Come on you two, stop fighting and give your mother a hug."

Both Leo and Liam flung their arms around her and lifted her off her feet. She hugged them back and felt happy. She had her family with her, that's all that mattered at the moment. As she regained her feet, she pushed everything else to the back of her mind and led the way to the kitchen.

An hour later, the three were sitting on the lounge floor munching on pizza, garlic bread and potato wedges. All had cans of beer, and they were happily engrossed in The Polar Express Christmas film on the television. Caroline was cosy and chilled out. No matter how old her children got, they still enjoyed watching seasonal movies with their mum. She hoped it was something they would never grow out of. Her thoughts drifted, and she imagined her boys married to lovely girls. She pictured bright grandchildren, all of them gathered in front of the TV watching Christmas films.

Her mobile rang, her work ring tone. Leo looked up and sighed. He pressed pause on the remote, and Caroline pulled herself up and grabbed her phone from the coffee table.

"Won't be a minute."

She told her sons as she took the call and wandered from the room. The number was unknown, but she had an inkling who it would be, and didn't want to talk in front of Leo and Liam. Especially since Gregg was not much older than her boys, just a boy himself she thought.

"Hello."

She tried for professional but her voice came out too breathy.

"Good evening Caroline. I said I would call."

It was him and her nerves jangled, her body reacting to his voice in a way she wasn't used to, and didn't want it to.

"Um, yes you did. Look, I have my sons 'round. We're eating and watching a film, I can't really talk right now."
She said. Gregg chuckled, deep and sexy.

"Are you trying to brush me off Caroline?"
He replied, his voice husky and alluring. He didn't sound at all cross though, and Caroline imagined his teasing smile.

"N…no, not at all. In fact I think I really do need to talk to you…"

"Hurry up mum"
Leo peeked around the door whispering loudly, making Caroline jump.

"About your manuscript."
She said into the phone whilst nodding to her son. Gregg laughed and Caroline felt her knees go weak. How could a man so young be so enthralling.

"What time shall I call you back?"
He asked. Caroline thought for a moment. Leo and Liam would go home about ten. Even though they both had flats within walking distance of her home, she would insist they not stay any later because of the weather.

"I'll call you. Ten thirty."
She left it vague as Leo was still waiting. He would think she meant in the morning, Gregg would know she meant tonight.

"Your son is listening. Ok, I will be waiting. Goodbye for now."

"Yes, thank you for your call."
Caroline replied, achieving professional at last.

"Client."
She told Leo as she passed him into the lounge.

"Mum?"

He said, and she looked back at the question in his eyes. She hadn't pulled off the act.

"It wasn't Frank was it?"

He asked gently. Caroline pulled him to her and wrapped her arms around him, even though he towered over her.

"No my angel boy. It wasn't Frank. I promise you I am done with him."

She leaned back and looked up into eyes that were hurt and worried. She held out a hand and felt Liam take it.

"My darlings, I've taken him back too many times. That has hurt us all and I should have seen his true self years ago. Did see it, but chose to ignore it. I've put me first when I should have put you two first. It's taken a long time, but I swear he will not ever be a part of my…our…lives again. I truly am done with Fuck Head Frank. It was a client on the phone. A new one. I went to the office yesterday and even though I was supposed to be on holiday, there were submissions. One interested me. I didn't think the author would call me so soon."

It was partly the truth. The stuff about Frank all true, Gregg's submission so, so. The rest skipped over. No matter what happened between her and Gregg, she wasn't going to tell the boys. They smiled, appeased at her words.

"So got any ice cream in the freezer?"

Liam asked and Caroline giggled.

"Go and sit down, I'll get it and we can finish watching the movie. But…I'm sending you both packing in a while, I don't want you out late with that lot coming down."

She said, indicating with her head the falling snow visible through the window.

Caroline sat wrapped in her fluffy dressing gown, her feet curled beneath her sipping a glass of wine. Leo and Liam had both texted her they were home safe and sound, and she was now feeling relaxed and comfortable. She swung her mobile between her thumb and forefinger, not so certain now she should call Gregg.

The sound of her work ring tone had her jumping and sloshing wine down her gown.

"Shit."

She grumbled, pressing the answer button.

"Hello Caroline."

Gregg's so sexy voice took away her agitation and brought all her senses alive. She took a deep breath.

"Hi."

She managed her mouth going dry with nerves.

"You said you would call at ten thirty. You didn't."

Caroline glanced at her clock. It was only just after that and a little bubble of annoyance popped out of her.

"It's just gone half past. I was just about to."

Gregg laughed, pleased he had invoked a reaction. Caroline huffed out a sigh of frustration. This boy-man was going to drive her insane. So hang up and ignore him, she told her herself, but knew she would do no such thing. As annoying as he was, she wanted to hear his voice, wanted to feel his lips against hers.

"Caroline, speak to me."

He said softly. Again Caroline was reminded of a vampire, hypnotic and tempting, drawing her in. She couldn't resist him.

"What about?"
She tried for cool and failed. He chuckled.

"How about your decision."
He said. Caroline panicked. What decision? She hadn't made one yet. But she knew she was lying to herself, she had decided. What she didn't know was how she would broach the subject. Once again, it seemed Gregg could read her thoughts, even over the phone.

"I can have a car pick you up tonight and bring you to my house. I will have my doctor and his nurse waiting to do all the necessary checks first thing in the morning. We'll know all the results the day after. Whilst we wait, we can get to know one another…better."

"I…I…don't…can't. Wait, where and for how long?"
Caroline stammered, all sorts of questions flying through her confused mind. Calmly and gently Gregg replied.

"My house, the one I am staying at now is in the middle of Dartmoor. And for as long as you want. Remember what I said Caroline. We won't do anything you're not ready and willing to do. I want you to give and ask for what you want."

"But…the snow. It's deep here, the moor will be impassable."
She said, barely registering the rest of his words. Gregg chortled.

"Do not worry your pretty head over such trivialities. Just be ready in an hour."

"Um…what do I bring?"
Caroline asked.

"An overnight bag. That's all you will need for now. I have to arrange your lift so I will see you very soon."

The last words were mesmerising and Caroline's insides went to mush. Then as soon as the line went quiet, she began to shake. She was stupid she told herself, for even thinking about going. Memories of the fear she felt in the office that morning had her adamant she wasn't going anywhere, especially the middle of the moor. Then his beautiful face came into her mind, and her steps were already leading to her bedroom.

Her overnight bag was on her bed half filled, before reality shook her and she stopped.

"What the hell are you doing? You're an idiot. Irresponsible and totally fucking off your head."

She yelled at herself out loud, dumping the contents of the bag onto the bed. But as soon as she had done that, she heard Gregg's voice in her head. It was magical, spellbinding, and her hands stuffed everything back in the bag of their own volition. Like in a trance, she went to her bathroom and gathered toiletries. Before she knew it the bag was packed and zipped up.

Caroline paced her sitting room. She had put on, and taken off her boots and coat three times since she had lifted her overnight bag and laid it on the sofa. At the moment they were off. She was again determined not to go when Gregg's driver arrived. She had thought about ringing Derby, but knew exactly what her friend would say. And anyway, she wasn't going.

She stopped treading back and forth and looked out the window. The snow had ceased, but it coated everything. Headlights bounced off the glistening white, and a big black car glided to a stop outside her home. The wide path surrounding the marina was meant for access only, but it seemed Gregg's driver had ignored the rule.

A man in a black coat, gloves and hat alighted. He paused, looked at her house and purposely made his way towards it. He didn't seem to be having any difficulty walking in the deep snow. Caroline's heart began to beat faster. The man looked big and was getting bigger the closer he got. Thoughts of devils and demons crossed her mind, and all of the old folk tales of moorland magic and mystery flooded her already stretched nerves.

Caroline decided not to open the door a second before the bell rang. She hung back inside the lounge doorway hoping he would simply give up waiting and go. But the bell rang a second time. Still she didn't move. Her mobile trilled, her work ring tone. She grabbed it, her head telling her not to answer, her heart already guiding her finger to the button.

"Caroline, answer your door please. It's impolite to leave Hal standing in the cold."

Gregg's voice came over the phone, patient as though speaking to a child.

"Um…I'm sorry. I'll open it right away."

Caroline replied. Gregg thanked her and hung up. Caroline stamped her foot in agitation.

"Damn that boy chick. His bloody Hal can stand there all fucking night. I'm not answering."

She mumbled to herself. Then as though being pulled by an invisible thread she did the opposite and opened the door.

"Good evening madam. Are you ready?"

Caroline almost giggled as she turned to get her bag and coat. He sounded like the actor David Niven playing his best butler part. But Hal, just the name made her want to burst into hysterics, Hal, was so big and wide, he looked more like one of those wrestlers off the TV, instead of a personal driver.

Hal reached out a hand and took her bag. He then stood back to politely let her go ahead of him. Caroline took one step out of her house and felt the ground move under her. She had no traction on her boots and the path was slippery. She flung her arms wide as her feet began to slide out from underneath her. Then strong arms were holding her up and lifting her from the snow.

"I think I had better carry you madam."

Hal said. Before she could object, he had swept her into his arms, bag and all and was walking sure footedly back across the snow to the car.

Caroline gasped, terrified Hal would lose his footing and they would both crash to the snowy ground. She felt a rumble close to her chest, and realised Hal had chuffed out a short laugh. Could this man read her mind too? She thought.

"Don't worry. You're very safe."

Hal told her, confirming her belief, at the same time knowing it was ridiculous. Maybe she was just giving off vibes that these men had a knack of sensing. Unnerving as that was, Caroline did actually feel safe.

They reached the car without mishap and Hal lowered her to the ground. She waited whilst he unlocked the doors and politely held the back one open for her. Caroline climbed into the big car, having to use the running board. The interior was black too, but the seats were covered in soft leather and were as comfortable as an armchair. Caroline settled herself and buckled her seatbelt. Hal stepped into the driver's seat, turned and rested one arm along the backrest. He had an envelope in his hand.

"Master Taylor-York asked me to give this to you before we set off."

He said in his oh so posh voice. Caroline took it to mean she had to open it straight away. Inside the envelope she found a single sheet of thick ivory writing paper. She bit back a giggle trying to escape. Who wrote letters these days? She thought, but kept it to herself. Unfolding the paper, she saw beautiful flowery, almost feminine and very old fashioned writing. Caroline stared for a moment thinking. If she hadn't heard his voice, tasted his kiss and felt the hardness of his body, she would still believe he could be a woman.

Without thinking, Caroline lifted the paper to her nose, closed her eyes and took in a deep breath. A scent, very male and very sexy invaded her senses, and for a few seconds she just breathed the aroma. Remembering she wasn't alone, she opened one eye. Hal was sitting facing the windscreen, silent and still, waiting patiently for her. She took one more sniff and then began to read.

My dearest Caroline.

Before Hal begins to drive, please would you text your family and friends. Tell them you will spending two days with an eccentric client going over a manuscript. Please also tell them you will have no phone signal, but will call from a satellite phone to let them know you're safe. Because you will be Caroline. I promised you that, and I always keep my promises.

I say two days, that my dear is just the beginning, as I can guarantee you more time if you request it. I am certain you will.

Yours

Gregg.

Caroline had a sudden desire to flee from the car. His words, the way he wrote had vampire flooding her brain again. This man could not possibly be just thirty years old. He sounded like someone from the mid eighteen hundreds, or the very latest, the turn of the century.

"And I don't mean this one."
She whispered.

"Excuse me madam. Did you say something?"
Caroline shook her head, but he couldn't see her.

"Uh, no, it's alright. Just looking for my phone."
She was delving into her handbag for her phone at the same time telling herself she should be running. Knowing she wouldn't, she grabbed her phone. Despite the ripples of silky fear that ran along her nerves, she was also bubbling with excitement and anticipation.

Caroline quickly sent identical text messages to her sons and Derby. She hesitated for less than a second before pressing send. Then she stuffed her phone back in her bag.

"Ok Hal. I'm ready. We can go."
She saw Hal nod briefly and start the engine. It purred, and Caroline barely felt movement as he pulled away from the house into the snowy night.

CHAPTER 10.

The car headed away from the city, leaving bright Christmas lights and crowds behind. They passed a group of carol singers, and Caroline lowered the window just a tiny bit to hear their voices. The sound brought to mind Christmas day. Did she want to spend it with Derby and her little family? They would be loved up, and Melody would only just be finding the festivities interesting this year. She was very happy for Derby, but she was also miserable for herself.

She should be loved up on her honeymoon, spending a luxurious Christmas day with her husband. She gritted her teeth. No she wouldn't begrudge Derby her cosy and comfortable day with Geoff and their daughter, and she wouldn't inflict her wretchedness on them. She would find something to occupy her Chri stmas day. That thought led to Gregg's letter. She still held it in her hand. She switched on the interior light and read it again. Two days, with the promise of more. What did that mean? She sighed. Gregg was an enigma, one she wasn't sure she wanted to unravel. So why are you driving across miles of moor to spend time with him? She silently asked herself. Shrugging she turned her face to the window.

They were now out on open moorland. Snow stretched as far as the eye could see. It was a beautiful sight but at times terrifying. The deeper in they went, the thicker the snow became. At times, drifts eight feet high had swept across the narrow roads, reducing them to thin ribbons of track. Yet the big car glided between the gaps, and Caroline suspected they were on sleigh runners rather than tyres.

"The car is fitted with snow tyres."

Hal said, making her jump. She took a breath in annoyance.

"How did you know what I was thinking?"

She snapped and immediately regretted it.

"I'm sorry for snapping. But please, how did you know?"

She met his eyes in the interior mirror.

"You were looking out of the window with a serious frown. You were also gripping the edge of your seatbelt. I guessed you were concerned that the car might skid. I assure you it will not. I have driven in snow all over the world, at times much worse than this."

Caroline made herself relax. She looked at the hand holding the seatbelt and saw it was white where she had held on so tightly. She let go and shifted back into her seat.

"I'm sorry. I've never been in snow this heavy before. And I've certainly never been in a car in snow this deep."

"It's perfectly alright madam. There's a built in screen and DVD player on the back of my seat if you want to watch something and relax. It will be a while before we get there. If you lift the armrest between the seats you will find the DVDs. Also, below the screen is a pull down tray, and next to that a pocket with two thermos flasks. One has coffee, the other tea. There are packets of milk, cream and sugar too."

Caroline smiled at him and he smiled and nodded back. She lifted the armrest and pulled out a few discs. She found a film she knew she liked, and after a moment of searching, worked out how to insert it in the player. A small remote was clipped to the screen and a couple of buttons later, the film began to play.

At first Caroline concentrated on the movie, a cup of tea held between both hands. But it couldn't hold her attention. Her eyes wandered again to the window, and this time she forced herself to relax and enjoy the sweeping winter scene. Deadly as it was, it was also very beautiful, stark white against the darkness of the night sky.

Across some of the fields, she could make out odd tracks where farmers had trudged their way through. Occasionally a distant farmhouse could be seen, smoke curling upwards from warm fires inside, squares of soft light from windows. She hoped the inhabitants were all safe, the animals too. She'd read and heard news reports from past winters, of fatalities caused by ice cold weather, and then it hadn't been anywhere near as bad as this year. Tilting her head upwards, she looked at the sky. It was still heavy with cloud suggesting even more snow.

As the car hummed its way over the snow and ate up the miles, Caroline wondered for the first time where they were going. Dartmoor wasn't that big, compared to other moorlands, and she already felt like they were in its heart. Then the car began to slow, gently and easily. Hal made a left turn between tall wrought iron gates and they were on a narrow road. Trees lined the road, their branches leaning inwards heavy with snow. It was like driving through an icy arch. Caroline ducked, even though she was inside the car, she had a feeling that the weight of the snow was going to bring the trees down on top of her.

"You're safe madam. Those old trees have held up for many years."

Hal said, as he looked at her in the mirror. Caroline gave a nervous giggle.

"They just look like they couldn't bend any further without toppling over."

"Believe me, they've seen worse weather than this. Not just snow, but gales and rain. They're tough old wood."

Caroline frowned to herself. She couldn't guess at how old Hal was, but he certainly didn't appear very old. How did he know what the trees had seen? She shuddered despite the warmth of the car.

"I've worked for the family for many years, and I've studied the history of all of their homes."

Hal told her, and she suspected he had again sensed her feelings from looking at her in the mirror.

"You're very perceptive Hal."

She said. Then his words clicked.

"How many homes do they have?"

She asked in a shocked voice. Hal laughed.

"It's my job to read peoples emotions. They have several."
He said no more, leaving Caroline wondering.

The tree lined road eventually opened into a circular driveway and Caroline got her first sight of Gregg's home. It was huge. Typically made of stone, and Georgham, Caroline guessed. It reminded her more of a fancy hotel than a house, and that made her nervous. The driveway had been mostly cleared of snow, though the house itself was topped with a thick layer covering the roof. Chimneys poked out, and smoke curled up. Bright lights from the windows and over the front door welcomed. Caroline thought of glowing open fires and warmth and that soothed her.

Hal brought the car to a gentle stop in front of wide steps leading up to a wooden front door. He slipped from the driver's seat and opened her door. Caroline took the hand he held out and gingerly alighted. The cold air bit into her cheeks and caught her breath. She shivered and wrapped her arms around herself. Her coat was still on the backseat. Hal realised he should have forewarned her, and quickly pulled off his overcoat and placed it around her shoulders.

"I am so sorry madam. I should have told you to put your coat on as we arrived."
Caroline smiled, the big coat almost weighing her down.

"Please, it's not your fault. I should have realised how much colder it would be out here than in the city. But I think maybe I should put my own coat on, yours is a bit too big."

She looked at Hal and felt completely at ease. He looked back and they grinned at one another. He reached into the back of the car and lifted out her coat. They swapped, and feeling like she was walking on air, she moved towards the front door, Hal behind her with her overnight bag.

As they approached the steps, the door opened as if by magic. Then Caroline saw a tiny woman who looked to be in her sixties, holding it open. She had a cheerful welcoming smile. She stood back to allow entry and waved a hand towards the interior.

"Welcome to Trewen House. I am Gwyn, housekeeper."

Caroline stepped into a large hallway with a central staircase. There were wooden doors and hallways leading off and Caroline wondered how big the house actually was.

"Master Gregg asked me to show you to your room and get you settled. It's very late now, and he would like you to get some rest. He asked me to tell you he'll see you tomorrow."

Caroline smiled nervously at the little lady. She was so small she had to look down and Caroline wasn't very tall herself. Gwyn took Caroline's bag from Hal. Caroline was about to protest, but the woman lifted it without effort and turned towards the stairs. Caroline glanced back at Hal and he gave her a nod of encouragement.

Caroline followed Gwyn up the stairs, which opened onto a wide landing. She was led through a heavy door, into a room that Caroline could only describe as palatial. The honeymoon suite at the Waterside wasn't a patch on the elegance that was before her. Every movie she had ever watched that had rich country estates, rolled into one. The bed totally dominated the room. It was large, antique and had sumptuous velvet hangings. Gwyn laid Caroline's bag on an ottoman at the foot of the bed and indicated toward a closed door.

"Your bathroom."

She said, leading the way. Caroline stepped into luxury. The room was huge. Right in the centre, raised and accessed by steps, was a bath. It was square, deep, with padded edges. Behind a glass screen open at each end, she could see a shower. Jets poked from the four walls, and Caroline's heart skipped at the thought of two people sharing. Behind another door was a toilet and two basins, a long lighted mirror adding the final touch.

Back in the bedroom Caroline strolled to the windows. They overlooked snow covered fields. There was a deep cushioned window seat and a small high back armchair, both upholstered in rich velvet in front of the glass, so the view could be thoroughly appreciated. Caroline imagined being curled up with a book in her hands.

"This is your dressing room."

Gwyn said, bringing her back to reality. Caroline stepped through yet another door. Inside she found rows of hangers, drawers and dressing table. What shocked her was the clothes on the hangers. She lifted a dress, it was her size. She opened a drawer and found silk underwear, again her size. There were also shoes, her size. Caroline gasped.

"Master Gregg had it all delivered this evening."

Caroline wanted to run. She felt trapped in some sort of bizarre nightmare, something from a horror movie. Gwyn put a hand on her arm and squeezed gently. Caroline nearly shrieked.

"Don't be afraid dear. Just enjoy it. Maybe once you've met Amy, you'll feel more comfortable."
Trembling, Caroline managed a reply.

"Who…who's Amy?"
Gwyn smiled kindly, and some of Caroline's fear eased.

"She will be your personal assistant whilst you're here. She's young, nineteen and will look after everything you need. You will meet her in the morning."

Caroline gave a sigh. She wasn't sure Amy would, or could give her the reassurance she craved, but she would wait and see and hope.

"I'll leave you to get settled. Is there anything I can get you, a hot drink maybe?"
Caroline shook her head.

"Oh, and there's a satellite phone on the bedside table. Master Gregg said to remind you to call home."
Gwyn said turning for the door. Caroline wanted to scream not to leave her, but the little lady was already closing the door behind her.

Caroline eased herself into the armchair and put her head in her hands. She was on the very edge of hysteria. She gave a little sob and tried to get herself under control. Visions of the clothes destroyed her efforts. Why had Gregg told her to bring an overnight bag when everything she could possibly need was already here. Feeling restless, she stood up. She could see the phone Gwyn mentioned. She should call the boys and Derby, but what would she say. She decided to leave it for now.

She went into the bathroom and stepped up to the edge of the bath. It really was very deep, almost a pool. There was a step halfway down to access it, that could also be used as a seat. When full, she guessed it would reach her thighs. Sighing, she lowered herself to the padded surround. She rested her elbows on her knees and mulled over her situation. She took a very deep breath. All she could do tonight was try and get some sleep. She wouldn't be seeing Gregg until the morning and she did feel safe.

Back in the bedroom, she opened her bag and pulled out a nightshirt and her toiletries. She readied herself for bed. She took a final look out of the window, but all she could see was a blanket of white cloaked from above by the night sky. There were no lights, yet isolated as she was, the winter beauty lulled her. She drifted to the big bed and slipped between the covers. She kept the drapes open and could see the sky as she snuggled down. He eyes began to close, and her last thoughts before sleep took her, was what will the morning bring?

Caroline woke suddenly. It was still dark outside. She blinked and sat up. She felt fresh and awake. A small clock on the bedside table told her it was quarter to seven. Stretching, she pushed back the covers and slid from the bed. The room was wonderfully warm, despite its size.

Flipping on lights, she padded over to the window and looked out. The night had changed the landscape. More snow had fallen and drifted into mounds. The driveway was covered and trackless. She settled on the cushioned window seat and drew up her knees. She could see the treetops bending, but the windows kept out the gusty wind that was blowing. She shuddered a little, feeling totally cut off from the world.

It was like she was the only person left alive, and it unnerved her.

A knock on the door made her jump. She leapt from the seat and dragged the door open. A young woman in jeans and sweater stood outside. She was smiling warmly. She had soft brown eyes and caramel coloured hair. She looked so normal, Caroline's mood was instantly soothed.

"Hi, I'm Amy. You're Caroline. I'm here to help you."

Caroline stood back and let the girl come into the room. She bounced in and flipped her hair over her shoulder as she turned to face Caroline.

"Gwyn says you're nervous. Hmm, I can see it in your eyes. Well, everything's fine. Gwyn and Hal, they're old school. You know, trained in the etiquette of the aristocracy. They've both worked for the Taylor-York family for like, well ever I guess. But me. Well I'm with this century. I'm still well trained, just not so…stuffy. They still call Gregg Master and Sir, but I just call him Gregg. He'd like them to do the same, but they can't get out of their old habits."

Caroline felt her lips turning up at the corners. Amy was fresh and delightful. Gwyn was right, she felt reassured. Nothing bad could happen with a modern bubbly girl like Amy present. Amy swept her arms wide around the room.

"Like it?"

Caroline nodded.

"Very much."

"Gorgeous isn't it. You should see the rest of the house and the grounds. I love working here. Sometimes I go to the other houses, but mostly I stay here. It gives me the chance to study the old buildings on the moor. My hours here are…well, not exactly regular. But they're not long either, and the pay is very good. It means I have time to do my studying, combine my job here with my love of the moor. Gregg's really supportive. He gives me time when I need it, but I don't take advantage."

Caroline found herself having difficulty keeping up. Everything Amy said triggered a set of questions that remained silently in her head. Maybe when she saw Gregg, she would be able to ask some of them and get answers.

"So I'm to run you a bath, get you in a gown and take you to the Doctor's room."

Caroline felt herself pale as all the air went from the room.

"Caroline. Are you ok?"

Amy said as she rushed to her side. Caroline felt her knees weaken and she reached for the ottoman, sitting before she fell.

"Oh…um oh. Look, I'm so sorry. I thought you knew the plans."

Amy dived for the bathroom and returned with a glass of water. She held it to Caroline's lips and let her sip slowly. The cool liquid revived her and the colour came back to her cheeks.

"About the doctor yes, just not the timing. And I didn't know who knew."

Caroline managed to murmur. Amy knelt in front of her.

"Everything between these walls stays here. Don't be embarrassed, please. It must have sounded dreadful, the way it came out. For that I'm sorry.

Gregg's personal doctor and nurse have like a surgery room here. They're professional and look after all of us, not just Gregg. They are both also very nice and easy to talk to."

Caroline felt a little reassured. She took the glass and drained it. Then she stood up.

"It's fine. Just a bit of a shock. All this, is…rather strange. Does…Gregg, do…have, Jesus, it is embarrassing. I'm not the first, I guess. He does this a lot?"

Amy shook her head.

"Actually no. I mean, yes he's had women visit here and stay before, but not like you."

Caroline frowned, assuming she meant her age. Amy quickly realised her mistake.

"Oh what I mean is, all this. The clothes, the sending Hal to collect you, the doctor. He hasn't done any of that before. Usually he brings them back with him, or they turn up after an invitation, only for a night or just dinner. With you, it's different. He hasn't told us anything about you or anything. Just gave us instructions to be there for everything you need."

She was gabbling now and Caroline felt very confused. So Gregg had brought other women to this house, for dinner and sex. But no one her age? Did she get that right, she wasn't sure she understood any of what Amy had said. So she took a deep breath and decided to take the visit as it came. She would bathe, see the doctor and then perhaps when she finally saw Gregg, she would know what she was really doing here.

CHAPTER 11.

The bath was deep and calming. Amy had filled it almost to the brim, and dropped scented bubble bath into the running water. Now Caroline laid her head back against the padded edge and closed her eyes. It was so big she could extend her legs fully, and so deep she almost floated. The steamy air and scented water drew out the last of the tension in her muscles and she dozed.

"Um…not to hurry you or anything, but we sort of need to get going."

Amy spoke from the doorway, startling Caroline. She sat up quickly sloshing water over the side, watching it cascade down the steps.

"Oh I'm so sorry. I didn't mean to make you jump. Here, let me help you."

Amy said, stepping into the room and grabbing a fluffy white bath sheet. She held it up in front of the bath. Caroline stayed under the water and foam for a few seconds. She wasn't used to standing naked in front of strangers, and it unnerved her all over again.

Amy stood waiting patiently and Caroline sighed. She couldn't stay in the water. Feeling very embarrassed, she stood up and took the towel from Amy's hands. But then she was stuck. She couldn't step out of the bath holding the bath sheet around her, it was too high. Amy sensed her conundrum and lifted another towel from the stand.

"Climb out, it doesn't matter if that towel gets wet. Then when you're ready I have a dry one for you to wrap yourself in."

Caroline felt foolish. The girl was only being helpful, and she, a forty seven year old woman was being bashful. She smiled.

"No. I'm sorry. I'm being daft. You're here to offer a helping hand, and I'm getting all wound up about you seeing me starkers."

With that she threw the towel around her shoulders and stepped up to the edge of the pool like bath, then held out a hand to Amy for balance. The girl grinned and supported her as she climbed out.

Caroline wrapped herself in the fresh towel and Amy went to a cupboard in the wall. From it she took a soft towelling bathrobe and draped it over her arm. Once Caroline was dry she held out the gown. Now, completely comfortable with her nakedness, Caroline dropped the towel and slipped her arms into the robe. She smiled to herself. She could get used to this.

Amy led them back into the bedroom and continued on to the dressing room. Caroline was about to follow, but the girl was already on her way back. She held out a pair of white silky panties, and again

Caroline felt her face flush. Maybe she couldn't get used to having what she could only describe as a ladies maid. This was the twenty first century, surely only the Queen had someone to dress her. Amy waited, holding the panties. Caroline shrugged and held out her hand. Amy passed the garment to her and she slipped them on.

"Are we done?"

She asked irritably. Amy smiled.

"Gregg asked me to treat you like royalty. He just wants you to enjoy yourself."

Caroline drew her brows together in a tight line. Gregg said. She hadn't even seen him yet and already he was annoying her. But it wasn't Amy's fault. She was simply doing as requested. It wasn't fair to take it out on her.

"Amy. I really am sorry, again. This is all very strange to me."

Amy nodded knowingly.

"It's fine, really. So can I take you to the doctor now?"

Caroline grinned.

"Lead the way."

After handing her a pair of leather soled slippers, Amy took her back down the main staircase and led her along a corridor. For several minutes, they wound their way this and that, and Caroline began to understand the size of the house. If Amy hadn't been with her, she would have got lost. A giggle tried to erupt, but she forced it back down. How could a person get lost inside a house?

She was still wondering this when Amy stopped outside a door. She tapped and opened it. Inside was an office, completely out of contrast with the rest of the property. Where they had passed dark wood doors and panelling, this room was white with modern furniture. There were two desks with computers on each. Two filing cabinets rested against a wall next to another door. A man in a suit stood at one desk, and a woman dressed as a nurse sat at the other. She stood up as they entered.

The man came around his desk and held out his hand. Caroline began to shake as she took it.

"Hello. I'm Doctor Ryan Clements. This is my nurse stroke assistant. Delia."
The nurse came to Caroline's side and held her hand out too.

"I'll leave you to it. Delia, please call me when Caroline's ready to be taken back to the main house."
Amy said from behind Caroline. She swung around, terrified of being left alone. Amy saw the panic in her eyes.

"Don't worry. I can't stay with you. You understand this is private and completely confidential, but I won't be far away. Just relax and soon it will be all over."
Amy smiled reassuringly and stepped out of the door, closing it behind her. Caroline turned back to the doctor and nurse, both were smiling kindly, but her trembles didn't cease.

"Please, sit down. Make yourself comfortable."
Doctor Clements said, indicating a chair in front of his desk. Nervously, Caroline did as he asked. Nurse Delia placed a glass of water in front of her. She then went to a trolley and began arranging various pieces of

equipment. Caroline tried to see what she was doing but the doctor was speaking again.

"So you're fully aware of why you are here?" He asked. Caroline nodded.

"Good, good. Now as Amy said, all of this is completely confidential. Just the same as if you visited your own surgery. The history and tests we take will be filed, and I can pass them to your own GP if you want. The results will be given to you only. What you do with them is up to you."

Caroline looked up at his last words.

"So…so, you won't tell Gregg?"

The doctor smiled gently. He leaned forward and placed his clasped hands in front of him.

"Caroline, I am a doctor first and foremost. I may be Gregg's personal doctor, but my oaths remain the same. He might want you to go through this, and personally I agree with him, for both your sakes. But any information about you is for you only. How you deal with it together is your business. I'm not here to judge, and I'm certainly not here to do Gregg's bidding."

Caroline leaned back in her chair and relaxed for the first time since entering the room. She hadn't known what to expect. But her imagination had filled in the gaps. She had some notion of a gnarled old man with fuzzy hair and glasses. He would have an accent, something like German or Scandinavian. There would be metal instruments and old fashioned equipment. And he would run straight to Gregg with everything he found out about her. Doctor Clements laughed.

"I'm not Frankenstein."

Caroline gasped.

"Your face tells a very good story."
He said.

"And I sure am not Igor."
Nurse Delia stated, as she pulled a chair next to Caroline. She had a tablet on her lap and crossed her legs in readiness. Caroline burst out laughing, believing this wasn't going to be as bad as she'd thought. Probably better, she told herself, for her own peace of mind. What Frank had done to her was deplorable, better she know if there were any consequences.

Doctor Clements began by asking her some very personal questions about her sexual history. Nurse Delia tapped quietly on the tablet as she answered. Caroline was embarrassed. Not by the questioning, but how naïve she'd been trusting Frank for so many years. It also made her very sad, having to relive every time the bastard had cheated on her.

Telling it all in one go also reminded her how many times it had happened, and with so many women. She then had to admit that there could be others she didn't know about. Probably were, that Frank had lied when she'd questioned him. Saying that out loud brought a flush to her cheeks. Nurse Delia stopped taking notes and placed an arm around her shoulder. Caroline felt tears threaten and forced them back. She wouldn't shed anymore over Frank.

Once the questions about her sex life were over, Doctor Clements asked about her general health and family medical history. He then left her with the nurse and disappeared into the other room. Nurse Delia took her blood pressure, temperature, weighed her and measured her height. Caroline found herself wanting to giggle again, silently asking herself questions. What did how tall she was have to do with what Gregg had planned? And what did Gregg have planned? Nurse Delia was speaking and she had missed her words.

"Sorry, miles away there."

"I said, all done out here. Could you follow me through to the examination room."

Caroline's nerves flooded back in at what she knew was now about to happen. She'd had gynaecological checks before, of course she had. Various screenings over the years, all normal practices for a woman. But this one felt so much more intimate. She took a deep breath and purposefully strode through to the examination room. She swept her eyes around the room taking it all in. It was typical of every doctor's room she had ever been in.

Nurse Delia took her behind the curtain surrounding the examination table. She helped her out of her robe and undies, and then placed a blanket over her. Then Doctor Clements was there. He now had on a white coat. That at least made Caroline feel more comfortable.

"Ok Caroline, just lay back and relax. I'm going to have a look and then take some swabs. It won't take long."

Caroline did as she was asked, breathing steadily. Doctor Clements proceeded with the checks, and Caroline actually thought he was more gentle and sensitive than any other doctors she had seen. True to his word, it was over fairly quickly. He disappeared from the cubicle, and nurse Delia held her robe for her.

"We just have to take a little bit of blood, then we're done."
Nurse Delia said. Caroline nodded in relief.

Once everything was completed, Doctor Clements explained to Caroline that he would have all her results the next day.

"I'll be back personally to go through them with you. Now you know which tests we have taken don't you?"

Caroline nodded, a tiny thread of fear snaking its way to her heart. It was all good and well having the tests done, but what if one came back positive? What if one of the dreaded incurable ones came back positive? She pushed the terror deep down. She wouldn't dwell on it. Frank had told her he used protection some times, with the young ones anyway. He didn't want to chance fathering a child. She had no idea about Tania, but guessed she probably had kept herself for Frank only, like she had. She thought the mature women she'd seen reacting on her wedding day had probably been cautious. They were all married or with partners, and again pregnancy was possible, so hopefully, she was safe.

A tap came on the door and Amy poked her head in.

"All done?"

She asked with a beaming smile. Caroline was pleased to see her. Amy meant normality. Caroline looked questioningly at Doctor Clements who nodded. She stood up, thanked the doctor and nurse and departed, relieved it was over.

"Not too bad was it"

Amy stated as Caroline followed her back through the house. Glancing over her shoulder to Caroline she said.

"Gregg lets all his staff use his doctor. When I came here I asked Doctor Clements to check me over. I mean, I've always been very careful, but it's good to get a check up now and then. The clinics are ok, but they're busy and so impersonal. But here, well it's much better. So anyway, I know what it's like."

Caroline didn't really know how to reply, so she stayed quiet. Amy was so young, but casual sex was a part of today's world. She knew her own sons had had girlfriends, knew sex had been a part of their relationships. She wasn't shy of talking about sex, had encouraged her boys to be open with her about it. It was just, she had spent so much of her life taking it seriously, and still look where it had got her.

Before she knew it, Amy was passing through the door to her bedroom. Whilst she had been gone, the bathroom had been cleared up, and her overnight bag stowed away. She didn't know if Amy or some other member of staff had done it.

"Everything you need is in the dressing room. I've put your bag and toiletries away, you won't need them. "

Amy told her. Caroline thought she really must try and not show her feelings so openly on her face. Too many people seemed to be reading her lately.

"So what happens now?"

She asked, instead of commenting on Amy's words. Amy pointed to the bed. Laid out was a set of blue satin underwear, jeans and a very thick white jumper.

"Gregg has a treat planned for you. But you will need warm clothes. I'll go and get boots and outdoor wear whilst you dress."

Amy left her by herself, and for a while Caroline just stood by the window looking at the scenery. The sky was still dull and thick with cloud, but it wasn't snowing. The wind had picked up though, and she could see fresh powder being swept into drifts across the fields and woodland. She shivered, even though the room was lovely and warm. She was sure they would get cut off from the rest of the world, be snowed in until it all thawed. If things went badly wrong with Gregg, what would she do stuck here with no one?

Dropping her shoulders, Caroline padded to the bed. She stripped off the robe and undies, looked about for a laundry hamper but couldn't see one. She laid the garments on the bed and donned fresh ones. As she was straightening the jumper, a tap came on the door. She called out "Come in." and Amy pushed open the door. She had boots in one hand and a thick fur coat draped over her arm. Caroline winced.

"Please tell me that's not real."
She said. Amy giggled.

"No chance. Gregg would go mental if anyone turned up wearing real fur. He hates all that stuff. But it is the best made faux fur you can get."
She held out the boots. They were soft leather with a fur lining and exactly Caroline's size.

"I only met him briefly. How did he know all my sizes?"
Amy shrugged.

"I don't know. He's very astute. When I started working here, I had a new complete wardrobe delivered to my room, all my size. He just knows."

An irrational little prick of jealousy stabbed at Caroline. She didn't even know the man, yet she felt like he was hers, that she was special. Gregg hadn't given her any signs to make her believe that, just a kiss and hint of more to come. Yet she didn't like the idea of him knowing other women's sizes, even those who worked for him. Caroline lowered her eyes. She absolutely didn't want Amy to read her face this time. It didn't work.

"Caroline. Gregg is good to the people who work for him. Yes he bought me clothes, but not like anything you have here. All mine are work gear. Even the underwear, nice, but not fancy, or sexy."

Caroline sighed. She seemed to be doing a lot of that lately. This young woman didn't deserve her jealous thoughts. Gregg had brought her, Caroline, here for a reason. Even though she hadn't set eyes on him yet, everything so far had been done especially for her, organised by him. Whatever she had thought of him at the office, and since, he was obviously a very nice man who cared about others.

CHAPTER 12.

Amy held the fur coat out and Caroline slipped her arms in. It was perfect. It came midway down her calves and had a large collar that covered her neck. Amy also handed her a matching Cossack hat, scarf and gloves. Inside she felt overdressed, but knew the temperature outside would be close to, if not below freezing.

"Ready?"

Amy asked. A rumble from Caroline's tummy made Amy laugh.

"Sounds like you are. Don't worry, no one has forgotten to give you breakfast. We don't plan on starving you. It's just Gregg said he had it sorted, so…" Caroline smiled at the young woman, not sure that she could eat even though she was hungry.

Descending the stairs, Caroline felt excitement building. She had no idea what Gregg had planned, but the anticipation gave her energy. As she reached the bottom step, she saw him for the first time since arriving, standing by the front door. He was dressed for the outdoors too. A very masculine, thick black leather jacket clung to his wide but slender form. He had on tough tread boots, a black wool beanie hat and thick gloves. He watched her as she stepped towards him.

She felt his piercing blue eyes bore into her very soul, heating her inner centre. He smiled, his perfectly straight, perfectly white teeth gleaming wickedly. Inside she felt her most feminine muscles clench, as desire began to spread through her to the softest spot between her thighs. She wanted to throw herself at him, rub up against him and feel his hardness. His smile widened, he knew her thoughts, she was sure.

"Hello Caroline. I hope your day has not been too difficult for you."

He looked down at her as she reached him. She didn't remember him being so tall. He towered over her, strength emanating from him. She breathed in his aura, well aware she was acting like a teeny bopper meeting her favourite pop star. But she couldn't help herself.

"Caroline."

His voice whispered softly close to her ear. She opened her eyes, not realising she had closed them. He was bending forward, down. She could feel his warm breath against her cheek, soft like a summer breeze. The scent of roses seemed to penetrate her senses, but she knew that couldn't be, because she could smell his wonderful masculinity. She didn't know if it was cologne, or just his natural odour, but it was mighty powerful.

She heard a deep devilish chuckle. Dragging herself back to reality she finally looked at him. He was grinning.

"Are you ready?"
He asked.

"For what?"
She replied, her own voice barely audible. He huffed out another laugh.

"For my outdoor surprise."
He said matter-of-factly. His jovial tone brought her to her senses. She straightened. Gregg held out a hand and Caroline took it. He then opened the door. A blast of freezing air hit them full in the face, but the coat and accessories kept her warm. Gregg tugged her hand and she stepped outside with him. She gasped. Standing on the driveway was a sleigh. Two white horses puffed clouds of breath as they stamped in the snow eagerly. Hal was holding the reigns, keeping the spirited animals from galloping away. At least that's how it appeared to Caroline.

Gregg trod sure footedly down the steps, leading Caroline alongside. She took them more tentatively. Gregg laughed, loud and boyishly.

"Don't be afraid. I won't let you fall."
And suddenly she knew he wouldn't. She felt herself give in and relax, though his hold on her hand remained firm but not painful. She looked up at him. His face pale and chiselled, glowed in the cold like a star. There were no rosy patches on his cheeks, like she suspected there would be on hers, only his porcelain skin, shining against the backdrop of snow. He was breathtakingly beautiful.

When they reached the sleigh, Gregg pulled Caroline in front of him. He placed his hands on her waist and half lifted her into the passenger seat. He went around the other side and hoisted himself up. He grinned at her again.

"Here, put this around you."

He draped a fur rug around her shoulders and tucked it in at her sides.

"I do hope you don't object to fake fur. I cannot stand the use of animals for fashion."

He said. Caroline was shaking her head before she found her voice.

"On no. I actually said something along those lines to Amy, when she brought me the coat."

Gregg tilted his forehead and gently touched his to hers. She felt his floppy blonde hair against her cheek, soft as silk, and sighed. He touched his lips lightly to her skin, and a tremor of wanting travelled like a wave down her throat, into her breasts, and settled throbbing at the juncture of her thighs. She felt her nipples harden inside her bra, the satin caressing the sensitive tips as she breathed deeply. A warm wetness seeped into her panties and she shifted her hips, stimulating her arousal. She swallowed, her eyes closing in readiness for a fuller kiss. Then there was icy cold air.

Caroline opened her eyes and looked up in frustration. Gregg was leaning back grinning at her. He knew exactly what he had done to her.

"Time to go."

He said wickedly and took the reigns from Hal. Caroline slouched back in the high backed leather seat. She was angry. She was like butter in his hands and she objected to that. She was the grown up, she should have enough control. But no, she was acting like some over eager, hormonal teenager and she was furious with herself.

Determined to stay cross, Caroline pulled the rug up under her chin and watched Gregg ease the horses around the driveway. She wouldn't enjoy herself. She would just let him drive around for however long he wanted, and sit there uncooperatively. But as they wound along a snowy track at the back of the house, the changing scenery grasped her attention.

For a while they glided along with hedges either side of them. The breeze, quite strong was lifting snow from branches, tossing it about. To Caroline it looked liked invisible beings were having a snowball fight. The hedges gave way to open fields and here Caroline could see the mounds of snow that had drifted in the wind. It was beautiful, like miniature alps. In the distance, she could see a woodland. Soon they were sliding underneath tall trees. Their canopy of white creating a snow cavern, and images of Santa's Grotto came to Caroline's mind. It was so magical she could almost believe she was in a fantasy world.

Under the cover of the trees, Gregg slowed the sleigh until it glided to a stop. The horses chuffed and puffed, but stayed calm. Gregg reached behind them and lifted an old fashioned hamper. He rested it on his knees as Caroline looked on curiously. He lifted the lid and pulled out two china mugs. He held them both in one hand whilst he pulled out a thermos too. He closed the lid and used it as a table. He unscrewed the thermos and the steamy aroma of hot chocolate drifted towards Caroline. He poured each a mug and handed one to her. She hugged it in both hands, sipping the delightful beverage.

"What did your family say when you called?" He asked. Caroline was surprised. It wasn't what she'd expected him to say.

"Uh…I didn't ring them. It was too late. The boys and Derby would have been in bed. "

Gregg tutted and shook his head slowly. Caroline felt like a naughty child. Without a word, he reached behind the seat again and drew out a small backpack. From it he took a phone.

"Call them now please. They will be wondering about you."

Caroline frowned. She hadn't wanted to call as she didn't know what to say. It wouldn't matter what the time of day was, she knew the boys would speak to her, and Derby would be at home now. It was one of the days she didn't work. Still it rankled that Gregg seemed to know she was lying.

Gregg held the phone out to her, a smile on his lips. She wanted to snatch it from his grasp, but knew that would be childish, and he would probably laugh at her for doing it. So she simply held her palm upward and he laid the phone in her gloved hand.

First she rang Leo and dreaded him answering. He did with a questioning tone to his hello. He didn't recognise the number.

"Hi sweetheart, it's me mum."

She said, trying to keep her voice light.

"Oh hi mum. Where are you calling from. I don't know the number that came up?"

"I'm at that client's house I texted you about. Just wanted to let you know I'm safe in case you were worried."

She told him brightly, acutely aware of Gregg close by.

"Mum…you're not with Frank are you?"
Leo asked, his voice full of concern. Caroline was shaking her head and frowning before she answered.

"Darling, no. I swear. I told you he's gone for good. This is work, like I said."
Gregg was staring at her with raised eyebrows and a cheeky smile. She turned her body away from him slightly.

"I'll keep in touch, I promise. And do not worry, I am fine."

They said their goodbyes and Caroline dialled Liam's number. He was more relaxed and calm than Leo had been. He didn't question her, just accepted her words, happy that she was getting on with things. Derby was a different matter.

"Did you call the clinic?"
Was her first words after Caroline told her she was at a client's house.

"Not yet. This, client," She looked at Gregg over her shoulder. "is rather eccentric."
He snickered. Caroline pursed her lips in irritation.

"Yes, a bit nutty I think."
She told Derby, thinking, take that Mr Oh So Smiley.

"Ok. But don't leave it too long. It's important Caroline. And keep in touch. I don't know where you are, and that makes me nervous, especially in this weather. Your text said you would call from a satellite phone, so you must be somewhere there's no mobile mast. Be careful please."

"I will, I promise. At least this phone means I can call anytime without worrying about a signal. So you don't have to. And just in case you are wondering,

I am not with Frank. Leo asked and I promise you like I did him, I am most definitely not with Frank."

"I wasn't going to say that…well yes I was. So, good to know. Look Caroline, whatever you're doing, enjoy yourself, and keep me posted."

Caroline agreed, said goodbye and hung up. She held the phone close for a few seconds chewing her lip. She hated not telling Derby everything. She hadn't exactly lied about anything, but she had been evasive. Gregg touched her arm and she jumped.

"Everything alright?"

He asked with concern. Caroline sighed and nodded. Gregg took the phone from her fingers and placed it back in the bag. Then he lifted the hamper lid and took out a container, opening it. Caroline's stomach growled, as the aroma of hot bacon wafted towards her.

"Mmmm."

She said, as he handed her a crusty roll filled with crispy smoked bacon. He took her mug and refilled it with more hot chocolate, as she bit into her breakfast. Gregg watched her as she ate. She swallowed, nervous again.

"Aren't you eating?"

She asked. Gregg nodded and took out his own roll. He bit into it heartily and she was reminded of her own sons. Where yesterday, Gregg had appeared older than his years, this morning he seemed young and boyish. It confused her.

"You have a question?"

He asked, in between bites. Startled he had read her once again, she replied.

"Are you really thirty years old?"

He finished his roll and leaned towards her.

"How old do you want me to be Caroline?"
He whispered, his eyes intense.

Caroline could feel herself drifting closer to him, her bacon and hot chocolate completely forgotten.

"Finish your breakfast."
He told her grinning. Once again infuriated, Caroline straightened up. She took another bite and chewed with fury. Gregg laughed, the sound ringing through the trees. Caroline almost expected to see snow avalanching from the canopy above.

Feeling frustrated and out of sorts, Caroline finished her food and leaned back in the seat of the sleigh. She had no idea what to think anymore. Her brain wouldn't work properly. Every time she seemed to have it under control, it made her body do things she didn't expect. Right then, she was torn between being angry with Gregg for teasing her, and wanting to throw herself into his lap and be teased even more.

"Who is Frank?"
Gregg asked quietly, sending icy spikes shooting into her thoughts. She lifted her eyes to his. Tears glistened on her lashes.

"I'm supposed to be on my honeymoon. That's why I wasn't taking submissions."
She blurted out. Her words seemed jumbled to her and out of context to his question. Gregg took one of her hands and held it. Though they were both wearing gloves, she could feel his heat.

"Tell me."
He coaxed softly. Caroline dropped her chin and felt a tiny sob escape her lips. She had no idea why she wanted to cry at that moment, but she was barely

holding back a flood of tears. Gregg tilted her face up. His eyes met hers, full of churning emotions.

"Please."

He said, no louder than the wisp of a breeze, his words breaking through her reluctance. Then she was pouring it all out. Even the part about wanting Doctor Clements to check her over. It felt like she talked for hours, but the whole sordid story was over in minutes. When she was finished she felt drained.

Gregg pulled her to him and wrapped his arms around her. Then the floodgates opened, and she couldn't hold back the tears. She cried, not loudly, but the sobs shook her body like an earthquake. Gregg pulled one of his gloves off, and she felt his long fingers stroke her hair under her hat. It was gentle, caring and in no way sexual.

She clung to him, gripping his jacket in her fists. All she wanted then was comfort, and that is what he gave. As the tears began to subside, Caroline's breath hitched as she tried to draw a lungful. Finally achieving steady breathing, she raised her reddened face to his. He looked down, his eyes boring into her. Instantly she no longer wanted comfort. She lifted her mouth and he covered her lips with his.

She wound her arms around his neck and pulled him to her. His tongue pushed between her lips and as it touched hers, fire ignited in the deep well of her womanhood. She deepened the kiss, taking it to the next level. Hungrily she nipped at his lower lip and flicked his tongue with hers. The hot wetness of his mouth flooded down through the centre of her and pooled in between her thighs. She moaned, craving more.

Gregg lifted her onto his lap and cradled her, all the while plunging her mouth with his tongue. Through the folds of clothing and fur rug, she could feel the hardness of his manhood. But he didn't press or push. She however, did not have as much control. She rolled her hips against his erection and felt intense pleasure burn into her soul. He wound his fingers into her hair, the hat falling to the snow. He took his lips from hers and she felt bereft, only to feel fire when they pressed against the hollow of her throat. His tongue caressed the spot under her earlobe, and trailed down the line of her jaw. Her breathing increased and she pressed down into his lap.

Then he pulled back. Caroline grabbed for him, but he lifted her from him and settled her back on the seat. She wanted to scream, lunge at him. She glared at him, her eyes stormy with passion and anger.

"What the f…hell was that?"

She cried out. She had no idea why the expletive stayed silent on her tongue. Anyone else would have had the full backlash of her usual tirade of foul language. But Gregg, with all his Englishness, stemmed the flow where no one else could. Breathing hard she stared, eyes like ice.

"It's not time."

He said calmly, as though nothing had happened. Caroline couldn't believe his words. She threw her hands in the air.

"What's that supposed to mean?"

She hollered.

"Please don't shout Caroline. It's unbecoming."

His words infuriated her even more. She opened her mouth to let out a stream of abuse, when his blue eyes drilled into her. Like a marionette, her mouth clamped shut. She could see emotion in his gaze, bridled but swirling.

"You are not in the frame of mind I imagined for such intimacy. I'm sorry. This is my fault. I asked you about your ex-fiancé, I should not have let what followed happen."

Caroline sat speechless and emotionally drained. Once again Gregg was being the adult and she the wanting teenager. She slumped back in her seat and pulled the rug close about her. Embarrassment began to creep under her skin, burning holes in her cheeks and staining them bright red. Gregg gave her his penetrating stare and she felt wretched.

"Caroline, enjoy this time. Do not be embarrassed."

She wasn't sure his words were making things better or worse, so she remained huddled against the leather.

Without another word, Gregg took up the reigns and clicked the horses into motion. They glided over the snowy terrain and deeper into the woodland. For a while Caroline simply sat in misery, not wanting to even attempt to enjoy the ride. But then the scene in front of the sleigh gradually began to change.

The air was much colder, and long glistening icicles hung from the branches overhead. The shrubbery was a lot denser and smothered in pure white snow. Santa's Grotto came back to her thoughts, as the arching trees shone with tiny pin prick lights. Even though it was day, the clouds were so thick they blocked out what little sun there was. The canopy also shielded the woodland from sunlight, thereby allowing the fairy lights to brighten the ice cavern.

Caroline slowly sat up straighter, her interest in her surroundings sparking. She looked up and around her at the beauty of nature, enhanced by a little technology. Curiosity got the better of her bad mood and she turned to Gregg smiling.

"This is wonderful. How did you manage to get the lights in the trees?"

Gregg gave her a grin.

"I get what I want Caroline, and pretty Christmas lights were what I wanted."

"Oh."

Was all she could think of for a reply. Gregg tilted his head back and laughed, the sound echoing around them.

"Don't laugh at me please."

She said, trying for haughty. It didn't work. Gregg looked at her sideways.

"But you are so delightful, especially when you are cross."

"I am not cross…"

She snapped and then shut her mouth quickly. He was grinning again and she realised he was goading her. She took a deep breath, closed her eyes briefly and said.

"I'm sorry for snapping, I don't mean to. It's…you…your…I don't know. Something about you gets under my skin."

She knew she hadn't expressed herself well. He irritated her, at the same time he aroused her, and that confused her, which in turn made her mad.

Gregg chuckled and clicked the horses on a little faster.

"Just under your skin?"

He questioned. Caroline frowned, not sure how to answer. It seemed he didn't need a reply as he pointed a finger forward.

"Ah, here we are."

Here, was a log cabin, and Caroline nearly choked on a laugh. This was obviously the cabin Gregg had described in his first chapter.

As he drew the horses to a stop outside the door, he looked her full in the face. His gleaming eyes drilled into her thoughts. She tried to look away but was once again hypnotised by his stare.

"You recognise this place?"

He whispered. Caroline nodded.

"First chapter."

He grinned.

"One has to write about one's experiences."

He stated. Caroline let her laughter escape and it felt liberating. Maybe this was going to be fun after all, she thought.

"Now you are the one laughing at me."

He said in a mock sulky voice. She stared into his eyes and saw he was teasing. Maybe this reading someone else's thoughts wasn't so hard, she told herself, and swore she saw him nod, barely.

Gregg took his eyes off her, and Caroline felt like a spell had been lifted. He hopped to the ground and came to her side of the sleigh. He held his hand out and she took it. Holding her firmly he helped her step out of the sleigh safely to the ground. The snow was deep and her boots sunk, but then Gregg was lifting her as Hal had done. She didn't resist. Effortlessly and sure-footedly, he carried her in his arms to the cabin door. Without putting her down, he unlatched it and stepped across the threshold.

The inside was warm. A bright orange glow came from a log fire and in front of that was a fur rug. Caroline giggled as Gregg lowered her to her feet.

"So where's the champagne?"
She asked jokingly. Gregg raised a hand and indicated a table. On it was an ice bucket with a bottle sticking out. By its side were two silver goblets and a bowl of strawberries. Caroline gasped.

"No."
She said, backing to the door a little. Gregg frowned in concern.

"What's wrong Caroline?"

Her expression must have given her thoughts away, for Gregg stepped back too, away from her. He held up his hands, palms out.

"Oh, I'm so sorry Caroline. This…" He swept a hand around the room. "is not an enactment of my novel. And believe me, I only meant the description of the cabin, not the rest. That was imagination."
Caroline felt her fear departing. She took a tiny step towards him.

"So…so what are we doing here?"
She asked.

"It's just a treat for you. As well as the champagne and strawberries I have chocolates too. The rug is so much more comfortable than a sofa, and less formal. I want to know more about you, and I know you have questions for me."

Gregg moved slowly towards her, and stopped just before his boots touched the toes of hers. Caroline looked up into his beautiful face, and knew he was telling the truth.

"Let me take off your coat and boots. Then you can settle, get comfortable."

He said in his deep alluring voice. Caroline let her arms drop by her sides, drinking in his Godlike face. As he unbuttoned the fur, her mind flipped like a coin. One side said run, vampire, the other said stay, Adonis. Whichever he was, his hands were touching her as the coat slid from her shoulders. She closed her eyes and sighed, waiting, hoping for his lips, but they didn't come. Instead he led her to the rug and gently pressed down until she felt it beneath her. Then he knelt in front of her and tugged her boots from her feet.

Caroline leaned back on her hands and felt the fake fur between her fingers. It was thick and luxurious. Gregg was still kneeling. He took one foot and gently slid her sock off, repeating the process with her other foot. She scrunched her toes in the rug and felt its depth, warm and soothing. Gregg stood up and went to the table. He quickly returned with the champagne and strawberries. He lowered himself next to her and unwrapped the foil from the wine. Caroline half laid down, propping herself on one elbow as he popped the cork. The champagne frothed and fizzed over the neck of the bottle, but Gregg already had a goblet for it to flow into.

He handed Caroline the glass and poured a second for himself. Then he lifted his.

"To getting to know one another."

Caroline sipped the wine. It was delicious. Tiny bubbles trailed from the bottom of the goblet to the surface, and though Caroline didn't know much about champagne, she knew enough to know it was a very good one. She took another sip.

"Mmmm, I really do love champagne."
She said.

"So that's the first thing I know about you. Caroline likes champagne."
Gregg said and Caroline laughed. The wine, the rug and the warmth from the fire was relaxing her. She found she was enjoying herself. She took a strawberry from the bowl and bit into it.

"So what about you?"
She said.

"I really like champagne too."
He said. Caroline grinned, savouring the fruit and the wine.

"I mean, tell me about you. For instance, what made you submit to me, or did you just send a bulk submission to every agent in the book?"
Gregg emptied his glass and refilled it, topping hers at the same time.

"Only your agency."
He told her. He sipped from his glass and Caroline thought he wasn't going to tell her any more. Then he spoke again, softly.

"In all honesty, I have no idea what drew me to your website."
He shrugged.

"I've studied acting and art at university, but have never found a niche. I thought I would try my hand at writing. Well…that's not really where my talents lie either."

Caroline looked at him full in the face. She would make no apologies for being good at her job. She didn't yet know this strange young man before her, but guessed he had a very privileged life. She would not add to that by cow-towing to his every wish. His attempt at being an author was appalling, and she would maintain her professional status on that.

Gregg leaned toward her a little, his eyes locking on hers. Caroline was now getting used to this action, but still found it difficult to look away.

"You are very good at what you do Caroline. I wouldn't dream of insisting you take me on as a client. Your judgement is important to me, so I accept my novel is not good enough to be published."

Caroline nodded.

"In any case, your job is no longer what interests me about you."

Caroline felt the atmosphere change immediately. Here we go again, she thought. Her jeans suddenly seemed too tight between her thighs, and her jumper too hot. Gregg laughed.

"Not yet."

Was all he had to say to damper the fire deep within.

Taking a very deep frustrated breath, Caroline tipped her goblet and drained it. She held out the glass to be refilled and Gregg obliged.

"So tell me more about you then."

She said flatly, and Gregg grinned infuriatingly.

"I'm an only child. My parents live most of the time on our estate with my Grandmother. I prefer to divide my time between this house and…other places. Do you like to dress up Caroline?"

His last sentence completely threw her. It was so out of context, that she had to take a moment to register what he was asking.

She trailed her thoughts to the outfits she had hanging at home. Some were from fancy dress parties, others, she would wear for Frank. He liked to watch her prance about as a maid or nurse, and even a dominatrix. During those times he enjoyed being tied to the bed with black fur handcuffs and silky scarves. Then he would get aroused watching Caroline play with a huge dildo, but only by stroking it and sliding it between her breasts. In all the years she had known him, she had no idea why he was so pleasured by the act. She shrugged.

"Well, I've been to quite a lot of fancy dress parties, so, yes, it's fun to dress up."

Gregg sipped his champagne, a smile creasing the corners of his eyes. Caroline knew she hadn't exactly answered his question, but chose to play ignorant. Maybe that way she would get to the bottom of this very complex man. Gregg huffed out a laugh. He was reading her mind again she was sure.

"That's not quite what I meant and I think you know that."

He said, laughter in his voice.

"So explain Gregory, please do, because I have no idea where this is going."

"Gregory? Hmmm, you have quite a little spark in you don't you Caroline?"

Caroline sat up and turned her back to him. That way he couldn't possibly read her. If he couldn't see her eyes or her facial expressions, then surely, he wouldn't be able to determine her mood, thereby what she was thinking.

"That won't work."

He whispered so close to her ear she jumped. She hadn't heard him move. Her insides trembled and a vein pulsed in her neck. Visions of a deep bite and gushing blood flooded through her, and once again all of the movies she had watched came to the front of her mind. She leaned back slightly, waiting for the excruciating pleasure that his teeth would give. But it never came, just a soft stroke of his fingers against her cheek.

"Look at me Caroline, please."

His honey voice murmured. She couldn't resist. He was turning her magnetically, her head first then her body following. He was so close she could feel his warm breath on her face. The goblet slipped from her fingers as she raised her hands to pull his head towards her. He came willingly, his lips hovering close to hers.

"What do you want me to do?"

He asked so softly Caroline almost believed she had heard it in her head.

"I…I, don't know."

She stammered. Gregg touched her lips so lightly, but they burnt into her soul. It was a peck, nothing more and then he was gone.

"Soon. Then you will know and I will give."

Caroline lowered her eyes and moaned. She didn't think she could take any more. Her body throbbed in so many places, yet she knew he was right. She had given of herself freely to Frank, had almost done it again on Monday, had, to a certain extent. She was raw and confused and very close to being at the end of her tether.

"Here try these."

He'd moved and come back and she hadn't even noticed. How did he do it? Her imagination kicked in again, and all manners of magic sped through her. She looked up at his words, expecting to see him in his nonhuman form, but it was just Gregg, as he always looked. He was smiling and holding out a crystal dish full of chocolates. They were so tempting she had plucked one from the bowl before she could blink. She placed it on her tongue, closed her eyes and sucked the sweet treat with relish. Chocolate could always ease her tension.

She heard a chuckle and opened her eyes. Gregg was watching her closely.

"Good?"

He asked, tilting the dish towards her. Caroline nodded and took another chocolate. This one was filled with a creamy centre and she murmured her enjoyment.

"Chocolate does quite a lot for you?"

"Oh yes. It's my only vice really."

Caroline told him as she swallowed and took another. Instead of eating it in one go, this time she bit into it, savouring the flavour. Soft pink fondant left a trail across her lips and she licked it with her tongue. Gregg was watching her intently, his eyes flicking from her mouth to her eyes and back.

"That is something to note."

He said, almost to himself. Caroline frowned, uncertain of his meaning. She finished the chocolate and pushed his hand away.

"No more. I might be a chocoholic, but I do know when to stop."

"Fair enough. It's time anyway."

Caroline sucked the remaining chocolate from her fingers and frowned. What did he mean now? She sighed and waited for him to tell her. But as usual he was going to keep her in the dark. Only when he stood up and reached for her boots did she have an inkling.

"Hold up your feet please."
He said. Caroline pursed her lips, but did as he asked. He deftly slipped on her socks, then her boots, and held out his hand. She took it and he pulled her up. Then he held out her coat whilst she slipped her arms in. He placed the Cossack hat on her head, and completed the outfit by wrapping the scarf around her throat. Caroline inhaled a deep breath as his fingers brushed her throat, but it didn't last more than a second.

"Ready?"
He asked, and Caroline saw somehow he had put on his own outdoor wear without her knowing he had done it. She nodded and Gregg opened the door to a blast of icy air and fresh snow falling.

CHAPTER 13.

The sleigh glided effortlessly over the snow. The horses didn't appear to be at all bothered by the large flakes dropping from the sky, and Caroline wondered if they were magical creatures too. After all everything else so far had seemed other worldly. Gregg glanced at her and smiled. She stuck her tongue in her cheek, and wondered how on earth she could keep her thoughts to herself.

The ride back was just as enjoyable despite the falling snow. It transformed the woodland from icy grotto, to a winter wonderland of ever changing scenery. Each flake that fell was so big, Caroline could make out its intricate pattern as it floated before her eyes. When it landed, it stayed in its form for some time, until it joined its partners in creation.

The undergrowth had taken on new shapes, as the snow piled higher and higher. The track had narrowed and the sleigh runners were gouging deep ruts in the fresh powder. Yet Caroline felt no fear of being stranded. Gregg sat by her side, guiding the horses, radiating a warmth that was in contrast to his alabaster paleness. She almost reached out her fingers to touch his skin, imagining the feel of cold hard porcelain, knowing his flesh would in reality be warm and pliable. His glance had her resisting her urge, his eyes telling her he knew what she had wanted to do.

Without realising, Caroline saw the house come into view. The snow was still falling heavily and the scene before her was breathtaking, just like a Christmas card. The roof was pure white, as were the window sills, piled high with fresh snow. Icicles were clinging from every ridge, and lights shone yellow and invitingly from the windows. Gregg eased the sleigh to a stop in front of the steps. Hal came out of the front door as though he knew the exact time of their arrival.

"Good afternoon Sir, madam."

He said so politely. Gregg smiled at the older man as he hopped to the ground.

"Could you please see to the horses Hal?"

"Of course Sir."

He replied as Gregg helped Caroline from the sleigh. As soon as she stepped away, Hal led the horses around the house and out of sight.

"I do wish he would call me Gregg."

Gregg said, a look of affection in his eyes. Caroline looked at his eyes. They were not the icy piercing blue she was used to. As he watched Hal depart with the sleigh, she saw they had gone a deeper softer shade. She had never known anyone who could change the hue of their eyes with their mood, yet it appeared Gregg could do just that.

"You're very fond of him, aren't you?"

She said, as Gregg took her arm and guided her towards the house.

"Yes I am, Gwyn too. They have both known me since I was a child. Actually Gwyn was my nanny."

Caroline shouldn't have been surprised by this information. She wasn't from a background that employed people to raise their children, but Charles had been. Yet it still amazed her that certain traditions remained in wealthy households, that she believed should have been left behind before the first world war.

Keeping her thoughts to herself, she let Gregg hold her arm as she ascended the steps to the front door. A tiny giggle tried to escape, as she imagined herself on the ground, on her arse, feet splayed inelegantly as she lost her footing on the slippery surface. She felt Gregg grip her arm a little tighter. She sighed inwardly. This man was in her bloody head. He glanced down at her, a smile creasing his lips and she knew she was right. Maybe I should wear a foil cap, to keep him out, like they do in the alien movies. She felt his chuckle rumble in his chest, and was completely unnerved as they entered the hall.

Amy and Gwyn were there to greet them. Gregg was already unwrapping the scarf from her neck and lifting the hat from her head as he spoke.

"Amy, please take Caroline to her room and help her change. Can you then bring her to the conservatory?"

Amy smiled and nodded. She indicated with her head for Caroline to follow, but as she moved, Gregg caught her arm.

"Let me take your coat Caroline, you won't need it."

His eyes had gone back to ice blue, diamonds flashing on the outer ring. She didn't know whether to be relieved or afraid. His grin told her he sensed her confusion.

Dragging her own eyes away from his, Caroline followed a waiting Amy up the stairs. Once inside her room she slumped down on the window seat and stared at the falling snow.

"Are you alright?"

Amy asked kindly. Caroline turned from the window and nodded.

"A bit confused if I'm honest."

"About Gregg?"

Amy asked and again Caroline nodded.

"Do you want to talk about it?"

The young woman said. Caroline shook her head. At that moment she wouldn't be able to talk about her feelings to Derby, let alone this very nice, very kind, very young girl before her.

"Well, I'm here if you change your mind. I'm sure Gregg just wants you to have a good time. Now, are you cold, do you need a bath?"

Caroline burst out laughing. It seemed Amy's solution to everything was a bath. Amy looked at her perplexed, and Caroline shook her head.

"I'm fine. Not cold and no bath needed."

Amy smiled.

"Cool. So ok, you get out of those jeans and jumper and I'll go and get your change of clothes."

Caroline was baffled as Amy disappeared into the dressing room. She was still sitting on the window seat when she returned.

"Oh…um, is something wrong?"

Amy asked with a tiny frown. Caroline stood up, sighed and pulled the jumper over her head.

"No, not at all. Just taking a little breather."

Amy grinned as she handed Caroline a dress and cardigan. Caroline took the garments, a look of pure astonishment on her face. Amy couldn't really expect her to wear this? The dress was cotton and strappy, the cardigan thin and light.

"The conservatory is very hot. You won't want winter wear. Probably not even the cardigan, but that's just to cover your shoulders on the way down."

Of course, Caroline thought. Why wear normal clothes in December, when the temperature is well below zero outside. Feeling very foolish she slipped out of her jeans and into the dress. It hugged her figure perfectly, and it felt so soft and comfortable. Amy nodded approval, went back to the dressing room, re-emerging with a pair of soft, low heeled shoes. Caroline pushed her feet into them and they cushioned her toes. She held her hands out.

"Am I ok?"

She asked.

"Maybe a touch of makeup."

Amy replied. Caroline gasped, lifting her hands to her face. She had no makeup on at all. She hadn't even thought about it earlier. Even when she went to the shops, she usually applied a little mascara and lipstick. Yet today that had completely slipped her mind.

"Oh God, I must look a fright."

She muttered. Amy shook her head.

"In fact you're glowing."

Caroline didn't believe her for one second. Amy took her shoulders and steered her into the dressing room. She placed her in front of the full length mirror and Caroline took in her reflection. Her skin was pale but not wan. Her cheeks were rosy as though covered in a layer of blush. Even her lips looked full and pink. Her hair, which she was certain would be lank and dull from the hat, fell to her waist, wavy and fluffy. She was shocked.

"This has got to be a trick mirror."

She mumbled and Amy giggled.

"No that's you, I promise."

"But I don't…how?"

Amy shrugged.

"Gregg only buys the very best skin care and hair care toiletries. What you had in your bath this morning, is reputed to be the leading brand to maintain youthful looks. I'd say it works."

Caroline's cheeks brightened with embarrassment. That Gregg had supplied her with 'anti-wrinkle' toiletries, for that's what she determined they were, was humiliating.

"Oh Caroline, Gregg isn't trying to turn you into a twenty something. He is just very sensitive to other people's needs. What he does is for them, not himself."

Caroline wasn't sure she believed her, but kept her thoughts to herself.

She scanned the dressing table and found a collection of top brand cosmetics. Amy's words took on a little truth as she examined a couple of items. None of them specified they were for more mature skin. Relieved, she applied a light layer of foundation, a perfect colour match for her skin. She brushed her lashes with mascara and swiped a sheen of lip gloss across her lips. Then she turned to Amy who smiled her approval.

"So to the conservatory."

Caroline said, pointing to the door. Amy laughed and Caroline joined in, feeling much more relaxed.

Again Amy led Caroline down the staircase and along corridors of dark panelled wood. Caroline believed she was traversing a maze, one which she would be lost in without a guide. Just when she thought they had got lost, the corridor opened onto a hall. In front were two very high glass doors beyond which Caroline could see greenery.

Amy pushed open one of the doors and Caroline felt warmth float over her. The house wasn't cold, but she had been glad of the cardigan. Now as she followed Amy into the conservatory, she peeled it from her arms, already more than warm. Beneath her feet was a tiled pathway that curved between plants stretching way above her. Then they reached the centre. Gregg was standing next to a fountain and stepped forward to greet them.

"Thank you Amy."

He said, holding his hand out towards Caroline. Amy smiled and left them.

Caroline automatically placed her hand in his. He tugged her forward very gently to his side. The water in the fountain bounced off the marble edge and a soft spray settled on her bare arms. It was warm too. She sighed with pleasure.

"This is beautiful."

She said, her voice barely loud enough above the water. Gregg gave her his charming smile and led her around the fountain. On the other side was a cane sofa, upholstered in plump cushions. In front of the sofa, a marble table was laid for afternoon tea.

"Would you like to see the rest of the conservatory before we eat?"
Caroline nodded eagerly. He took her hand and led her along the pathways.

The conservatory was huge, much larger than Caroline imagined. The glass walls reached high up to a curved ceiling. Strangely, she could make out the clouds in the sky, could see the snow still falling. But none settled on the roof.

"It's heated."
Gregg said, reading her expression.

"Oh, amazing."
Gregg pointed out the various tropical plants and trees, explaining each one and its place in the miniature eco-system. Some had unusual fruits hanging from their branches, and Gregg told her many were quite rare.

A large, predominantly bright blue butterfly, fluttered past Caroline's face.

"We have quite a collection of tropical butterflies too."
Gregg said proudly. He pointed to a branch, and another gloriously coloured one gently flapped its wings. He held out his hand, and the insect opened its wings and fluttered to him, like he had beckoned.

"They know me, trust me."
He said quietly as the butterfly settled on his palm. Caroline was awed. This man was more than any man she had ever known, despite his youth.

The butterfly took flight and Gregg continued with the tour. He was very knowledgeable about everything in the conservatory. Caroline found it all interesting and delightful. Finally they came full circle back to the fountain. Gregg, still holding her hand, guided her to the sofa. He gently pushed her down until she was sitting.

The table in front had delicate, flower patterned china. Caroline heard a sound she didn't at first recognise. Then Gwyn appeared on the pathway pushing a trolley. She stopped at the table, smiled at them and then left. Caroline raised her eyebrows. Gregg said.

"Our tea."

"But of course."

Caroline murmured and she heard Gregg chortle, which she totally ignored.

"Caroline, relax. Enjoy yourself."

Humph, easier said than done, she thought. But she settled back against the cushions and tried to do exactly that.

Gregg took a teapot from the trolley and poured golden steaming liquid into cups standing in matching saucers. He handed one to Caroline.

"Just how you like it. Black and unsweetened."

"How did you know that?"

Caroline gasped, taking the china with an unsteady hand.

"There are many things I know about you."

He told her, his voice low. Caroline sipped from the cup, trying to keep her hand from trembling.

"But you only met me yesterday."

She stammered, her voice higher than usual.

"Caroline, don't worry."

He said so gently. She sighed and sipped her tea. Of course she would worry, but since there appeared to be nothing she could do about it, best she try and loosen up.

She actually found it easy, once Gregg had fully unloaded the trolley. There was a serving plate of neatly cut sandwiches, and a tiered cake stand loaded with tempting sweet treats. Gregg sat by her side and handed her a plate. He then politely offered her the sandwiches to choose from. She took two and felt him watching her.

"Please don't watch me eat. It's really off-putting."

He grinned, but turned his head away. Caroline bit into a sandwich and watched him instead. See how you like it, she thought. She heard his laughter as he piled his plate high. Caroline took a deep breath and let it out slowly, nibbling on her food. Gregg, his manners impeccable, still managed to devour twice as many sandwiches as she, in less time.

After their sandwiches, Gregg refilled the cups. He nodded his head towards the cake stand.

"Go ahead."

He told her. So she did. She picked up a cake covered in whipped cream and bit into it without reserve. The cream touched her nose and she felt like a child.

"Here, let me."

Gregg said, holding a linen napkin. She ran her tongue over her lips, but leaned towards him slightly. He dabbed at the remainder on her face and she giggled.

"Don't think anyone has done that before. Well not since I was little and my mum did."

Gregg gave her his ice blue stare.

"This is just the beginning Caroline. I promise you so much more, if you are willing."

Words were forming on her lips, but he continued.

"Just not today."

Caroline finished her tea and sat back on the sofa. She couldn't respond to his words because she had no idea what to say.

"I asked you a question in the cabin, but you…evaded answering."

He broke into her thoughts.

"I don't think I did. What question?"

Caroline frowned. Gregg stared at her and sipped his own tea.

"Do you like to dress up?"

He asked again.

"Oh, that question. Well I did answer."

She said, her eyes wide and innocent. He laughed, the sound echoing through the plants and bouncing off the glass.

"Not entirely truthful, Caroline."

"Well, I have costumes at home which I have worn to fancy dress parties. Like I told you."

She tried again. He was already shaking his head as she finished her sentence.

"But…do you like to dress up?"

Quietly he enunciated each word. Caroline shrugged as she leaned forward and placed her cup and saucer on the table.

"I…I don't think I understand you."

She said.

"Fancy dress, for a party, is taking on a themed image. It fits with everyone else, and is to enhance the enjoyment of the occasion. People only look like what the costume portrays. To dress up, is taking on a character, be that person and all their traits."

Gregg told her. Caroline pressed her lips together.

"Did you learn that at university studying acting?"

Gregg shook his head.

"No, that's something I worked out for myself."

"So you ask all your female friends to dress up?"

Caroline asked, putting on a sarcastic tone as she emphasised the last two words.

Gregg grinned. He laid his own cup down and took both her hands in his. He stroked her thumbs with his own and gave his piercing look.

"No Caroline. As I told you in your office, I like sex very much. But that doesn't mean I have had a lot of women. In fact, my list is quite short compared to some my age I know. Most of my experiences have been relatively conservative. The last girl I was with, was six months ago. It was a short relationship and I had no inclination to experiment. When I met you, all of that changed. I saw something in you, something so lost, and it hit me. I wanted to help you find you, and I'm certain my plans can do that."

"What are your plans?"

She whispered.

"Wait until tomorrow. At first, I intended to take you. Like I said with protection, but I wasn't going to wait."

He shrugged.

"I changed my mind. I want to find things out first. Then I'm sure my plans will have the most effect."

Caroline took a deep breath, held it and let it out slowly. This young man before her was confusing her. She thought back to her words to Derby. Maybe he actually was nutty. He certainly sounded it. Perhaps this was all some weird and crazy piece of theatre, some play script he was experimenting with, like the novel. She mentally shook herself. No, he wasn't mad, she was sure of that. He seemed far too together and calm, to be some barmy rich kid who had nothing better to do.

Gregg chuckled and gently squeezed her hands. His eyes boring into her were reading her yet again.

"I am as sane as you are Caroline."

She shut her eyes, and felt him shake as he snickered at her attempt to block him out. He gave her hands a little wiggle and she opened her eyes.

"What?"

She snapped, which only made him laugh more.

"You are trully wonderful when fired up."

She tried to snatch her hands from his grasp, but he held them firm. He leaned towards her, drawing her to him. Lightly he kissed her forehead, and once again, Caroline's temper dampered.

"I still want an answer."

He whispered.

Caroline pulled herself away from his contact. She couldn't think straight when he was so close. He let her go, waiting. She plucked another, smaller cake from the stand and bit into the confection. The sweetness soothed her nerves and gave her time to formulate her answer. The outfits in her wardrobe that had never been worn in public flashed across her mind. The toys Frank had enjoyed watching her play with. Her old vibrator, that no one had seen her use, not even Frank. Did she like to dress up? She didn't know. All of it had been at Frank's request and she had complied. That thought sprung another. What had Frank asked his other women to do.

“I can see this subject has upset you Caroline.” She jumped at his soft words. She had been so engrossed in her own wonderings, and he had been so silent, she had almost believed she was alone.

“Oh, um…no. not upset. Just a couple of things I was reminded of.”
She tried t o brush it off.

“Caroline, look at me.”
Gregg urged. She did.

“I’ve told you. Anything that makes you uncomfortable will not be proceeded with.”
Caroline bit back a giggle. The way he spoke was strange, even for someone of aristocratic background.

“Where do you come from?”
She asked and Gregg actually looked a bit taken aback. That at least made him appear human.

“Well I was born at the estate, in Yorkshire. But I have travelled extensively. Why?”

“Oh.”
Caroline didn’t want to tell him what was on her mind for fear of offending him. And she definitely didn’t want him to know how her imagination had him labelled as a vampire, or other inhuman being.

“Um, no reason really.”
She said, averting her eyes. She knew the lie hadn’t got past him, but he didn’t push the question, again turning back to his previous query.

“Dressing up?”

Caroline folded her hands in her lap, and stuck her tongue in her cheek, formulating an answer. Finally she took a breath and began.

"Right. Well, Frank used to like me to dress up in a few outfits…"
She stopped, a deep blush staining her cheeks. Gregg covered her hands with one of his.

"Don't be embarrassed. I won't judge."
He coaxed. Caroline swallowed, cleared her throat and continued.

"It wasn't really role play. He liked me to do the same stuff in any of the costumes."

She hesitantly went on to explain about the toys and what Frank would get turned on by. When she was finished she looked at Gregg. He gave her his stare.

"So did you like being in the clothes, doing what you did?"
Caroline turned her head to one side and lowered her chin to one shoulder.

"It didn't…do…anything for me. I mean, once he…started making love to me, then yes. But before that, it was just…mechanical."
She expected to see disappointment in his gaze. But he tilted her chin up and smiled.

"Caroline I promise, if you choose to dress up for us, you will have as much pleasure from it as I will. We will enjoy it together."
It took a moment for his words to register. That he had said 'us' and 'we' excited her. Suddenly, whatever Gregg had planned no longer seemed frightening. She had no idea what his plans entailed, but now she was actually looking forward to them, wherever they took her.

CHAPTER 14.

Gregg lifted her hands from her lap and kissed the palms, feather light and arousing. Yet Caroline held herself in check. As she began to heat up inside, she knew he wouldn't take the simple kiss any further. He had promised more, just not then and she believed him. The anticipation excited her further.

"I want to show you another part of the house that I'm sure will delight you."

He told her, standing and pulling her to her feet.

"But first, a change of clothes. You look beautiful in that dress, but it's not suitable for other rooms in the house. We keep the fires burning, and of course we have central heating, but the ceilings are high and the rooms can feel a little chilly. I'll walk you back and call for Amy."

Caroline felt strange. On any normal day she would wear office clothes and then change into casual at home. Occasionally she would dress up if Frank was taking her out. She had a decent wardrobe, but not so many clothes to be changing several times a day. Still, she would let Gregg spoil her, there was no one else to do that.

Amy was already waiting in the main hall when they arrived. Caroline thought Gregg had either sent instructions mentally, or he had the day so perfectly planned to the last minute.

"Please take Caroline to her room and help her change."

He said to Amy, who nodded. Then he stepped back.

"I shall see you shortly."

He told Caroline and waited politely for Amy to lead her up the stairs. Once inside the room, Caroline spoke.

"Tell me you weren't waiting in the hall the whole time."

Amy giggled.

"Of course not silly. Gregg arranged for me to be there at that precise moment."

Caroline sighed with relief. That at least told her one thing, he wasn't sending out thoughts for his staff to capture mentally.

"So what am I to wear for this event?"

She asked Amy.

"Sit down, relax, and put on your gown. We're not in any rush this time."

Caroline tossed her head from side to side, stripped off the dress, and wrapped herself in the long satin gown laid across the bed. She padded over to the window and plonked down on the window seat. No rush this time, she thought, as she gazed out the window at the winter scene.

It took her breath away. Inside the conservatory she hadn't noticed the day passing by. Now she realised it was late enough for the sun to start setting. The sky was clear and bright, having finally beaten the snow clouds into a retreat, leaving deep red slashes on the horizon. Caroline watched as the lowering sun began to remove the colour from the world. The red deepened to purple, and finally as the sun dipped beyond sight, the purple became deepest dark blue. Tiny pin pricks of starlight popped up, and the moon glistened silver, competing with the brightness of the snow.

Caroline gave in to the beauty of the winter sunset, and settled herself more deeply into the cushion of the window seat. Wrapped in her gown she was warm and cosy, so relaxed her arms hung limp in her lap. She could stay where she was all night, just watching the silent, still world outside.

"Don't go to sleep."

Amy's gentle voice roused her. Caroline turned her head and smiled at the young woman.

"It's so beautiful out there, don't you think?"

Amy nodded.

"I love the moors in all seasons. It's unique and wondrous. There's always something new to see and discover."

She told Caroline, passion in her voice.

"But, right now, here's your outfit."

She stated pragmatically. Caroline sighed and slipped from the seat. Amy was holding up a hanger. When Caroline saw what she was to wear, she burst into laughter.

"Are you serious?"

"Oh yes. Gregg was very specific."

"Oh I bet he was."

Caroline replied, holding out her hand for the garment.

As before, Amy led Caroline down the stairs and along the halls. Caroline wondered if she would have time to find her own way around the house. When it seemed like they were going in circles, Amy stopped at high, double wooden doors. Instead of opening them she turned to Caroline.

"Just go right in. Gregg will be waiting."

Amy smiled, and leaving her alone, walked back the way they had come.

Caroline was nervous as she took the handle of one of the doors. What was behind it? What would be waiting? All of the old horror movies flooded into her brain. The room would be cold, lit by candles only. It would be bare, but for an ancient coffin in the centre. Gregg would emerge, a dark cloak wrapped about his shoulders, his face pale as death. Long fangs smiling wickedly.

Caroline gave herself a mental shake and told herself to stop being ridiculous. Still she trembled as she turned the door handle. She was surprised it opened easily. She had expected it to squeal and the door to be heavy. She stepped through the opening and gasped. The room was as far from her imaginings as it could be.

A huge bright fire gave off warmth and glowing light. Surrounding it were several plump sofas and armchairs, with side tables. But what had made her gasp, was the deep shelves of books. She was in a library.

"Amazing isn't it?"

Gregg's deep voice penetrated her surprise. She looked to where he was standing near a shelf, a book in his hand, and laughter burst from her lips.

"You…you're…we're matching."

She exclaimed. He came forward to greet her, his eyes so blue against the firelight, his smile dazzling.

"And the most appropriate attire for a relaxing time with books."

She giggled as he stopped in front of her. She put her hand out and plucked the sleeve of the red, holly patterned onesie, identical to the one she was wearing. She looked down and Gregg was wearing santa slippers, the same as hers.

"You're crazy."

She chuckled.

"But I'm right."

He said, throwing an arm over her shoulder and leading her to the rows of books.

Caroline was in her element. Not only did Gregg's library contain a wide selection of books, it also housed some very old and rare ones. Some, so valuable they were locked in alarmed glass cases. Caroline stared, longing to hold these treasures. Gregg leaned in close and she heard the sound of jangling. She looked over her shoulder and he was holding out a small ring of keys.

"Go ahead. Indulge your desire."

He said so softly. For once Caroline was exceedingly glad he could read her mind, as she took the keys from his hand.

"Explore Caroline. I'll be by the fire. I have already chosen my read."

Gregg left Caroline to browse. In her cosy onesie, she unlocked the glass cabinets, and lifted the precious books carefully and examined them. She held them lovingly and sniffed the leather bindings, inhaling the history of each and every one. Books were her life, but she had never seen and held any so precious.

Knowing she could spend a life time in this room, and knowing she had limited time, Caroline sighed and replaced the rare books, re-locking their secure beds. From there, she strolled to the shelves and randomly picked out books reading the blurbs.

Some were her kind of read, others just interesting, because they were books. She discovered authors she had never heard of, and wondered if Gregg took a particular interest in those. It made her squirm a little. She was like most literary agents, who only took a real interest in her own clients, the known authors, or those who could be endorsed by the known, or others in the industry. Maybe she should change her habits a bit and take a gamble on some of the unknowns, she thought as she selected a book.

She read the title, it was catchy. She turned it over and read the blurb. That was interesting, enticing. The author, she didn't know. But she took the book and padded over to an armchair. Gregg was sitting in the opposite chair. He glanced up from his book and smiled.

"Found something you like?"
He asked, firelight bouncing off the sparkles in his eyes. Caroline nodded and held up the novel.

"Ah, good choice."

"Do you particularly champion unknown authors?"
She enquired. Gregg placed a finger between the pages of his book and leaned forward.

"Not really. I just don't only choose books from the well knowns. I find a lot of books from authors all over, who have never made it into the mainstream publishing world. If I think they are good and interest me, I buy them."

"Is that why you chose to have a go yourself?"
Gregg smiled and shook his head.

"No Caroline. To be honest, I was bored. Thought I would try my hand."
He leaned forward even more.

"I'll let you into a little secret. It's not even finished."

Caroline raised her eyebrows. He had taken quite a gamble himself doing that. Every literary agent and publisher made it quite clear on their websites that submissions should only be sent when a manuscript is complete. Many these days, also require it to be polished and even professionally edited.

"Well, well, well. Cheeky aren't you."
She told him light-heartedly. Gregg grinned boyishly.

"You asked me why I chose you."
Caroline nodded. Gregg leaned back and closed his brilliant eyes for a moment. Then he popped them open and once again bore them into her.

"I sat here one morning, mulling over what to do with the day, and my little story leaped into my mind. First the sketch. I'm good at drawing."
He stated. Caroline smiled. She definitely agreed with that.

"So, I took a notepad from the stationery draw over there." He pointed to a desk in a corner. "And wrote the first chapter. The second and third followed…in a similar way."
Caroline giggled.

"I'd say."

She said. Gregg's eyes flashed, but he was smiling at her.

"Then I ran out of steam. Had no idea where to go from there. I booted up my laptop and thought I should do a bit of research, find some writing techniques. The key words in my search engine included results for agents. Having no idea what your profession really offered, I clicked on yours."

Gregg laid his book on the side table and stood up. He crossed to her and knelt on the floor in front of her. He covered her hands with his.

"I cannot explain what it was about your site that intrigued me. Then, it wasn't even the photo of you, or your bio. But something about your professionalism struck me. It was like you were talking directly to me. I knew then I wanted to really make an effort with the novel. I've never finished anything, not even university. I know that makes me sound like a spoilt brat, and I suppose that's what I am. But this time I wanted to try."

He gazed into her eyes. As she looked back, she saw the colour darken and soften, just as they had done when he spoke of Hal and Gwyn. Gone were the diamonds and penetrating stare, replaced by a different emotion. Caroline felt a prick of guilt. His novel would never have made it.

"I'm so sorry Gregg."

He placed a finger to her lips.

"Sh. It's fine. I know, should have known before, I'm not a writer. Besides, after I met you, it just didn't matter anymore. I maybe spoilt, but I do care about other people, and giving you pleasure, in any form is enough for me."

The diamonds were back, glittering and flashing. Caroline sucked in a breath and Gregg chuckled devilishly. His finger still rested on her lip and she longed to take it in her mouth, bite it and suck on it.

"Not yet."

He whispered. Caroline took a breath and let it out slowly. It helped calm her. He stood up and returned to his seat.

"Relax and enjoy your read. We can continue this discussion over dinner."

Caroline blinked. She hadn't even thought about food. The day had been so strange and fulfilling, at times extremely frustrating too, but she couldn't quite believe so much had happened in a few hours. Dinner would be very welcome and she wondered how that would pan out. She guessed another outfit. She couldn't imagine Gregg would slum it on the sofa in his onesie with a tray on his lap. She would be happy with that, but she was also excited at the prospect of dinner with this glorious man opposite her.

Caroline lifted her feet and tucked them under her. She would do as he asked and read the novel she had chosen. It wasn't a thick book and she could speed read, it was part of her job. But she did want to do it justice. So she opened it and paged to the first chapter. If she liked that one, she would take her time with the rest of the book.

It took her only a very short time to get through the first chapter and she very much liked what she read. Gregg was right, it had been a good choice. She didn't think she would have time to read the whole thing then, not properly, with the attention it deserved.

"This is good. I want to enjoy it, not speed read it. So would it be alright to take it to my room for later?"

Gregg glanced up at her words.

"But of course Caroline. You don't have to ask. Everything in this house is at your disposal."

Feeling like royalty, Caroline beamed.

CHAPTER 15.

Caroline was deeply absorbed in the novel. It wasn't her usual choice of book, but the author had a style she found fascinating. Some of my clients should take a leaf out of this author's book. She told herself, laughing inwardly at the idiom. Maybe I should contact the person and ask to see some more of their work, if they have any. She said to herself.

"You are enjoying it, aren't you?"

Gregg said, startling her. She looked up from the book and nodded.

"Yes, and it makes me feel rather guilty and inflexible. I always used to think I would give anyone who can write well, a chance. But I'm no different from the rest of the agents. I bin most of the submissions I receive, some of which show promise. But because they are a high risk, I don't take a chance on them and try and take them further. This…you, have opened my eyes."

"Then my seriously bad, unfinished manuscript did some good then."

He replied. Caroline pressed her lips together.

"When I get back to work, I'm going to make an effort to find out about this author. I don't suppose you know her personally?"

Gregg shook his head.

"No, sorry. I was simply browsing a tiny backstreet bookshop in York, an independent. I found the book in there. The author has used her own imprint and self-published. The owner of the shop only had that one copy on the shelf."

"Hmm, that's often the way it works. Even some of the big high street stores only carry one or two copies of most authors. Really, only the top ten get the most promotion and have dozens available."

She shrugged.

"That's the business."

Gregg studied her face, his exquisite blue eyes flicking across every feature. She didn't feel uncomfortable anymore.

"Time to change for dinner I believe."

"Oh…ok."

She said, taken aback at his sudden change in subject.

"Don't worry Caroline. We will return to this topic, over dinner."

He stood up and laid his book on the table by his chair. He stepped forward and held out a hand. Caroline took it and he pulled her up.

"Amy should be in the main hall waiting."

He linked her arm through his own and together they left the library.

"This house is like a maze."

Caroline murmured as they walked through the corridors. Gregg looked down at her and smiled.

"Wait until you see the estate. This place is positively tiny compared to that."

Caroline sucked in a breath. She hadn't thought beyond the two days Gregg had suggested. Hadn't known what to expect. But it seemed Gregg had further plans. She wanted to question him, ask what he meant. But that would mean discussing the doctor, and she wasn't ready for that. In fact, she hadn't really thought about it since this morning.

They reached the main hallway quite quickly. Caroline assumed it was because she was getting used to moving about the house. She remembered Leo at university. His first week there he had phoned every night, teary and lonely. He had felt lost. The campus was huge and he didn't think he would ever find his way around. Three weeks later, his calls had reduced to two a week and he was settled. He had friends, and could get around to his lessons without needing the little map in his induction pack. By the end of the first term, he told her the campus must have shrunk, because it took him no time at all to go from building to building.

"Amy, could you help Caroline change for dinner please?"

Gregg's voice broke into her thoughts as he handed her over to a smiling Amy. As they mounted the stairs, Caroline's feet didn't need to follow each of Amy's steps. She was at least remembering the way to her room. Inside, an outfit was already laid out on the bed, complete with underwear and lace topped hold-up stockings.

"Wow, that's gorgeous."
Caroline exclaimed. Amy nodded, grinning.

"Your bath is ready too."

Caroline soaked in the deep pool of a bath, enjoying the scented bubbles. Amy had insisted on washing her hair and then left her alone. She closed her eyes and rested her head on the padded edge. She could get used to this, she thought. Then another thought crept in, invading her peace. This wouldn't last. It wasn't like Gregg was going to propose and they'd get married. Of course not. He wanted some fun and she was his target. Whatever his plans were, and for how long, it would all come to an end.

"So enjoy it whilst it lasts."
She said aloud, angry with herself.

"Don't be so damned serious. Have some fun yourself and let whatever comes after take care of itself."

"Everything ok?"
Amy said from the doorway. Caroline stood up, letting the water and bubbles drip from her body.

"Yes Amy. I'm just having a little go at myself. Don't worry, I'm not mad, talking to myself. I'm ready to come out now."

No longer conscious of her nakedness in front of Amy, Caroline waited for the young woman to fetch her a towel. She stepped up to the edge of the bath and wrapped the fluffy bath sheet about her. Then with Amy's help, descended the steps. She followed Amy to the dressing room, sat before the mirror and let the girl comb and blow-dry her hair. Caroline then smoothed moisturiser over her face and applied fresh makeup, with suggestions from Amy.

Back in the main bedroom, Amy helped her dress. After donning the silky underwear and stockings, Caroline stepped into the dress. It was lace, cream with a black overlay that reached part way down her thigh and up the bodice. The bottom was cream, as were the three quarter length sleeves. It moulded her body, and was soft and comfortable. The final touch were black and cream suede high heels.

With her red blonde hair cascading about her shoulders, Caroline gave a twirl.

"Will I do?"

She asked Amy.

"Caroline, you look stunning."

She felt it too, as Amy once again led her from the room down the stairs. At the bottom, Amy took her along another unknown corridor.

"Gregg said the main dining room is far too formal. I mean, it's huge. The table can seat twenty. So he asked me to take you to what used to be the drawing room. It's a lot more cosy."

Amy chatted as they strolled. It didn't take long to reach the room. Amy pushed open a door and stood back for Caroline to enter. Gregg was standing by a long French window. He had his back to her, but turned as she entered. Caroline's breath left her. He was simply stunning. His blonde floppy hair fell to one side, his alabaster skin glowing in the firelight. He was wearing a black suit that fit his wide shoulders perfectly, narrowing to his slender figure. His white shirt was open at the throat showing the golden blonde hairs of his chest.

Stepping forward, he came to greet her. He took her hand and lifted her palm to his lips. His kiss, so light, burnt into her skin, sending tingling sensations straight down to her centre, igniting her most feminine point.

"You are beautiful."

Gregg murmured against her palm. Caroline took in a deep breath.

"So are you."

She whispered, barely able to speak.

"Come."

He said, tugging her hand and leading her towards a table near the French doors.

The table was intimate, just big enough for two. It was laid elegantly. But what really impressed Caroline was what it looked out on. The French doors had velvet drapes hanging open. Outside, Caroline could see a terrace, cleared of snow. Beyond that was a garden. The snow was piled high in drifts, obscuring most of the rows of hedges and shrubs, but it was still an amazing sight.

"I thought you would enjoy this more than the formal dining room. That is so big and has no view. Here you can look out at the big freeze, and stay completely warm."

Caroline nodded and smiled appreciatively at him, as he drew out a chair for her.

"Gwyn will serve our meal."

He told her, uncorking a bottle of wine and pouring her a glass.

Gwyn came in with the first course and set it before them. Caroline tucked in immediately. She was hungry and hadn't noticed. Gregg ate silently for a moment, but Caroline could feel his eyes on her. She expected to feel disconcerted, being watched whilst she ate, but actually didn't. Once the main course arrived, Gregg topped up their wine glasses and held his up.

"To us."

He said. Caroline clinked her glass against his and smiled.

The food was delicious. It fit perfectly with the winter evening without being heavy. Gregg took a bite, chewed and put down his knife and fork.

"I knew I wasn't supposed to send in my submission. Your website was very clear that you would be away. But I had it ready in an email and decided it couldn't harm. Even if I had to wait until you returned."

Caroline finished a mouthful and lifted her wineglass.

"If I hadn't gone into my office that morning, I probably never would have looked at it. I don't take much time off. Usually just a couple of days. There are always those who ignore the website and still submit."

Gregg's eyes flashed and he grinned.

"But because of my…failed wedding day, I decided I might as well go back to work immediately. My inbox had many submissions, and I guessed had I have actually been on my…honeymoon, by the time I returned there would be thousands. I would have binned the lot. But as there weren't that many, I went through them. The majority did get binned. Yours would have, but I was in a funny mood. Your pseudonym struck me as amusing. Then the sketch. I almost didn't look at the chapters. Was in fact, about to send a rejection email. Then I changed my mind. I thought, arrange a meeting, I have time on my hands."

Caroline picked up her fork and continued with her meal.

"Do you believe in destiny Caroline?"
Gregg asked softly. Caroline thought for a moment.

"I don't know. I didn't…then, now. Everything that has happened over the last couple of days is so…unreal."
Gregg smiled, his eyes glittering.

"And there lies your answer."
Caroline was confused, so she stayed silent. Gregg grinned. He knew exactly what his words were doing to her. For a moment she had the horrific feeling that it was all just a game to him. She shook off the sensation. If that were the case, then she would go with the flow and enjoy whatever was in store.

They continued with their meal, and it seemed to Caroline the subject was closed, as Gregg said no more about it. Gwyn brought in a tray of coffee, and Gregg said they would take it by the fire. He poured and handed her a delicate china cup and saucer, sat back and sipped his own.

"Well, I am certain this was all meant to happen. Especially after our first meeting."

"What makes you so certain?"
She asked curiously.

"Caroline, even though you were upset and very raw, would you have, at any other time, agreed to meet a complete stranger in your office, on a fine day, let alone one where the weather had virtually cut off everyone from their daily activities?"

Caroline had asked herself that very question the day she stood in Adele's office making Gregg's tea. She recalled the chill of fear that had flooded through her, the shock of finding herself vulnerable.

"No."

That one tiny word slipped between her lips.

"So we were destined to meet. If I'm honest, I knew the novel didn't have a chance. I read a lot Caroline. So I have some idea what constitutes good writing. I believe I was as driven to send that submission as you were to read it and contact me."

Caroline finished her coffee and took a deep breath. It was a lot to take in. She knew he was right. Too many things had happened since Monday for it all to be just coincidence. But could she really believe that some mysterious force was directing her life. Especially since so many years had passed with so much chaos.

Then Derby's words came back to her. Despite Frank's habitual cheating, he had given her and the boys huge chunks of happiness. Yes it had finally gone horribly wrong, but would she have had their lives any other way. Without realising, she was shaking her head, just a tiny bit.

"Destiny Caroline. It moulds our lives when we are least expecting it."

Caroline glanced up at him. His words were so mature and wise, she half expected to see an old wrinkled man before her. What she said next, popped out of her mouth involuntarily.

"Do you have a portrait hidden in your attic?"

Gregg leaned back and his laugh resonated around the room.

"I'm no Dorian Gray Caroline."

Caroline gave herself a mental shake. She really should stop letting her imagination influence her thoughts. Gregg gave her his stare.

"Do not be afraid of me Caroline. I wouldn't, couldn't hurt you."

"I'm not…I know."
She stammered, not sure she was telling the truth.

Gregg leaned forward and put his cup on the table. His eyes had changed again. They were no longer flashing diamonds, nor were they the deep blue of a calm sea. Instead they seemed to swirl, a whirlpool sucking her in. Before she knew it she was leaning forward too. Gregg laughed, more softly.

"Would you like to watch a movie?"
Caroline sat up straight, shocked at his sudden change of subject.

"Um, yes. If you'd like."
She said hesitantly. Gregg shook his head.

"Not if I want. If you want."
He told her gently. Caroline nodded.

"Well, um, then yes please. That would be very relaxing."

Gregg was on his feet holding out a hand. She took it and he pulled her up.

"You will want to change."
He told her. Caroline raised her eyebrows as she followed him through the door. He was right, she didn't think sitting in front of a TV would be very comfortable in a formal dress, but another outfit? Gregg glanced at her over his shoulder and grinned. Damn him, she thought. He was reading her thoughts again.

Amy was waiting in the hall. So the movie was on the agenda, Caroline thought.

"Could you take Caroline and help her change into something casual please."
He said to Amy.

"What sort of film would you like to watch?"

He asked Caroline. She was surprised. Everything else had been pre-arranged. She assumed the movie would be the same.

"Uh, anything."

He gave her a quizzical look.

"Oh come now Caroline. That's a little vague."

"Ok, something Christmassy then."

He grinned boyishly.

"Right. Amy, please bring her along when she's ready. I'll get it set up."

He spun around and bounced off down a corridor. Caroline giggled. For once he had dropped the sophistication and she found it a nice change.

In Caroline's room, Amy went to the dressing room and returned with a fleece lounge suit, and a pair of soft suede moccasins. Caroline stripped out of the fine clothing and slipped on the casual.

"So he had this planned too?"

She stated. Amy shook her head.

"No. He asked me to be available to help you change if needed. But I didn't know what time and if I would be."

"So how come you were already waiting?"

Caroline asked, surprise in her voice. Amy chuckled.

"You wouldn't have noticed. Gregg has a pager app on his phone. He can alert me very discreetly."

Caroline simply nodded.

As the other times, Amy led Caroline through the house. Caroline was curious to where they were going. Surely any of the rooms could accommodate a television and DVD player. Finally they stopped in front of another set of doors, which Amy pushed open. Caroline gasped as she stepped into a mini cinema.

Four rows of four, deep, plush seats faced a huge screen. Gregg was nowhere to be seen.

"He'll be in the projection room getting set up. Go and sit down, I'll leave you to it, he won't be long."

Caroline strolled down the aisle between the rows to the front. As in a public cinema, there was a carpeted space between the front row and the screen. She turned and saw a light from a window right at the back and above. Gregg waved through the glass, then he disappeared. A few seconds later he was by her side. He held out his arm, sweeping it across the room.

"Where shall we sit?"

Caroline pointed to the middle.

"There."

"You go and get settled. I will be just a moment."

Caroline padded to the seat she had chosen and sat down. There was plenty of leg room, but the chair was also wide enough to tuck her feet up if she wanted to. Like on an aeroplane, the seat in front, had a drop down tray in its back. Gregg reappeared and Caroline burst into giggles. He was carrying a card bucket of popcorn, and two large paper cups. Caroline pulled down the tray in front of her seat and Gregg placed the goodies on it.

"I have some chocolate in my pocket too."

He told her, taking the seat next to her and pulling down his own tray. He took out the chocolate and handed it to her.

"Now enjoy."

He said shuffling into his seat and taking her hand in his.

Caroline thoroughly enjoyed the film. It was one of her favourite Christmas movies. A romance with all the magic of Christmas added. She knew it was quite lengthy, but didn't feel at all tired, even though the day had been very long and full. She munched on popcorn and chocolate, sharing with Gregg, surprised she had any room for the confectionery, and sipped Coca Cola.

In part of the film, a couple made snowmen and snow angels as they fell in love. Caroline felt a tear prick her eye, but refused to let her emotions get the better of her. She felt Gregg squeeze her hand gently. How could he sense her mood in the dark of the cinema, but she pushed the question away. It no longer mattered how he did it, he just did.

The movie came to an end and Caroline stretched. She had no idea what the time was and didn't care.

"Good?"

Gregg asked. She nodded and yawned, quickly covering her mouth with the back of her hand.

"Oh sorry."

"Don't be. It's been a very long day. Come, I'll take you to your room."

Caroline's heartbeat quickened. Gregg's eyes gleamed, shining like beacons in the dark.

"Not tonight Caroline."

He whispered. His words should have extinguished the fire that was beginning to burn, but the sexiness of his voice only inflamed her.

"Soon, I promise."

Caroline wasn't entirely appeased as they made their way along the halls. They came to the stairway and Caroline stopped. Gregg looked at her questioningly.

"Could you just open the door, let me see the snow."

He grinned and complied. Icy air swept into the hallway. Caroline stepped forward and rubbed her arms. She looked out at the stillness of the night. The grounds were dazzling. The snow reflecting starlight.

"Makes me want to go out and jump in it, like a kid."

She whispered.

"Then let's."

Gregg said, shocking her.

"But we'll freeze to death. It's got to be, I don't know, well below zero."

She exclaimed. Gregg laughed.

"No we won't. I'll take you to your room. In your dressing room you will find a full snowsuit and snow boots. I told Amy we wouldn't need her anymore tonight, so I'll leave you to change then come back for you."

Gregg said it so matter-of-factly that Caroline couldn't refuse.

Before she knew it, Gregg was knocking on her door and she was stepping through it, having donned the cosy snowsuit. He was dressed similarly, his suit being all black to her pure white one.

"You'll lose me in the snow."

She giggled.

"Never."

He told her seriously as they descended the stairs.

Caroline thought they would go out the front door, but Gregg led her along a corridor. Soon, they were back in the drawing room. He took her over to the French doors and pulled one open. She followed him onto the terrace and down to the lawn. The snow had reached the top of the terrace.

"There are three steps, but follow me."
He said, puzzling her.

Gregg let go of her hand and took several steps back. She watched him. He ran forward and at the edge of the terrace took a leap. He landed in the soft snow and turned to face her, laughing. He beckoned with his hand. Caroline didn't stop to think. She stepped back and launched herself forward, taking off at the last second. The snow cushioned her landing and she emerged from it squealing with delight. Her first thought was, this must be how our little dog felt.

Gregg grabbed her hand, and together they forced their way through the snow. For Caroline it was thigh high, but her suit and boots kept her warm and dry. Gregg steered her towards what looked like a clump of bushes, easing in between a gap. They were so covered, it was difficult to make out their shape. Then Caroline gasped in wonder. At the centre of the clump was what should be a triple basin fountain. But the water had frozen as it had fallen into cascades of glistening icicles. His breath puffing out in wisps, Gregg spoke close to her ear.

"We forgot to switch it off when the snow began to fall. But it makes a wondrous sight doesn't it?"
Caroline could only nod. She hadn't ever seen anything so beautiful, it took her breath away.

The snow wasn't quite so deep near the fountain, the shrubs having caught most of it. Gregg led her around the stone and their boots crunched. It was such a delightful sound Caroline laughed. She felt very childlike, lifting her feet, stamping her prints in the snow. Each one left a deep impression, each scrunch ringing out in the silence of the night.

Gregg took her to a clearing and pointed.

"Shall we make a snowman?"

Caroline nodded eagerly, and together they rolled two big balls, heaping one onto the other. There was too much snow about to find stones for his eyes, but Gregg plodded to the edge of the clearing and returned with bits of branch. He stuck two small ones on the snowman's face and added larger ones for nose and mouth. The stars and moonlight in the clear crisp sky, lit up their creation.

A tiny bubble of mischievousness grabbed Caroline. She took a small handful of soft snow and rolled it between her palms. Then she drew back her arm and tossed it at an unsuspecting Gregg. Her aim was true. He spun around in surprise. She laughed.

"You, little demon."

He said, his wicked grin wide.

In a flash, Gregg had pulled her to him and deposited her in the snow. She gasped, but held his hand firm, pulling him down with her. They rolled, Caroline clinging to him, both full of laughter. He came to a stop on top of her, and as he looked down, his eyes flashed. She put her hands on the back of his head and pulled his mouth to hers. He didn't resist. She opened her lips and his tongue penetrated deep. She could feel his hardness instantly, through the snowsuit and pressed her hips against him. He pushed lightly and she wriggled, desire swamping her. Devouring his mouth, all Caroline could think of was the pleasure she was getting from this heavenly man.

Gregg kissed her deeply, enjoying the feel of her tongue and her body pushing up to his. She rolled her hips and he barely held on. But he wouldn't lose control. He would let her take what she wanted then, let her have some release, but his own desire could wait. He had so much planned, and part of his enjoyment was the wait. So he plunged her mouth with his tongue, and held her hips against his own. Caroline pushed and wiggled harder, panting as her climax approached. Even with the thick snowsuits between them, when it came it was powerful. She squealed against his lips, threw back her head and arms in the snow, and let out a scream of pleasure.

Gregg pushed hard, intensifying her orgasm. He so badly wanted release himself but wouldn't let go. Her satisfaction was all that mattered then, and he watched in delight as her face shone with passion. Seconds, that seemed like hours later, Caroline slumped, her breath coming in rapid puffs. Gregg lifted his body a little from hers, and looked down into eyes filled with rapturous emotion.

"That was…that was amazing."

She panted. Gregg smiled.

"You are beautiful when you come."

He whispered. Caroline felt her cheeks burn in the icy air. No one had ever said anything like that before. She felt she should be embarrassed, but found she wasn't.

"Thank you."

She simply said. Gregg lifted himself off and rolled to her side.

"Not quite snow angels."

He said and she laughed.

"No, but it was heavenly."

They both lay in the snow gazing at the starlit sky above. No more words seemed necessary. The air around them was pure and silent. The snow muting any sound that may have been made, even by a creature of the night. Caroline felt satiated. She felt no need for her vibrator, even though it was tucked away at home, the orgasm had been that satisfying. She didn't think Gregg had come. He hadn't shown the signs, and she was reluctant to ask.

"It was for you Caroline. My time will come. I'm not disappointed."

His voice penetrated the silence.

"Oh."

Was all she could say and he huffed out his deep, sexy laugh.

Gregg bounced to his feet and leaned forward, offering a hand to Caroline. She took it and allowed him to pull her to her feet. The freezing air finally found its mark on her cheeks and she shivered.

"Come."

Gregg said.

"I already did."

She replied, unabashedly. He gave her a sideways glance, his eyes gleaming wickedly.

"Naughty Caroline."

Came his honeyed voice, barely louder than a breath of air.

With his hand firmly holding hers, Gregg took them back to the French doors. The warmth of the room hit them welcomingly. Gregg closed the door on the night, Caroline giving a last look at the beauty beyond.

He took her to her room and kissed her cheek chastely, before saying goodnight and waiting until she had entered her bedroom and closed the door.

Caroline leaned back against the solid wood, closing her eyes. She was a little too hot in the snowsuit, so began peeling the outfit off where she stood. She padded in socked feet to the ottoman and laid the suit over it. In her hurry to change, she hadn't noticed the silk pyjamas laid out on her bed. She smiled. Amy had thought of everything.

Caroline didn't feel tired despite the lateness of the hour. Her bedside clock told her it was nearly one thirty. She strolled to the window seat and looked out. Clouds were beginning to float across the sky. Some wispy and light, others thick enough to block the stars, the moon peeking in and out. Caroline thought it would probably snow again.

She readied herself for bed and slipped under the covers. She closed her eyes, the pillow soft beneath her head. She was quite sure she wouldn't sleep, wasn't ready to sleep. But the warmth and comfort of the big bed, had her drifting off before her mind could register she was doing so.

CHAPTER 16.

Caroline came awake refreshed and stretching. The clock on the bedside table said eight. She had slept deep and well. She threw back the covers and trod to the window. Clouds raced across the sky. The fields had changed where fresh snow and wind had whipped up more drifts. A knock on the door startled her.

"Caroline."

She heard Amy's voice, light and soft. Caroline opened the door and the girl stepped in.

"Sleep well?"

Caroline nodded.

"Gregg says he'll meet you for breakfast at nine."

Caroline felt a little bubble of excitement at the prospect of seeing him. Then another thought doused the thrill. The doctor, he would be back to give her the results. For most of the previous day she had been able to forget about the ordeal. Now it was the only thing she could think of.

"What's wrong?"
Amy asked with concern.

"Nothing. Well, results today."

"Oh. Look Caroline, whatever they are, the doctor will give you the best advice."
Caroline shrugged. She wasn't bothered about that. The only thing she could think of was how it would affect her relationship with Gregg. After yesterday, and especially their intimacy in the snow, she wanted more. Wanted all. She wouldn't have that if the news was bad.

Dressed in stretch jeans and cosy jumper, Caroline was taken to the drawing room, where Gregg sat waiting. Through the French doors, Caroline could see the terrace was now covered in snow. Gregg stood as she approached, and as ever the gentleman, held out a chair for her. The table had a plate of croissants and preserves, a teapot and a pot of coffee.

"There's hot food there. Would you like me to get you something?"
Gregg asked, indicating a small, wheeled hot trolley. Caroline smiled, her mouth watering.

"Bacon?"
Gregg grinned.

"Now that's what I call breakfast."

He stood up and went to the trolley. Whilst she waited, Caroline poured herself a cup of black coffee. The aroma was powerful. She sipped from her cup and stared out at the morning. Then it came to her, and she sucked in a breath. Gregg returned, placing a hot bacon roll in front of her. He saw her expression.

"Caroline. What's wrong?
Her breakfast forgotten, the cup still held near her mouth, Caroline blinked.

"The snow."
Words stuck in her throat. Gregg covered her hand with his, as he retook his seat.

"The snow what Caroline?"

"The doctor."
Was all she could manage in reply.

Gregg's grip relaxed. He lifted her hand and folded it into both of his.

"It's alright Caroline."
She looked at him puzzled, not sure what she had even said. He seemed to understand though.

"They will fly in."
He told her.

"Huh. What, who…fly in?"
She shook her head to get rid of the muzzy feeling inside. Coffee slopped over the cup onto her hand. It wasn't so hot to burn, but it did bring her to life. She lowered the cup and it rattled against the saucer. Gregg was massaging the back of her hand with his thumb.

"Caroline look at me."
He commanded. She did.

"The doctor will not have any trouble getting here. They are not restricted by the road. Doctor Clements and Delia will fly in by helicopter. We have a pad that Hal always keeps clear. They are due at eleven."
Caroline blinked again, his words finally breaking through. She took a deep breath and held it. Then she let it out slowly.

"I'm so sorry. You must think I'm demented or something."

Gregg roared with laughter, breaking any further tension she held. She smiled and suddenly noticed the plate in front of her.

"Bacon roll, yummy."

Gregg shook his head and leaned back in his own chair.

"Not quite, but maybe close."

He said cheekily, taking his own roll and biting into it.

They lingered over breakfast, Gregg offering her fruit and yogurts too. Caroline nibbled on a handful of grapes and listened, whilst he told her about the house.

"This is mine. We came here when I was a child. It belonged to some friend of my grandmother. Had been in her family since it was built. I loved it as soon as I saw it. The York estate is the family home. It is enormous, beautiful, but rather impersonal. Really too formal for me. My parents however, and grandmother of course, still live way back in the last century, and will change nothing. They even insist on having a full staff. Mother likes to remind anyone who will listen, that we are related to the Queen, and should therefore be served as such."

"You wanted me to know."

Caroline said when he paused for more tea. Gregg snickered.

"I did, didn't I. Trying to impress you."

Caroline lifted one shoulder.

"Royalty doesn't impress me. You did though."

Gregg gave his blue eyed diamond stare.

"Well I am very glad I did."

He offered the coffee pot and she nodded. He refilled her cup. Settling back in her chair she hugged the cup in two hands, waiting to hear more.

"I was only thirteen when grandmother's friend died. She was a strange old lady, hardly spoke to me. You know, children should be seen and not heard, kind of stuff. So when I was told she had left me the house in her will, I was completely shocked. So were her nephews. She had no children of her own, and the two boys assumed they would inherit. Caused quite a stir in our circle. But there was nothing they could do. Her solicitor had written and witnessed her will. He attested she was of sound mind, and that was that. I was, as you can imagine, very happy."

Caroline raised her eyebrows.

"Wow. You're very lucky."

"Well, the house needed a lot of attention, especially modernisation. But it was a delight to get it to how it is now. I turfed out a lot of furniture and so on. Had new carpets and curtains throughout. Installed the cinema and changed some of the rooms around. Now it's just perfect."

Caroline couldn't agree more. She gazed around the room and the snowy outside scene. She knew she hadn't seen all of the house, but guessed it would be as enchanting as the areas she had already been to.

"I'll take you around later."

Gregg said, making Caroline jump.

"I wish I knew how you do that."

He huffed out a laugh, but didn't answer. Caroline studied his face for a few seconds, his grin widening as she did.

A knock on the door broke the connection. They both looked up as Amy poked her head around.

"He's here."

She said lightly. Caroline suspected it was to ease her nervousness, but it didn't work.

"Thank you Amy. Could you take Caroline along please, wait for her and bring her back here after."

Caroline stood up shakily. Gregg took her hand for a moment.

"Don't worry Caroline. I have a feeling all is well."

She nearly giggled at the formality of his tone. She gave him a tiny smile and walked towards Amy.

Going to the doctor's room was worse this time. Despite Gregg's assurances, Caroline felt she couldn't be that lucky. After what Frank did to her, she was sure there would be some consequence. Still, she stood up straight and waited patiently as Amy tapped the door. Delia answered and with a smile stood back to let her in. Amy gave her an encouraging nod.

"I'll be right out here."

Caroline entered and Doctor Clements stood up behind his desk. He was dressed in a suit and looked every bit the professional doctor.

"Sit down Caroline please."

He said. She did so mechanically. Delia sat next to her with her tablet resting in her palm. Caroline clenched her hands in her lap, sitting straight backed and knees together, she waited.

"All of your tests came back clear."

Doctor Clements said. Caroline let out the breath she had been holding. She put her palms to her cheeks and felt tears under her fingers.

"Oh…oh my God."

Was all she could say. Doctor Clements smiled.

"I'm pleased to say, you have been very lucky, especially from what you told me about your ex-fiancé. Either he didn't pass anything to you, it can happen, or somehow, he's been lucky too."

Caroline was shaking. She had so prepared herself for the expected bad news, that this good news was more of a shock.

"Would you like me to bring Amy in?"

Delia said kindly as she stuffed a handful of tissues into her hand. Caroline nodded. Delia stood and opened the door. Amy came straight to her side, kneeling down.

"Oh Caroline, I'm sorry."

Her breath hitching, soggy tissues pressed to her cheeks, Caroline let out a half sob, half laugh. Amy frowned, puzzled.

"It's…I'm ok. All clear. The tests…nothing."

She stammered. Amy choked back a laugh and wrapped her arms around Caroline's shoulders.

"That's brilliant. I thought…the tears. Come on, let's get you back to Gregg."

"I can't see him like this. I bet I look like a raspberry."

Delia handed her a glass of water. Caroline drank thirstily.

"We can pop to your room first and you can put on a bit of makeup, ok?"

Finally, the news penetrated her frozen brain and excitement seeped in. Some of it was just pure joy at knowing she was healthy, another part of it was anticipation at what would come next between her and Gregg.

Once Caroline was feeling more herself, her cheeks now back to their normal colour, Amy led her back to the drawing room. As soon as she entered Gregg came towards her.

"Told you."

He said, pulling her towards the table where a fresh pot of coffee stood, invitingly.

"What, how…?"

She shook her head, knowing she wouldn't get an answer if she asked. He held out a chair and pressed her shoulders down. When she was seated he leaned towards her.

"Your face and eyes are shining. Had it been bad news, it would show."

Caroline wasn't sure she liked being read so easily, and was about to say so when Gregg bounced to the other side of the table. He sat down and poured her coffee. He looked so pleased though, Caroline bit back the words that wanted to spill. Enjoy all of this, now you can. She told herself as she sipped the coffee.

"After our coffee, you should call home."

Caroline paused drinking. She had no idea what to tell the boys and Derby. Gregg smiled.

"Are you ready for an adventure Caroline?"

She raised her brows.

"Um…I'm not sure. What do you mean?"

"Do you trust me Caroline?"

"Yes."

The word popped out without thought. She barely knew this young man, but she did trust him. She didn't know why, he just made her feel calm and secure. Gregg leaned across the table and stroked the back of her hand with his thumb. Tiny sparks of electricity tingled the skin he touched and she melted.

"Make your calls. Tell them what you wish, but tell them you will be spending the rest of the month, new year too I think, with your eccentric client."

Caroline gasped. She hadn't known what to expect, but his words hit her deep. A whole month with Gregg. Where? Here on the moor. She thought.

"Not just here, but places you will love, I guarantee. And all with phones so you can keep in touch with anyone you choose."

Caroline was nodding in agreement without realising she was doing so. Gregg leaned back and grinned.

"That's settled then."

Even though Caroline had no idea what was settled, if anything.

CHAPTER 17.

After coffee Amy took Caroline to her room. Caroline went straight to the window seat and Amy disappeared into the dressing room. She returned with a fresh set of clothes and laid them out on the bed. Caroline giggled. She'd only been in the jeans and sweater a few hours. But she didn't complain.

"I'll leave you to make your calls and get changed. Gregg said he would come for you himself."

Caroline thanked the girl as she left, closing the door behind her. Caroline picked up the satellite phone and nestled herself on the window seat. The frozen expanse of countryside was blinding, but she still looked out as she first dialled Derby.

"Caroline. Are you alright?"

Derby asked as soon as she heard Caroline's voice. Caroline felt herself smile, visualising Derby's frown.

"Derby, I'm fine. Better than fine really. It's been a very odd couple of days, and to be honest, I can't quite work out how to describe it."

"What do you mean Caroline, where are you?"

"Still out on the moor. But I think not for long."

"Caroline. Tell me what's going on."

Derby demanded and Caroline sighed.

"Look, I would really love to be able to sit with you and curl up with hot chocolate and tell you it all. But, it really is complicated."

"Frank came 'round."

Derby cut in.

"Oh. What did he want?"

Caroline asked, enunciating the word 'he'.

"He cried, promised all sorts and begged me to tell him where you were."

"About right for him. What did you say?"

Caroline was biting the inside of her cheek to stop from laughing. She could imagine Derby's response.

"I told him to shove his promises where the sun don't shine. And I told him to leave you alone, and where you were, you were better off without him."

Derby stated. Caroline did laugh then.

"Thank you Derby. He'll get the message eventually."

"So, what is going on Caroline."

Caroline took a deep breath.

"Like I said, I'm with a client, a new one. He, yes a he." She said as Derby gasped down the phone. "Is…Derby, he's something else. I can't explain. Look I'm just going to say this quickly. I'm staying with him from now until the new year. And before you say anything, I absolutely do know what I'm doing."

There was a quiet pause on the phone and for a moment Caroline thought they had been cut off. Then she heard Derby sigh, ever so lightly.

"Are you having some sort of rebound affair Caroline? And what about the whole STI stuff?"
Caroline laughed gleefully.

"First the STI stuff is sorted. When I get home I promise I will tell you all the details. As far as a rebound affair goes, it will be. Hasn't yet, but I'm pretty sure that's where it's heading."

"Be careful Caroline, your heart is still fragile."
Caroline gazed out of the window. Was it really? She wondered. She took a breath and let it out.

"Derby, I don't think I am fragile. I was, three days ago, totally breaking apart. But, since I've been here I've had time to really look at myself and the relationship I had with Frank. Yes I loved him, and it still hurts. Yes he's done so much for me and the boys over the years, good stuff. But looking back I think…no I know, I settled. That's the only way I can describe it. We were comfortable, habitual. I couldn't see a life without him, and I let him take advantage of that. I wasn't really stupid, just…well the boys were happy and I thought I was too. We clung together, and now I think, because I was too afraid to let it go and start again."
She paused, pulling her feet underneath her. Derby was quiet for just a second.

"And now?"
She asked gently.

"Now…don't know, but I'm going to have a great time finding out."

"Um…explanation please."

"This man, he's very different from anyone I've ever met. He's a…bit…younger than me." She didn't want to tell Derby how old Gregg was. "And he makes me feel alive. That's the only way I can explain. We haven't… had sex…yet. But it is going to happen. And well… I just know it's going to be out of this world when we do. He does something to me that I have never felt before, not even with Frank."

"That I do get."

Derby replied. Caroline remembered being told how her friend had felt when she found Geoff. How he could set her pulse beating rapidly with just a glance. Gregg did that and more to her.

"So Derby, I could spend hours talking about this, but right now, I want to just enjoy it. I promised I would call and let you know I'm ok, and I will keep doing that until I'm home. Then you will get the whole story. For now, it's mine, and sorry, I don't want to share." She giggled. "I've got to tell the boys something yet. God, don't know what I'm going to say to them."

She was babbling and knew it. Derby detected it in her voice.

"Caroline, I wouldn't dream of telling you how to live your life. And if you are absolutely sure you're ok and happy, then that's good enough for me. I'd say I would tell the boys, but I think, hesitant as you are, you want to talk to them yourself."

Caroline could feel herself nodding even though Derby couldn't see.

"Got to girlie. And yes, promise you I'm really buzzing. This is going to be good for me, however it pans out."

They said their goodbyes, after Caroline swore to keep in touch regularly. Then she sighed. Now for her sons. She really didn't know what to say to them. She tapped the phone whilst she mulled it over. Finally she thought she had something credible to tell them.

She called Leo first and followed up by repeating herself to Liam. She kept it light, telling them her new client was wealthy, and prepared to cover her expenses if she stayed and helped with the manuscript. She didn't mention the client was male, or how old. She didn't think she would get away with that. She told them both, it was doing her the world of good to be away, that she would have been anyway. They accepted her words, and like with Derby, she promised to phone regularly and let them know she was fine. Leo was more concerned than his brother, questioning her whereabouts. She eased his worry by telling him she wasn't alone, that the client had staff. Finally, she was finished with her calls and let out a long breath. It hadn't been easy, but then nothing in life was. She laid the phone down and began to change.

Almost as if on cue, a knock came on the door just as Caroline finished putting on her makeup. Of course it would be Gregg, she told herself as she opened the door. He stood smiling and Caroline couldn't help but smile back. All the worry over the tests and results was behind her. Now, she felt young and eager to have her adventure.

Gregg held out his hand and she took it.

"You look lovely."

He told her. She gave him a tiny shrug. She was only in patterned leggings, a long cowl necked jumper and soft soled boots, very casual. But the compliment made her glow and feel twenty years younger, just not so naïve.

Gregg led her around the parts of the house she hadn't seen. It still seemed enormous and she was sure she would get lost without him. In each room, he explained how it used to look, and what he had done to refurbish. They came to the kitchen which had every most up to date appliance, but also had a door leading to a cellar. Caroline hesitated at the opening. Despite her self-assurances that Gregg was safe, again all of the old scary movies pulsed through her heart. Gregg sensed her hesitancy.

"Don't be afraid Caroline."

He whispered, his voice silky soft and his eyes piercing. Caroline shivered and Gregg grinned.

"Whooooo."

He teased. Caroline frowned, he was mocking her. Gregg flicked a switch and white fluorescent light flooded the stairway and as far into the cellar as she could see. Gregg let out a deep hearty laugh, and led the way down.

"It's where we store the wine."

He said lightly. Caroline felt very stupid, as she followed him through the racks of bottles. Gregg pointed out various wines and Caroline was impressed he knew so much.

"Derby and I, we just go to the supermarket and grab whatever's on offer. I mean I know what I like, but I'm not a connoisseur or anything."

"It doesn't matter Caroline. I just happen to find it interesting, and of course I can buy whatever I like. So I do."

Of course you do, she thought. Then felt churlish.

"Choose any bottle Caroline, or bottles. We can have any you want for dinner tonight."

"Oh…I wouldn't know where to start."

Gregg stopped suddenly and pulled her around to face him. He stood close and Caroline thought he might kiss her, but he didn't.

"As I said, it doesn't matter. I know your choice will be perfect."

"Ok."

Caroline said, pulling away from his closeness. She turned and plucked two bottles from the racks.

"These then."

She held them up, one in each hand. Gregg leaned forward and read the labels. He straightened and nodded.

"As I said, perfect."

He told her taking the bottles. Caroline believed he was mocking her again, but decided not to react. Humph, she thought, be your fault if one or both of them is corked. She heard him chuckle just ahead of her and stamped her foot soundlessly. Attractive as he was, he could be very irritating at times. Gregg held the bottles in one hand, and stretched out the other behind him towards her.

"Come along Caroline. The tour is over."

Caroline didn't think so. She hadn't seen his bedroom. She opened her mouth to say that.

"For now."

Gregg said as he stood back and allowed her to go up the staircase first.

Gwyn was in the kitchen when they reached the top. She was whisking something in a bowl, and smiled kindly as Caroline emerged.

"Gwyn, would you please serve these with dinner. Caroline chose them."

Gwyn nodded without comment, as Gregg placed the bottles on the counter.

"I think we'll have lunch in the little sitting room please."

"Ok Master Gregg."

She said, without turning from her task.

With his hands now free, he again took Caroline's and strolled slowly along a corridor with paintings on the walls. As they walked, he told her about the artwork. Caroline had never taken much interest in art, but Gregg again was very knowledgeable, and his enthusiasm was infectious. Before she knew it, she was asking questions.

Gregg took Caroline to the little sitting room. It was just that. Small, snug and cosy, a fire burning warmly. This room also looked out across the terrace, and had tall French doors flanking a ceiling to floor window. An intimate table for two nestled between the French doors, the view from the window marvellous. Gregg indicated small armchairs near the fire and Caroline sat down. Gwyn popped her head around the door.

"Is it alright to set the table?"

She enquired. Gregg beamed at the old lady, his eyes dimmed to the soft blue Caroline was beginning to understand. He waved his hand beckoning.

"Of course, come in Gwyn."

Lunch was casual and very relaxing. Caroline was surprised Gregg hadn't sent her off to change again, but he seemed content with her as she was. He had one arm resting along the back of his chair, his other hand wrapped around a cup.

"Caroline, where do you keep your passport?"

Caroline was taken aback by his sudden question.

"Um…actually it's in my handbag."

Gregg raised his eyebrows.

"Does your work take you out of the country frequently?"

Caroline giggled and shook her head.

"Not at all."

She looked down and a tiny sigh escaped.

"My…our, honeymoon was supposed to begin last Sunday. I put it in my bag the day before the wedding, so it was one thing I didn't have to think about. It's tucked away in the inside pocket. Why?"

"Where were you going?"

Gregg whispered, covering her hand with his. Caroline lifted a shoulder.

"The Seychelles."

She murmured.

"Very overrated."

Gregg stated and Caroline couldn't help but laugh.

"So back to the passport. Good it's here. We won't have to delay collecting it from your home."

Caroline leaned back in her seat and sipped her coffee. She gave him a sideways glance and saw he was staring at her, daring her to ask again.

"So?"

She couldn't resist. Gregg leaned forward, excitement lighting up his face.

"I have a villa on St Lucia. It's very beautiful in December. We can leave in the morning and stay, well as long as we choose."

He drew his brows together.

"Although, I think we should spend Christmas at the estate with my family."

Caroline took a panicky breath. Time with Gregg on St Lucia she could easily cope with, but Christmas with his parents? What on earth would they think of her, a forty seven year old mother, with their young thirty year old son.

"Caroline, don't worry. My family won't bite, well grandmother has quite a bark, but my parents are used to my ways."

Caroline didn't want to ask what that meant. She only hoped it didn't mean a stream of women attached to his arm. He gave her his stare, boring into her thoughts.

"I told you, there haven't been many women. And I've only taken a couple home over Christmas. My parents, well I suppose my father mostly, is quite cool. They don't ask questions."

She didn't know whether to feel reassured or more nervous.

"Anyway, it's days away. By the time we have been to the island, and had fun in the sun, you will feel very different."

Thoughts of fun in the sun certainly eased her anxiety. She hoped it meant what she wanted it to mean. Sun, sea, sex and cocktails. She felt stirrings at her centre, a low throb and almost wriggled in her chair. Gregg smiled.

"You won't be disappointed Caroline."

She chewed the side of her lip. How did he always know?

"So, I have to go and make some arrangements. Would you like me to call for Amy to keep you company?"

Caroline mulled it over. She decided she didn't need company. She was used to occupying herself.

"I think I would like to just go to the library. Spend the time with your books."

"Ok. Would you like to find your own way there?"

Caroline nodded eagerly. He stood up and took a phone from his pocket.

"Take this in case you get lost. It has a pager app."

He opened the app and showed her how to call for Amy.

"But won't you need it?"

"I have others. Now, turn right outside the door. You shouldn't have any trouble finding the library, but please call for Amy if you do."

He leaned towards her and gave her a tiny peck on the lips. Light as it was, Caroline felt the fire inside flare. She was excited and longed to pull him to her, wanted him to take her right there. He grinned, knowing her thoughts.

"Later Caroline."

He left her to finish her coffee. She didn't linger, keen to find her way to the library.

It actually was easy. She followed the hall and soon came across the tall doors to the library. Inside it was so quiet, the fire giving a cosy glow to the room. Caroline spent time browsing, found a novel and curled up in an armchair. She buried herself in the book and was soon lost in the story.

Caroline came awake when a light tap touched her shoulder.

"Hello sleepyhead."

Gregg's soft voice whispered close to her ear. She blinked, sleep confusion being replaced with joy at his beautifully chiselled face.

"Oh, I must have dozed off."

She stretched, the book slipping to the floor. Gregg retrieved it and held out a hand.

"Come, Amy's waiting to help you get ready for dinner."

"Wow is it that late."

He smiled.

"Not really, you have plenty of time. There is no rush.

Amy was in her bedroom when Gregg left her at the door. She already had a bath prepared and her evening outfit laid out. Caroline felt refreshed after her nap, and stepped into the bath, luxuriating in the feel of the softly scented water. She soaked and imagined St Lucia. It had been her first choice for the honeymoon. But Frank told her he and Tania had gone there for theirs, that he wanted the Seychelles. She had given in. It now made her wonder, where else Frank may have taken his other women. She shrugged in the water.

"I do not care anymore."

"Talking to yourself again?"

Amy grinned at her as she laid out towels. Caroline giggled.

"Just a bit, but don't tell anyone, they'll cart me off to the asylum."

Dressed in an expensive chic outfit, Caroline met Gregg in the drawing room. Again he too was dressed for dinner. They ate and chatted and Caroline asked about the planned trip.

"We will take the helicopter to Newquay airport, and from there, private jet to the island."
Caroline was shocked. When he told her he had arrangements to make, she assumed booking flights. She sort of expected first class, but by no means a private jet.

"I fly about quite a lot."
He shrugged. Then he leaned forward, the gleam very bright in his eyes.

"Are you enjoying the wine?"

Caroline was taken aback at the change of subject. She hadn't really thought about it, just sipped during the meal. Now, taking another small sip, she nodded.

"Yes, it's very nice."
Gregg grinned.

"Do you want anymore, or are you ready for the adventure to begin?"
Again the change of subject surprised her. She held the glass in front of her.

"How will the adventure begin?"

Gregg stood up and held out his hand. She placed the wine glass on the table and took his hand.

"In my room."
He said, his voice sexy and alluring. Caroline swallowed, her breath caught. So this would be it, she thought. Finally she would get what she had been waiting for, him.

With no further words, Gregg led her from the room. He took her up the stairs and along a hallway. He stopped outside double doors.

"Are you sure Caroline?"

She couldn't speak, her mouth had gone dry. She nodded, and his eyes flashed their diamonds. He opened the doors and let her enter before him. What she saw was so unexpected.

Where every other room had been redesigned to classic country, Gregg's room was totally opposite. It was ultra modern, predominantly in shades of white. A huge circular, white leather bed stood in the centre on a raised dais. White satin sheets and plump pillows were the only covers, and Caroline suspected the room had a sophisticated temperature control unit somewhere. Creamy white carpet with pile so thick her heels sank, stretched from wall to wall. A feature wall of deep aubergine surrounded the fireplace, the only colour in the room. Caroline was awed. She turned and laughed, clapping her hands like a child.

"It's wonderful."

She gasped. Gregg smiled and strolled to a white table. He lifted a decanter of golden liquid and poured a measure into a glass.

"Go ahead Caroline. Explore."

"First, can I have one of those please?"

She asked, indicating his drink.

"You like whisky?"

"Yes I do."

She did, but she also suddenly felt very nervous. Gregg gave her his knowing look and poured. He handed her the heavy crystal tumbler and she took a sip. Closing her eyes she murmured.

"Mmmm, smooth, a perfect malt."

"You know your whisky."

She opened her eyes.

"Better than my wine."

He chuffed out a laugh.
"Explore."
He said.

CHAPTER 18.

Caroline pushed open a white door and stepped into Gregg's bathroom. It was totally masculine. All white tiles, glass and chrome. An impressive multi faucet shower took up one wall, but it was utilitarian, not luxurious as hers was. She lifted a bottle of cologne and sniffed. It smelt of him. She touched the robe on the hook and let the fabric slide between her fingers. But she didn't linger.

Back in the room, Gregg was sitting on a chair by the fire. He smiled as she walked past him, having spotted another door. She pushed it open and saw it was a dressing room identical to hers. Rows of clothes and shoes lined both sides. Many more than her own sons had, put together. A full length mirror hung at the far end, and as Caroline approached, she noticed a door knob protruding. Feeling wary, wondering what was on the other side, she grasped the handle and pulled. The whole mirror opened towards her, lights coming on automatically.

Inside was a duplicate dressing room. This one however was far from anything she had ever seen.

"Oh my God."

She whispered to herself. The rows were lined with clothes, but they were costumes from various periods and themes. There were drawers of accessories and wig stands with numerous colours and styles. On a dresser was an array of makeup. To Caroline it was like the wardrobe of a theatre.

"Impressive, isn't it?"

She squealed, and jumped at the closeness of Gregg's deep voice. Whisky leapt from the glass and trickled across her wrist.

"Oh Caroline. I'm so sorry I startled you."

Gregg said, grabbing a handful of tissues from the dresser, soaking up the drink from her hand. Caroline shook her head.

"It's fine, but what is all this?"

Gregg looked about the room.

"Well quite a lot of the outfits are my own fancy dress costumes. I've been to so many. I like to try and get authentic dress for them, the wigs and makeup too. Many have been period parties. Those though." He pointed to a row at the end of the room. "I had those delivered especially for you. I had no idea what, if any you would like, so I just bought…everything."

Caroline took a sip from her whisky and strolled over to the clothes. She pushed a few aside. All were her size. There were nurses, army, police uniforms, fairy and elf dresses, sexy lacy negligees, and many more. She found matching shoes, bags, toy guns, stethoscopes and a variety of other bits and pieces. She stood and stared, unable to quite grasp what she was seeing.

"It's all for to you wear, or not."
Gregg said close to her. She turned her head and looked up at him.

"But you would like me to."

Gregg tilted his head down until he was almost touching her face. He smiled and his teeth gleamed. His eyes flashed their diamond ring and Caroline felt faint.

"This is your adventure. I told you, we will only do what you want, what you ask for."

"Oh."
Was all she could say. He wasn't some sort of control freak who wanted her pliant and obedient. She thought of something and checked. There were no handcuffs, whips or bondage restraints. She let out a breath. For that she was thankful. Frank had been a bit kinky about that stuff, but never on her.

"I could never have you, held down. I want to pleasure you, yes, but not with tethers."
He whispered. She shuddered as his breath tickled her throat, sliding down her skin like warm water. He chuckled.

"I'll wait in the bedroom. Be whomever you want to be Caroline and we will go from there."

Gregg spun around and disappeared through the mirror door. A flicker of panic washed over her, but vanished when she saw he had left both dressing room doors open. She gave herself a mental shake. Was part of the excitement these little thrills of fear that he could invoke. Was her desire for him sparked by his almost vampire, predatory traits? Yes, all of those, she told herself. But there was more, nothing she could put her finger on. So what are you going to do? She thought. Then decided.

Caroline stood the glass on the dresser, sat on the stool and searched through the makeup. She found what she was looking for and began to apply it. She picked up the exact hair accessory and clipped it in. Next she slid the hangers along the rails and found what she wanted to wear. On a small shelf, she discovered bottles of perfume. She sniffed each one and stopped at a scent that oozed sex. She dabbed the fragrance on her inner wrists, and where her pulse beat at her throat. If Gregg had chosen them, he would like it.

When Caroline emerged from the dressing room, Gregg was still sitting by the fire. He had dimmed the lights in the room, and with the firelight, the ambience was perfect. He watched her as she slowly walked to his side. His eyes penetrated as she neared.

"You are truly beautiful."

He whispered as she came to a stop in front of him.

"You like my choice?"

She asked huskily.

"Very much."

He said, sliding his hands up the inside of her thighs and pinging the lace tops of the fine black stockings she wore. Caroline resisted the urge to grab his hands and hold them at the juncture of her thighs. The rest of the outfit consisted of a black silk babydoll, trimmed with deep red velvet and matching full length negligee. Her eye makeup was dark and smoky, her lips glistening bright red. A rich red silk rose in her hair, and five inch, black, killer stilettos, completed the outfit.

Caroline curled her fingers in his hair, threading his silky blonde strands through her fingers. He closed his eyes and sighed.

"What do you want me to do Caroline?"

He asked, his voice full of promise. She leaned towards him.

"Open your eyes."

She commanded and he obeyed. His blue diamond irises sparkled at the view of her cleavage before them. She waved her shoulders, and her full breasts jiggled, just contained by the thin fabric of the babydoll.

"I want you to…pleasure me."

Her words came on a soft sighing breath.

In one fluid motion, Gregg stood and lifted her from her feet. He carried her to the bed, and laid her down in the ripples of silk. She lay looking up at his face as he leaned over her. Her eyes were swirling with desire, his giving off their devilish light. He placed a hand either side of her head and lowered his mouth to hers, hovering a bare millimetre from her lips.

Caroline arched her back to try and make contact. Gregg grinned and pulled back his head a fraction.

"Soon. I won't rush."

All Caroline wanted to do was rip his clothes from his gorgeous body, and wrap her legs around his hips, taking what she suspected was going to be very impressive. He laughed, his deep sexy laugh.

"My way will be better. Wait there."

Caroline felt bereft as he left her side. She closed her eyes and took a deep breath. She splayed her hands across the silk underneath her, the material sending waves of sensation through her body. She throbbed deep at her centre. She pulled her knees up and clasped her thighs tightly, the motion tickling her already very sensitive spot.

A soft dipping of the mattress had her opening her eyes. Gregg was back, she hadn't heard him. He was bare chested, but still wore his suit trousers. He sat by her side and took one of her hands, placing it on his chest. She could feel his fine hairs beneath her fingers, like gold dust glittering on his porcelain skin. She stroked and tugged them, very lightly. He gazed at her.

Gregg put one finger under her chin, then he slowly trailed it down her neck and between her breasts. She sucked in a breath. His featherlight touch was like a thin thread of fire. She arched, straining for more contact, and heard him chuckle.

Something warm and liquid flowed from her throat into her cleavage, and she smelt her favourite confection, chocolate. Gregg lowered his head and she saw his eyes spark. She waited. Then it came. His tongue flicked at the hollow of her throat, slid down and up. It followed the course of the melted chocolate, down between her breasts, where it idled, filling her with passion. He nipped the flesh of her breasts and Caroline moaned.

She lifted her body slightly, letting the negligee slide from her shoulders. Without taking his mouth from her breasts, he slipped the straps of the babydoll down her arms, stroking the skin with his fingers, gradually moving nearer to the outside of her breasts. She sighed with delight. He was very good at this, her mind barely registered and again heard him chuckle.

His tongue tracked back up her throat and finally reached her lips. Sweet wet chocolate touched her mouth as his tongue pushed inside. She took it, sucking and flicking, her hands knotting themselves into his hair. One of his hands slipped under her back lifting her towards him and the kiss intensified. Yet he was still sitting by her side.

Caroline ran her hands up and down his shoulders, the feel of taut muscles sending thrills to every nerve, as his tongue rolled around inside her mouth. Suddenly, he released her mouth and Caroline groaned.

"Patience."

He murmured. Caroline didn't want to be patient. She wanted him stripped and inside her, plunging her wetness.

"I won't deny you."

He whispered as he shifted from the bed, and Caroline feared she was speaking aloud, knowing she wasn't.

Seconds that seemed like minutes, her body on fire and vibrating with anticipation, Caroline finally watched him come back to her. He pulled the stilettos from her feet, and lifted the babydoll over her head. Now she was clothed only in panties and stockings. He still had his trousers on. He kneeled on the bed and looked down into her turbulent eyes.

"What do you want?"

He asked.

"Take off your clothes."

She said. He was about to comply, but she grabbed his hand, stilling it on the waistband of his trousers.

"No, let me."

Caroline twisted to her knees and Gregg shuffled further onto the bed laying back. Caroline tucked the tip of a finger under the button, sliding it back and forth. She heard Gregg take in a breath and smiled, pleased with herself. She rested her other hand flat against the zipper and was thrilled at the length of hardness underneath. She lightly stroked, up then down. Deftly, she unbuttoned his trousers and gently unzipped him. Gregg raised his hips so she could slide the trousers down.

Caroline flung them to the floor. She sat back for a moment and gazed at his erection, straining against his trunks. It was mouth-wateringly enticing. Gregg lifted onto his elbows and looked at her face, watching her desire spread across her cheeks.

"Go ahead."

He whispered.

Caroline slipped her fingers under the edge of his pants and inched them down slowly. As she released his cock, she gasped. He was huge, nothing like she had ever seen before. She felt the wetness in her own panties at what was coming, but now she didn't want to rush. She leaned over him, her hands either side of his head, draping her breasts until her nipples touched his chest. She undulated, teasing herself and him too.

Gregg took a full breast in each hand and rubbed his thumbs across her nipples. Caroline gasped and threw back her head, pressing into his palms. Suddenly, he rolled her to her back and closed his mouth over hers, kissing deeply. Then he lifted away.

"Keep your eyes closed and stay there."

He murmured. Seconds passed.

"Open your mouth Caroline."

He had moved with the lightness and speed of a lion. She complied. Gregg dangled a strawberry dripping with champagne just above her mouth. She tasted the wine, waiting for more. He gently laid the fruit against her lips and she bit into it, relishing the flavour. Gregg lowered his head. She knew he was there, sensed his move. Holding the ripe strawberry between her teeth, she raised her head a fraction, making him an offering. He closed his mouth over the fruit and together they sucked the juice and flesh.

Caroline could feel his pulsing manhood pressing into the flesh of her belly. She rolled her hips and heard him chuckle.

"I have more to play with."

He said softly. Caroline wanted desperately to lift her knees and have him between her legs, but she was also enjoying the game.

"Then play."

She commanded.

Gregg ran a single finger down her body, from her throat to the soft triangle of hair and stopped just before her most sensitive spot. She groaned. She felt the bed give slightly, but kept her eyes closed, waiting.

"Show me your throat."

He said, close to her ear. Caroline's pulse beat faster. Was this it? Is he really a vampire about to sink his fangs in? She asked herself. Despite her thoughts, she felt compelled to do his bidding, was so full of desire, longed for his touch, no matter where it came from.

Something light like dust settled on her throat where her pulse beat, but she waited, not moving. Gregg trailed her body with one hand, kneading the flesh lightly on the way, stopping at her belly button. She felt him lay a cool soft something in the dip, still she stayed motionless.

"Open your eyes."

His voice came from above her. She did, looking up at his pale beautiful face. Slowly he lowered his head to her throat and she sucked in a breath. His mouth closed over her beating pulse and she felt his teeth nip her flesh. It was erotic, her heart rate increasing as he began to suck, her eyes closing in bliss.

She heard him chuckle as he pulled away. Then a tepid liquid slid down her throat pooling in her cleavage. Gregg's mouth came back to hers. She expected to taste blood on his lips, so into her vampire imaginings, but instead there was the flavour of salt. Her eyes snapped open, but Gregg had already begun to trail his mouth down her body. He stopped between her breasts, his tongue lapping, then continued down to her tummy. He paused at her button, then lifted his head. Caroline giggled. He had a slice of lime between his teeth.

"Tequila."

He mumbled around the fruit.

Caroline eased herself onto her elbows smiling at him. Even though her entire body was throbbing and pulsing for release, Gregg's game was so enjoyable she could wait, knowing when the release came it would be mind blowing. She could still feel his erection against her skin and longed for it, wondering how a man so young had so much control. Even Frank couldn't hold on long at his age. The thought burst into her mind and she shoved it back hastily. She wouldn't let that man intrude on this time, her time.

Gregg slinked up the bed towards her mouth like a predatory lion, one hand either side of her, his legs straddling her body.

"Your turn."

He said, taking the lime from his mouth. He kneeled back on his heels, pinning her under him. His cock was aimed right at her face, huge and very inviting. Gregg dusted the inside of his own wrist with salt and offered it to her. She licked and he gasped. He held out the bottle of liquor. It had a shot pourer, so she tilted it upside down and let the tequila trickle out onto his organ. It twitched and Caroline's mouth watered.

Caroline's tongue flicked over her lips tasting the salt. Gregg watched her with eyes so blue, they were nearly dazzling. She rested her hands on his tight muscular buttocks and slowly pulled him forward, raising her head to meet him. She took one hand and ran a finger down his erection, feeling it quiver at her touch. She flicked him with her tongue, licking the tequila right along the length and closing her mouth slightly over his tip, sucking gently. Gregg arched his back, his blonde head thrown back in ecstasy. Then he pulled back, dragging her teeth a little on his flesh.

"The lime."

He murmured, and Caroline knew he was barely holding on. She took the same piece of fruit he had discarded and placed it between her lips. Gregg was now watching her. His eyes flashing with emotion. Caroline took some of the lime juice, then cast the slice away.

"Now."

She demanded.

Gregg inched back a little, taking her hands. He pulled her forward until she was sitting, he still straddling her. He wrapped his arms around her, so strong, so firm, taking her mouth in a devouring kiss. Then he pressed her down, into the silkiness of the sheets, sliding between her thighs. With one hand he snapped the thin thread of fabric holding her panties together. They came apart and were discarded. She felt his hardness close, and spread her legs. He hovered a moment over her, eyes penetrating. She gave a tiny nod and then he was inside her. Caroline gasped at his size. Her wetness giving him perfect access.

He slid in and out with slow deliberation, each plunge deep, filling her. Caroline's juices flowed, her internal muscles clenching and unclenching around his cock with each thrust. He placed one hand underneath her, raising her hips from the bed, deepening his force, whilst his other hand caressed the inside of her thigh. She raised her knees, linking her ankles to his calves and met him thrust for thrust. She tangled her hands in his hair and pulled his mouth to hers. He gave what she craved and more, using his lips fully, reigning kisses on her mouth and throat, nipping at her shoulders and sucking on her pebble hard nipples.

Caroline's hips rolled and Gregg pounded. Her breath was coming in gasps and she moaned with pleasure. She felt her orgasm mounting, ethereal, raised beyond anything she had ever experienced or imagined. Her whole body vibrated as she writhed desperate for release. Just when she felt she had reached her peak, Gregg braced himself on his strong arms, and thrust hard and deep taking her even higher. Then she came around him on a storm of passion.

She threw back her head grasping handfuls of silk in her fists. Her body shuddered and twitched, electric shocks of desire drawing a scream from her lips. Gregg poised himself above her for a mere second. Then he growled, deep in his throat as he came, thrusting faster and with intense power. Caroline felt his warmth spill into her, sending her over the edge again, even before she had returned. Her body juddered as did his.

She didn't think it would ever stop, didn't want it to stop. But as their orgasms subsided, the power inside her intensified and her heart skipped a beat. Gregg eased himself down and took her lips. His kiss was gentle, moving, and tears seeped from her eyes. He stroked her hair and wiped the tears away from her cheeks with his thumb.

"Sh."

He whispered so quietly, it was like a breath of wind.

Caroline had never felt passion so pure that it made her cry. She unclenched her fists and wrapped her arms around his shoulders, holding on. His light, now chaste kisses soothed her, even though she could still feel his hardness deep within her. Gradually her breathing settled to something near normal, and the tears slowed.

"Did you enjoy that?"

He murmured close to her ear. She nodded.

"It…it, was…amazing. More than amazing. Like nothing ever before."

He chuckled and nipped her neck.

"That's just the beginning of your adventure. But for now, you must rest. We have an early start tomorrow."

Gregg slowly pulled out from Caroline's body, the sliding motion sensuous and arousing. Caroline very nearly grabbed him, wanting to keep his warmth inside her. She knew he knew what she was thinking, from the wicked smile he gave her as he lay by her side, his eyes intensely looking into hers. Gregg lifted the silk sheet and laid it across them, planting a kiss on her shoulder.

Caroline rolled onto her belly, her red blonde hair fanning the silk around her. Gregg leaned on one elbow, his head resting on his hand. With his other, he gently massaged her shoulders.

“Go to sleep Caroline.”

His words a lullaby to her ears, had the right effect. She was so completely satiated, so relaxed, her body felt heavy as she drifted into calm and peaceful sleep.

CHAPTER 19.

Caroline awoke to the smell of coffee and a bakery, she thought. She stretched and sat up. Her body tingled all over. Three times during the night she had woken, hot, wet and ready. Gregg had given her everything she wanted each time, his unending stamina a delight.

"Good morning."

She looked towards his voice by the window. He was dressed in just a pair of lounge pants, his shoulder and chest muscles rippling as he poured coffee from a pot on a small table. Caroline felt stirrings between her legs. She heard him chuckle and knew he sensed her desire.

"Patience. We have a flight to catch. But I promise you, I have much more to give."

Caroline sighed, as she slipped from the bed. A silk robe, obviously meant for a woman, draped across a chair. She wrapped it around her and padded to the table. It was laid with a white linen cloth and set for breakfast. The bakery smell emanated from here.

Freshly baked rolls and croissants with butter and preserves tantalized her nostrils, and her tummy rumbled.

Gregg pulled out a chair for her, waited until she sat, then he offered the coffee he had poured, and grinned.

"Sounds like you have worked up an appetite."
Caroline sipped her beverage.

"Mmmm, that's lovely, and yes, I am rather hungry."
She said, taking a warm croissant.

"Amy will be waiting in your room to help you get ready for the trip. I'll take you there when you are ready."
Caroline felt her cheeks flush and Gregg gave her his knowing stare.

"Don't be embarrassed Caroline."

"I…um…I'm not really. So what do I take with me?"
She said, trying to avoid the subject. She didn't exactly feel embarrassed, not with Gregg, after what they had done. But she wasn't sure how Amy would react.

"Amy will only ask if you choose to tell. As for luggage, just yourself and your passport. Everything else is organised."

Caroline shouldn't have been surprised, but she still wasn't used to having her clothes chosen and laid out for her, or things taken out of her hands. She had been independent for many years, and lovely as it was, it still felt strange.

Amy was running her bath as Gregg opened the bedroom door and stepped back for Caroline to enter. He kissed her lightly on the lips and her body flamed.

"I will see you soon."
He whispered. Caroline nodded and made her way to the bathroom.

"Hi."
Amy greeted her chirpily, pouring bubble bath into the running water.

"Hi, that water looks very inviting."
Caroline replied. Amy stood up and walked towards her.

"All ready."

Caroline looked at the girl, trying to ascertain if she was acting differently. She gave herself a mental shake. It was her who was different. She smiled and stepped up to the bath, discarding the robe on the way. The water was warm, and deep as she lowered herself, felt it soothe her muscles.

"I think I've used muscles I didn't know I had."
She said to Amy. The young woman came and sat on the steps.

"You don't have to tell me anything Caroline, and I won't ask."
Caroline sank into the water and grinned.

"I know, and I won't go into detail, but he was bloody amazing."
Amy burst out laughing.

"I always thought, that under his English aloofness, was a hidden passion."
Amy replied. Caroline's brows creased. She had never thought Gregg aloof. But then she had only known him, God, she thought, just three days, today being the fourth. It felt like she had known him forever.

The bath eased all of the tension in Caroline's body and she emerged fresh and ready for the journey.

As she dressed, she looked out of the window. The snow was still thick and deep, but the sky was crystal clear. A beautiful December morning. She applied a light layer of makeup then turned to Amy.

"How do I look?"

"You're glowing Caroline. Whatever Gregg did…well, it did wonders."

Caroline blushed. But she did feel great, younger, fitter and energetic.

Gregg was waiting in the hall. He held out a light padded jacket.

"You will only need to wear this to the helicopter."

He told her, as he helped her into it.

"Have a brilliant time, Caroline. I hope to see you again."

Caroline felt a tiny prick of tears in the corner of her eyes. She liked Amy and would miss her. Also she had no idea where this adventure would take her, or where it would end.

"Thank you Amy. I do too."

She gave her a kiss on the cheek and a little hug. Then Gregg was taking her hand and leading her down a hallway.

Once they left the house, it was just a short walk to the helicopter pad. Caroline was however grateful for the jacket. The sun might be shining, but the temperature was bitter. Gregg put his arm around her and rubbed her shoulder.

"It will be warm inside."

He told her, even though she hadn't given any indication that she was cold.

Caroline didn't know what to expect, having never flown in a helicopter before. She found the experience invigorating. Gregg sat by her side, holding her hand. With his thumb he traced circles in her palm and it felt so erotic. He looked at her, his piercing eyes baring her soul.

"I'm looking forward to it too."
He whispered.

Flying by private jet was a new experience too. Again she had no idea what to expect. She had supposed it would be like travelling first class, though she hadn't ever done that either. She only knew what she'd seen in movies. She found it more enjoyable than she imagined, especially with Gregg lounging next to her whilst they sipped champagne. During the flight, Gregg gave her a light summery outfit to change into.

"You will be far too hot in what you're wearing."
He said. She changed in front of him, wishing he would take her in his arms and make love to her. But he only smiled knowingly.

The flight seemed to take less time than a commercial one, but Caroline suspected that was due to the comfort of the jet. It seemed no time before they were descending. Caroline looked out of the window and saw St Lucia below them. Lush rainforest and sandy beaches filling her with excitement. Gregg took her hand and she smiled gleefully.

"And so the adventure continues."
He said.

A big luxurious car took them to Gregg's villa. They passed through tall gates and up a winding road bordered by tropical plants. As they reached the house,

Caroline gasped. It was sheer luxury. Predominantly white, with large windows. Caroline couldn't wait to get inside and see the rest.

Gregg took Caroline's hand and led her inside. Beyond the main door was tiled open spaces, so different from Trewen House.

"Go ahead, explore."

He told her. Caroline felt like a child as she breathed in the warm air, and began.

The villa wasn't as big as Trewen, but it was so airy it felt just as spacious. From the main entrance she discovered the lounge. It was beautiful, opening onto a terrace and infinity pool. Lush gardens stretched down to a private beach, the bay protected by high cliffs. On either side of the terrace she could see raised pavilions, accessed by bridges from the upper rooms. It was all so breathtaking.

Gregg appeared by her side. He held a tall glass out to her. She took it and sipped fresh juice.

"This is…so beautiful."

She said.

"Come back inside. I will show the bedroom."

That one word had her eyes lighting up and Gregg laughed.

"You're insatiable."

He said, taking her hand and leading her into the house.

"Only with you."

She murmured.

Gregg took her up a tiled staircase and into the master bedroom. Caroline clasped her hands to her face at the sight before her. The bed was huge, but it was the view that took her breath away. One entire wall was glass, opening onto a balcony, where there was a jucuzzi and outside shower. Stepping out, Caroline could see the sea below, and bouncing gently on the water, a stunning yacht.

"Oh my God, this is heaven."

She squealed. Gregg joined her, laying an arm across her shoulder.

"Do you like the water Caroline?"

He asked. She beamed at him.

"I love the water."

"So the adventure recommences."

Gregg turned her into his arms and kissed her. She was pliant in his hold, the glass of juice still held in one hand. It wasn't a long kiss and Caroline was reluctant to let him go when he pulled back. He took the glass from her hand and placed it on a table.

"Come."

He said, leading her from the room and down the stairs. Outside, he bypassed the pool, and took a pathway between sweet tropical flowers, until they reached the beach.

Caroline kicked off her sandals and felt hot sand between her toes. Gregg, who had been wearing cotton trousers and T-shirt since they left Devon, grabbed her hand and led her down to the water. Without taking off any clothes, he plunged into the waves, Caroline following.

The water was wonderfully warm. Gregg dived under and came up wrapping his arms around her. He lifted her in his arms and pressed his lips to hers. She tangled her hands in his wet blonde hair, and took his mouth with veracity. Carrying her, Gregg emerged from the sea and laid her in the sand at the water's edge. Their clothes clinging to them, he settled between her thighs and pressed his already hard manhood against her. She moaned and strained, bringing her hips up to meet him.

He lifted her wet sundress and slid one hand up and down her inner thigh. She twisted, forcing his hand to make contact with her very wet centre. He pushed aside her soaking panties and plunged two fingers inside her. She braced her heels in the sand, lifting higher, her hips thrusting against his fingers. All the time his mouth devoured hers. She came on a mountain of pleasure, her hands grabbing handfuls of sand as the ocean washed over them.

He was still hard as her breath calmed and her orgasm abated. Yet she knew she wanted more. Gregg kneeled back, pulling her up. She could see his erection straining against the cotton of his trousers.

"What do you want Caroline?"

"You, naked."

He grinned and began removing his clothes. Caroline yanked her dress over her head and practically tore her own underwear from her body. When they were both free from the restraints of fabric, she kneeled in the sand. She placed her hands on his shoulders and pushed him backwards. He went willingly. She lifted one leg over him and knelt back on his thighs. His cock stood tall and big. Caroline wrapped both hands around him and gently squeezed. He pushed upwards, forcing his organ to slide through her fingers.

Taking one hand away, she stroked the golden hairs on his chest, trailing a finger down. He arched and she heard him groan. She gazed at his face. His eyes were open, their blue diamonds flashing. He was beautiful, and as she clasped his hardness, moving her hand up and down, she watched the pleasure cross over his face.

Gregg reached for her bare breasts and massaged her nipples. They were hard and tingled beneath his fingers. Caroline was more than ready. So aroused she didn't want to wait any longer. She inched forward, held herself on her knees then sank down onto him. He was so big.

She clenched and unclenched her internal muscles as she leaned forward, taking him deeper. She lifted up and plunged down, each thrust more powerful than the last. Gregg squeezed her buttocks, driving into her hard, as her hips rolled and bucked. He dug his heels in the sand, his body going rigid, his lips drawn back from his teeth. Caroline ground against him, harder and faster as he came, spilling his warmth into her, sending her over the edge. She threw back her head and screamed. Her orgasm hit her like a turbulent sea, pounding and washing over her, wave after wave. She was drowning and didn't care, gasping for breath, not wanting to let the feeling subside.

Still moving her hips back and forth, but with less speed, Caroline finally felt herself come down. Gregg was still holding her buttocks, still squeezing, but more gently. Gradually, she slowed to a stop and slumped forward to his chest. He held her and stroked her wet hair.

"That was out of this world Caroline."
He whispered.

"Me too. I don't want this to ever stop."

"I'm yours for as long as you want."

He said. She tilted her head to look into his eyes. They had dimmed, the blue, deep and soothing. She didn't know how to answer.

"I mean it Caroline. This adventure could last forever."

Caroline looked away. She wouldn't, couldn't think about what was to come, the future. It was all too uncertain, despite Gregg's claim that it was destiny. Gregg pulled her chin around, his eyes back to their piercing blue.

"For now, your thoughts are in turmoil. When you know, I'm here."

She nodded and pressed a kiss into the palm of his hand.

CHAPTER 20.

As Gregg led Caroline naked and dripping back up the beach to the villa, he told her the house wasn't staffed like Trewen was.

"I can take care of myself. But I do have security here. That's a requirement of our family. You won't see them, unless it is necessary, and I assure you they will not intrude. When I take you around the island, we will have a bodyguard, but here in the villa, it will be like we are alone. You can walk about like you are now, without ever having to fear anyone will see."

Caroline liked that idea, especially since Gregg's naked body was pure pleasure to look at, more pleasure to play with. Instantly, she felt stirrings inside, and couldn't believe she could want, no need, she thought, so much sex so soon.

For the rest of the day, they lounged by and in the pool, ate fresh barbequed fish and fruit, and made love. Gregg was powerfully virile, and every touch, every kiss, sparked her desire. Even when he licked his lips whilst eating, had her rubbing her thighs together, teasing herself.

The heat was wonderful, after the freezing cold of Devon. A light continuous breeze from the ocean kept it fresh. Gregg insisted on smothering her with sun lotion, and of course that immediately led to another round of pure unadulterated sex. The evening brought sweet smelling flowers to her nostrils, and the soft sound of breaking waves on the beach below. Laying next to Gregg, she closed her eyes, the sound and scents taking her into a deep sleep.

Their days on the island went by in a whirl. Gregg took her to the drive through Soufriere volcano, where they stood with other tourists admiring the sulphur springs, despite the smell. The only difference between them and the other visitors, was the big bodyguard that stood close by.

They spent a day hiking through the rainforest, Gregg pointing out the beautiful St Lucia parrot. He was so familiar with his surroundings, Caroline wondered how much time he spent there. As usual, he read her thoughts.

"I've had the villa for six years. It's an escape for me. When I'm here I spend much of my time exploring. Even though I have to have a bodyguard." He looked over his shoulder and grinned at Bryn, who grinned back. "I can still feel like I'm by myself. I know it seems that I am spoilt and self-indulged, and to an extent I am. But at times, my family, our lives are so monitored, that I just want to get away."

Caroline linked her arm through his and kissed his shoulder. When she first met Gregg, she had thought him arrogant and spoilt. But now she knew he was sensitive and very caring.

"When I need to get away, I just go for a walk." Gregg laughed.

"So do I. Just mine is usually thousands of miles from home."

On one particular day, Gregg took her to Piton Falls. He had organised a private visit, so they were able to walk alone down the garden path and bathe in the waters without others intruding. Of course Bryn was close by, but he gave them their privacy. It was the only time they didn't indulge in sex, even though Caroline would have willingly. But they both agreed it was a public place, and even though totally alone, not appropriate. They more than made up for it back at the villa.

Some of the best times of the visit was going out on Gregg's yacht. It was pure luxury and he handled it like a dream. They spent hours cruising around the island, the only time Bryn was not with them. Gregg told her it wasn't necessary as the boat had full tracking and satellite. They would be completely safe. They found tiny deserted coves and swam in warm shallows, snorkelling and observing the marine life. Caroline could see why Liam loved it so much. They sunbathed on the deck, drinking champagne, and of course explored every inch of each other's body. Every time Gregg made love to her, it was different, and every orgasm was as powerfully fulfilling as the last. She really did not want this adventure to end.

"It doesn't have to Caroline."

He murmured as he held her naked and trembling from her recent climax. She was still overawed at how he could read her thoughts.

"How do you do it?"

She whispered.

"Do what?"

He asked, but with a knowing smile.

"Know my thoughts."

He raised a shoulder in a tiny shrug.

"I don't really know. Intuition maybe."

She wasn't sure she entirely believed him, thoughts still hanging in her mind of his humanness. Then he lowered his head and the kiss turned into something more, making her forget what she was thinking.

Too quickly the days flew by. They had visited all over, swam in the ocean and enjoyed the islands National Day festival of lights. Each experience was exciting and new, but December was nearing its end and Christmas was very close. Caroline sighed as they gathered their things to return to the airport.

"That was very deep."

Gregg said softly.

"I know we have to go back, but it's so…unreal here."

"But the adventure is not over Caroline."

Caroline wondered what the adventure would entail, especially at his family estate. On the jet back, Caroline began to feel very nervous about meeting the regal parents and grandmother. Suddenly she wanted to speak to Derby, needed to hear her friend. She had only called her once from the island, the boys too, and felt rather guilty.

"There's the phone."

Gregg said in his usual knowing way.

"I'll be up front."

He said, though she hadn't requested privacy.

"Caroline, how are you?"

Derby asked brightly. Caroline had given her all sorts of reassurances that she was perfectly fine and safe. She still hadn't given much away about Gregg, decided that could wait until she saw her.

"I'm a bit nervous actually. We're flying back now and going to his family for Christmas."

She also hadn't told Derby how rich Gregg was.

"Oh you'll be fine. Your very good at meeting new people. Just enjoy yourself. Plenty of time for the real world when you do come home."

Caroline wished for a second she had told Derby all, then she would know and understand why she was feeling so tense. But her friend's voice had eased her nerves a little and by the time they finished chatting, Caroline was ready for the next step.

"Everything alright?"

Gregg asked as Caroline finished on the phone. She nodded.

"Yes, fine."

"What is it Caroline?"

She sighed.

"Being on the island, with you, it's been so…magical. Now we are not only returning to the real world, but I'm going to meet your family too. It's all very unnerving. I mean, have you told them about me?"

Gregg knelt in front of her and took her hands between his.

"I have told them I will be bringing you home for Christmas. That's all they need to know."

Caroline winced.

"They're not going to like it. I'm not sure how I would react if Leo or Liam brought home a woman old enough to be their mother."

Gregg laughed, kissing the backs of her hands.

"No one who saw you could ever imagine that. I certainly do not see you like that."

He pushed her knees apart and slipped between them, taking her face in his palms.

"You are a beautiful, intelligent woman. Any man of any age would give his right arm to be with you."

He kissed her, long and deep. Her body responded instantly. Somewhere she'd heard or read, that the altitude of a plane had an effect on libido, she believed it right then. Gregg's kiss intensified as he leaned in close. His chest brushed against her breasts, and her nipples immediately hardened. His hands glided under her jumper, up her sides and stroked the flesh just under her breasts. She pressed into him, wanting more.

"What do you want?"

He murmured, biting and nipping at her neck.

"You, here, now."

She gasped, drawing up her knees.

Gregg unzipped her jeans sliding them down her legs, discarding them to the floor. She grabbed the waistband of his jeans and yanked at the buttons, releasing his erection. She wriggled out of her panties and shoved his trunks down. The she pulled him into her. Every story she had heard about the Mile High Club was true. As the jet soared through the sky, she soared to a heart stopping orgasm, coming around him, more turbulent than the air currents beneath the wings.

For some time, they stayed where they were, Gregg still inside her. He kissed her gently and stroked her hair. It was for Caroline a moment to be treasured, the two of them half naked, joined in sex, up in the air, the cabin crew a tiny door away.

"It will be a wonderful Christmas Caroline, I promise."
He breathed in her ear between kisses, and she knew she believed him.

Caroline didn't want to move. She could still feel him, warm and wet, but the jet changed direction and she knew they would begin their descent. Gregg felt it too. He stood up and rearranged his clothing. He passed her panties and jeans, and whilst she dressed, he poured juice for them both. He handed her a glass and sat next to her, holding her free hand with his, as the jet tilted towards the ground.

CHAPTER 21.

Caroline watched out the window as the plane touched down. She could see snow in the distance, the airport having been cleared. The sky was quite grey, she already missed the sun. Gregg wrapped her in a thick fur coat.

"You will feel the cold more after the heat."

Caroline snuggled into the fur, her heart flipping at how thoughtful he always was, and was very grateful for the garment as she stepped off the plane. Freezing air bit into her cheeks and stung her eyes. Gregg took her hand and they jogged over to a waiting black car.

The interior was lovely and warm. Caroline settled on the comfortable seats and sighed. Gregg rubbed her hands.

"Are you warm now?"

"Mmm, yes thank you. It's toasty in here."

He smiled, put an arm around her shoulder and drew her to him.

"It's not far to the estate."

Feeling so snug and cosy, Caroline didn't care if it took all night to get there.

The snowy countryside whipped by as they travelled north. Gregg had given her some idea of where his family home was, but she didn't really know. As the car ate up the miles, Caroline gazed out on field after snow covered field. It seemed that whilst they were away fresh snow had fallen, promising a white Christmas for the first time in years. She smiled to herself. Her boys would be chuffed to bits about it. They were both spending Christmas day with a bunch of uni friends in a cabin. They would have a whale of a time, with snowball fights and building snowmen.

Suddenly she missed them desperately. So much so, she nearly asked Gregg to turn the car around and take her home. A phone was placed in her hands.

"Call them. You will feel better."

Caroline could not fathom how he did it again and again, but she was very grateful. She dialled first Leo then Liam. Just hearing their cheerful voices raised her mood. She didn't talk for long, and certainly made no mention of Gregg, just let them know she was back in England, and that she would call again soon.

"Thank you for that. I miss them so much. I mean they're all grown up, live in their own homes and do their own stuff. But I still miss them."

"Of course you do. You love them and they love you. Caroline I don't want you to be unhappy. If you would rather I take you home, then we can go now. I have to be home for Christmas, but we can pause the adventure and restart after Christmas."

Caroline leaned up to him and kissed him lightly.

"You are wonderfully thoughtful. But I don't want any break in the adventure. I am looking forward to spending Christmas and New Year with you. My sons won't be home, they're off to some cabin in the woods with a group of friends. Derby would have me at the drop of a hat, but I want to be with you."

Gregg pulled her close and grinned.

"I'm relieved. I wasn't keen on letting you go, even for a few days. But I would have if you'd wanted it. Christmas is going to be so much better with you by my side."

The car began to slow and Caroline looked out of the window. They approached a set of double wrought iron gates, which slowly opened as they neared. Here we go, she thought, as the car quietly rolled over a wide driveway lined with trees. It seemed to take a long time. A glow in the distance began to grow, and before long, Caroline could make out the Taylor-York house in the darkness. It was enormous, far bigger than Trewen House.

The car slowed to a stop at the front entrance. Curved stone steps led up to a front door, which opened. A man and woman both came outside.

"That would be Handsworth and Mrs Astley, the butler and housekeeper."

Gregg said as the driver opened their door. Caroline gasped, believing she had just stepped back into the previous century.

Gregg laughed at her expression as he took her hand and led her towards the house. It towered above her and Caroline couldn't guess how many rooms there were. She had accepted Gregg was rich, the private plane, helicopter, villa and bodyguards all signs of wealth. But until then, she had sort of put him in the celebrity rich category, not really thinking about his heritage. Now, the sight of the house, the butler and housekeeper, made her nervous. Gregg was not just rich, he was old money rich, royalty. How could she possibly compete with that?

They reached the top of the steps, Handsworth and Mrs Astley stepped to one side, backs rigid, hands behind them. Caroline wanted to giggle. This must be a production set, she thought. The whole scene reminded her of a series she had been watching on television set in the twenties. Except the two people before her were wearing twenty first century clothing.

"Good evening Master Taylor-York."

They both said, Handsworth closing the door behind them.

Gregg moved Caroline into the centre of the entrance hall. She stood presenting a calm she did not feel inside. Her eyes wanted to dart about, take in her surroundings. But something about the waiting couple, the way they looked at her, like she was something they would wipe off their shoe, riled her enough to maintain an air of decorum.

"The items I had delivered are in my suite?"

Mrs Astley brought her hands in front of her and lengthened her neck.

"I had them put in one of the guest rooms."

She replied haughtily, giving Caroline a glare. Gregg clamped his lips together and frowned. The look was not one Caroline had ever seen before, it was anger. He took in a deep breath.

"Caroline will be staying with me, in my suite. Is that clear? You will have the small bag taken there now. The rest in the morning."

Caroline was surprised at his tone. When he spoke to Hal and Delia, he was friendly and gentle, even when he asked them to do something. Yet, here, his tone was very formal, commanding.

"But sir, it's past midnight, everyone is in bed." Handsworth piped up. Gregg's head spun around, his face thunder. He kept his voice low, nearly a growl.

"Handsworth, I do not give a damn what time it is. Caroline is here with me. She is not a guest. It is not up to you to make decisions. I specifically requested the delivery should be taken to my suite. I do not appreciate arriving here to find that has not been done. So, either you or Mrs Astley will do as I ask now."

Mrs Astley gave Handsworth a tiny frown.

"Your grandmother told Mrs Astley to put the items in a guest room."

Gregg sighed.

"No excuse. You should know by now my grandmother does not rule me. Now we will go to my suite and one of you will bring the small bag, the rest in the morning."

He took Caroline's hand, and without another word led her off along a side hallway.

"I'm so sorry for their rudeness Caroline."

"It's alright Gregg. I'm a big girl, I can take it."

He stopped suddenly, swinging her in front of him.

"But you shouldn't have to, that's the point."

He let out an agitated breath, raised her hand and kissed its palm. He closed his eyes and sighed. Caroline got the feeling the kiss was to soothe him more than her. He opened his eyes and smiled down at her.

"Come on."

The hallway led to what Caroline could only describe as a wing of the grand house. It seemed Gregg's suite was actually a set of rooms in that one wing. She had found it difficult visualising the layout of Trewen House, this place, she would definitely get lost in.

"It's not so big really, once you know your way around."

Gregg said as he took her through a door into a sitting room. Caroline mentally disagreed. Even the sitting room was huge.

Gregg slipped her coat from her shoulders and gently pushed her down into an armchair.

"Relax. You must be tired."

Caroline's eyes swept around the room.

"I know, so very old fashioned and formal."

Gregg said. Caroline smiled at him as he crouched at her side.

"It's, just different from Trewen."

Gregg laughed at her diplomacy.

"It's ok Caroline. Unfortunately I don't have as much control over the décor here. My mother and grandmother are…used…to all of this and won't have it changed. Most of the furniture and so on, has been in this house for a couple of hundred years, all part of the estate. I have managed to change a few rooms in this part of the house, to fit with my lifestyle, and I think if father had his way, many more would be modernised too. But, well, I try not to be here too often, it's…sometimes…depressing."

Caroline turned sideways in the chair and took his face in her hands. She pulled his head towards her and gave him a gentle soft kiss.

"Don't worry. I am going to enjoy myself, with you, and no one will intimidate me."

A knock came on the door and Gregg called for the person to enter. Handsworth came in with a leather bag in his hand.

"Where shall I put it sir?"

"In the bedroom."

Handsworth glanced at Caroline, his lips pressed together disapprovingly as he did as Gregg requested. Caroline couldn't contain her laughter this time. She covered her mouth with her hand and snickered. Gregg's shoulders shook a little too. Handsworth returned from the bedroom.

"Will that be all sir?"

Gregg nodded.

"But in the morning, I want everything else brought here, do you understand?"

"Of course sir. Goodnight sir."

Gregg stood up and walked over to the man.

"Handsworth, I will not tolerate this rudeness. You will instruct Mrs Astley and all the other staff, that despite what my grandmother says, you will be polite to Caroline. At all times, not just in front of me."

Handsworth's cheeks reddened.

"Yes sir, I apologise miss, er madam…Caroline. Goodnight to you both."

He darted from the room and Gregg came back to Caroline.

"Hopefully that's put him in his place."

He said, kneeling in front of her.

"Your grandmother is going to hate me."
Caroline said, sadness in her voice. Gregg inched forward, leaning his elbows on the arms of the chair, enclosing her protectively.

"My grandmother dislikes anyone who is not born into money. But you don't have to worry about her."
He tapped one finger on her nose making her laugh.

"All of this." He waved an arm. "It all actually belongs to my father, and then to me. So although she likes to think she still rules the household, well she's getting on, so everyone indulges her. You will see tomorrow. She's rather, um, strange."
He said it with an affectionate laugh. Caroline's curiosity peaked and she found she was actually looking forward to meeting the old lady.

"But now, bed I think."

Caroline's heartbeat increased at his words. She ran her tongue over her lips, already aroused at what was to come.

"So what did you have delivered?"
She asked, standing up.

"Everything you will need for your stay here. The little bag." He pointed towards the bedroom. "Has what you will need for tonight."
Caroline grinned seductively. She turned her back to him, flashing her eyes over one shoulder. Slowly she lifted the edge of her jumper and raised it over her head, dropping it to the floor. She unsnapped her jeans and wriggled out of them, leaving them on the carpet too. In just her underwear, she turned a full circle, paused then darted towards the bedroom.

She heard Gregg laugh behind her, but she didn't hear his steps. In a flash he was beside her as she bent to the little bag.

"Not so fast, miss, madam, Caroline."

His voice filled with laughter and she joined in. He plucked the bag from her reaching fingers and held it high.

"What's in it?"

She said, trying to reach upwards, but he was too tall.

"Close your eyes."

He ordered, his voice beguiling. She melted, complying.

She heard the sound of a zip being undone. Then Gregg's warm hands were unclasping her bra and tugging her panties down. She opened her legs a little, expecting, hoping, to feel his finger probe her hot wet centre. They brushed her inner thigh and left. She took a breath, disappointed.

"Hold up your arms."

His whisper came close to her lips. Again she did as he asked. A flutter of soft silk slid down her body, tickled her already hard nipples and fell in a wisp about her thighs. A thin trickle of heavenly scent, slid down her throat into her cleavage. She breathed in the perfume, heady and hypnotising. Gregg's finger trailed a path from her lips to her breasts and Caroline stepped forward into his arms.

With her eyes still closed, she tangled her fingers in his floppy blonde hair, taking his mouth in a deep arousing kiss. He wrapped his arms around her lifting her from the floor, sliding her body up and down his. She felt his erection, straining for release.

"Now."

She murmured desperately. Gregg carried her to the bed and laid her down. She opened her eyes then and watched. His muscles rippled like liquid gold, as he threw off his jumper and made light work of his jeans. He dropped his trunks and Caroline raised her knees, ready to take him.

He leaned over her, just for a moment, his hands either side of her head. Then he was inside her, and she was wrapping her legs around his waist. It was quick, his thrusts pounding, her hips bucking, but the orgasm was still mighty. She came on a swirl of emotion, her hands grabbing handfuls of his hair, her tongue flicking against his. He plunged deeper, faster, then he came. His body twitched, his arms solid as he held himself rigid. Together they slumped to the bed, sated.

Gregg pulled the covers over them and curled her in front of him. He kissed her gently, and stroked the skin over her hip. She wriggled back into him. He was still partially hard and it felt so good.

"Sleep Caroline."

He whispered. She closed her eyes. His hand found hers and together they rested,

Caroline was alone in the bed when she awoke. She sat up, the covers pooling about her. She could hear voices in the room beyond. Gregg's she recognised, the other she did not. She slipped from the bed and looked about for something to wrap about her. She was still wearing the tiny silk babydoll, but it was so brief she didn't dare venture out of the bedroom in just that.

Before she could find anything, the door opened and Gregg came in. He was fully clothed and fresh. His blue eyes flashed at the sight of her.

"Breakfast is in the sitting room. I didn't want you thrown in at the deep end by eating with my parents and grandmother."

So that was the other voice, she thought, someone bringing breakfast.

"Here we have a full staff. Someone to do just about everything. It's too much really, but well, that's the way it is."

Once they had eaten, Gregg showed Caroline into a dressing room and bathroom. Everything she could need was already there. It seemed Gregg's command the night before had been obeyed.

"I can have someone sent up to help you dress." He said as he watched her soaking in a deep luxurious bath. She shook her head.

"No it's fine. I can manage. Besides, she wouldn't be Amy."

Gregg waggled his brows.

"Who said it would be a she."

Caroline flicked bubbly water at him, but he was too quick and ducked out of the way, laughing.

Fully dressed, with a light layering of makeup, Caroline let Gregg take her by the hand to meet the family. She was nervous as she followed him. He took her to a large sitting room overlooking formal gardens. An enormous Christmas tree stood in a corner, a fire blazing in a beautiful fireplace. The furniture was antique and regal.

A man, nearly as tall as Gregg and almost as handsome stood near the fire. He had his hands behind his back and smiled warmly when they entered. On a sofa were two women, neither smiling. Mother and grandmother, Caroline thought. Gregg pulled her close to his side.

"Father, mother, grandmother, I'd like you to meet Caroline."

Gregg's father stepped forward, his hand held out. She took it.

"I'm very pleased to meet you. Please call me Henry."

He was so like Gregg, Caroline warmed to him immediately. The two women remained where they were.

"My mother Elizabeth, and my grandmother Anne."

Caroline moved to the sofa and held out her hand. Elizabeth took it lightly, but Anne ignored her. Henry sighed.

"Mother do not be churlish. Caroline is with Gregg, be polite."

Anne gave a little snort and held up a reluctant hand. Caroline took it and gave it a tiny shake. She was not at all as Caroline imagined. Where Elizabeth was slender, elegant and formally dressed, Anne was frumpy. She wore a pair of woollen trousers that looked very old, with thick socks and slippers. A droopy jumper covered her plump figure, and her grey hair hung to her shoulders, wispy and dry looking. Caroline was quite shocked.

"Mother came in from the garden to meet you." Elizabeth told her. Caroline looked into the eyes of Gregg's mother, expecting to see disapproval, but the woman had a slight grin on her face.

"Oh, thank you."

Was all Caroline could say in reply.

"I'm going to give Caroline a tour of the estate." Gregg stated easing the tension.

"Well when you're finished, I can show her my garden."
Anne piped up eagerly.

Gregg nodded but made no comment. Caroline thought something odd was going on, but didn't want to ask then. Instead she let Gregg lead her from the room.

"We'll start inside, where it's warm, then I'll show you the grounds."

"What was that about. Your grandmother?"

"Oh she has her own walled garden she's very proud of. She likes to show it to .everyone."
Caroline still thought she was missing something but let it go. Anne was peculiar, haughty one moment, grinning the next. Maybe her age was getting to her, Caroline thought.

The entire estate was very impressive, similar to every stately home she had visited with her sons over the years. Large, high ceilinged rooms were furnished with antiques. Paintings and portraits hung on hallway walls and staircases, and drapes, thick and rich fell to the floor, covering wide windows. The grounds were equally opulent. Acres of woodland met formal gardens adorned with statues and fountains. There was even a separate building, housing a swimming pool. But Caroline was most impressed with the stables.

"Do you ride Caroline?"

"Phew, not since I was about seventeen. I mean, I learnt when I was little and kept it up, but you know, teenager stuff got in the way."

"Come and meet the horses."
He said, pulling her gently towards a door.

Inside there were eight stalls, four on each side. A beautifully groomed horse stood in each. Gregg stopped at one stall and laid his hand on the nose of a gleaming black mare.

"Black Diamond. She's my favourite."

The horse tossed her head at his voice as he stroked her. Caroline came close, nervously putting out her hand. The horse gave her the eye, but let her touch her coat.

"We can go out later, if you want."

Gregg said in a low voice. Caroline smiled.

"I'd love to if you have one that's not too feisty."

"Over there. Boy, he's gentle."

Caroline looked to where Gregg pointed. A glorious dapple grey gelding leaned his head over his stall. He was at least sixteen hands high, Caroline thought. She strolled over, leaving Gregg with Black Diamond.

"Hello Boy."

She said, holding out her hand. Boy nuzzled her palm, closing his eyes. Caroline laughed as the horse's lips tickled her flesh. He was lovely. She looked forward to riding him.

Gregg joined her and introduced her to the other horses. All were beautiful with shining coats. They exited the stable at the other end, and came to a hay loft. Caroline could smell the sweetness of the hay. Gregg took her hand and with a glance backwards, pulled her into the building.

He closed the door behind them and took her in his arms, kissing her hungrily. Caroline responded. Gregg walked her backwards to the bales of hay, and as the backs of her knees collided, lowered her down. He lay over her, deepening the kiss. She could feel his hardness and pushed up, exciting herself. Gregg unclasped both their jeans. Caroline wiggled out of hers, kicking off her boots and shoving her own panties out of the way. They were alone, but anyone could walk in. That made it all the more hurried and exciting.

When Caroline came, she bit down on Gregg's shoulder, stemming the squeal that so wanted to erupt from her mouth. The cry she longed to make, would be heard, and someone might think she was being harmed. Gregg pounded, and as he orgasmed, Caroline did again, still biting hard into Gregg's flesh.

After, when they were dressed, Gregg rubbed the top of his arm.

"Did I hurt you?"

She asked, still panting. Gregg grinned.

"It was well worth it. But I think I'll have to gag you next time we're within ear shot of anyone else."

He teased. Caroline touched the sore spot with a finger.

"I'll just use the other shoulder, you'll have a matching pair then."

Gregg laughed, picked her up and dumped her in the hay. She giggled and pulled him down for a lingering kiss. Her body already burned, wanting to rip his clothes from him again, but she abstained, not wanting to push their luck too far.

After lunch with the family, Gregg told them he and Caroline were going out riding.

"Oh please walk with me around my garden first."

Anne begged. Gregg looked to Caroline, who nodded in agreement. She would be kind to the old lady, let her show her, her plants. Anne stood up from the table.

"I'll get my coat and meet you both at the gate."

Gregg and Caroline strolled through a formal garden until they reached a high wall with a locked gate. Anne was already waiting, jangling a set of keys. She smiled at the couple.

"Come along."

She said as she unlocked the gate. She stepped back and let them go through.

"Wait, don't go any further."

"I know grandmother. I wouldn't let Caroline venture in by herself."

Caroline squeezed her lips together, wondering what she was walking into. Anne came to her side and tilted her head up, a wicked gleam in her eyes. She was a small round woman, and though Caroline wasn't tall, she felt like she towered over her.

"This is my poisonous garden. There are only two in the whole country, and mine has more species than the other one, more dangerous too. I have a special licence to keep and raise a lot of the plants. Some are so dangerous they could kill you."

"Now grandmother, play nicely."

Anne chuckled like an old witch, and Caroline was very glad Gregg had his arm around her.

Anne led them slowly along the pathways pointing out and naming all of the plants. With delight she imparted what the most dangerous ones could do, and giggled gleefully, when she described the impact of the milder ones. Gregg kept Caroline close to his side, especially when Anne stopped and talked about the plants that could harm from contact. As interesting as the tour was, Caroline was glad when the they came through the gate and Anne locked it back up behind them.

"I'm sort of glad that's over."
Caroline told Gregg once Anne was out of earshot.

"She's very dramatic, and…odd. Has been for years, well since my grandfather died actually, but she is harmless."
Caroline silently disagreed, wondering if one of Anne's plants had made its way into grandfather's tea. She brushed the thought aside as preposterous. No one poisoned people these days, she read far too many thrillers.

Anne and the poisonous garden was swept from her mind as she mounted Boy. Gregg was already in the saddle of Black Diamond, the mare dancing and prancing, eager to be given her head. Gregg held her in check, obviously a well accomplished rider. Caroline was just relieved Boy was happy to be guided by her, and walked gently when she squeezed her knees and turned the reigns.

They trekked through woodland and onto a track, leaving the snow covered formal lawns and beds behind. The trees had protected the pathway from most of the snow, as it was only an inch deep here. Gregg glanced over to her, grinning.

"Ready for a gallop?"
She wasn't, but did. Even though she was very out of practice, riding came naturally back to her. Boy encouraged by her confidence, lengthened his stride and soon she was flying behind Gregg, along the bridle path that bordered fields covered in deep snow.

The sun was beginning to set as they walked the horses back to the stables. Dismounting Caroline looked up at a clear crystal sky. A few stars were making an appearance, one getting brighter as the light dimmed. Realisation came. It was Christmas Eve. The boys would already be at their cabin, and Derby would be making mince pies with Melody and Geoff. She wasn't sad, just a bit anxious that she was so far away from those who knew and loved her.

Gregg took her to his suite and they stripped off their riding gear.

"How about a swim before dinner?"
He asked. Caroline was about to say it was dark out and the pool wasn't attached to the house.

"Oh not the family pool. I don't use that one. I mean here in this wing, I have my own. It's not as large, but I make do."
Caroline opened her mouth, but no sound came out. Gregg chucked her under the chin.

"Come on."

Caroline followed him down the stairs and along a corridor. At the end was a set of glass doors. Beyond she could see the shimmer of water. Lights came on as they entered, and spread out before her was the pool. It wasn't big, but certainly large enough for purpose. A jacuzzi bubbled in one corner and an open archway led off to another room.

"The gym's through there."
Caroline gasped. It was everything a person could dream of and more.

Their swim inevitably led to sex in the pool and again in the jacuzzi. Caroline couldn't believe how much she craved him, and he gave unreservedly. He was never tired, never ran out of energy, and she was surprised that she was the same. Vampire sneaked into her thoughts, but if he was, then she didn't care. He had done nothing ever to hurt her, had only made her happy and pleasured her. So whatever he was, of course he's human, she told herself, it didn't matter.

CHAPTER 22.

Caroline and Gregg met the family in the dining hall for Christmas Eve dinner. Despite having changed into a dress and low heeled shoes, Anne still presented herself to Caroline in a strange way. Elizabeth and Henry, however were friendly and kind.

Throughout the meal, Gregg's parents chatted and asked a few questions. Caroline got the impression Gregg had told them not to grill her too much, and for that she was grateful. Anne was not so polite.

"How old are you anyway?"

She demanded.

"Mother, that is really not your business."

Henry admonished her. Anne gave Caroline a glare, but she did notice Elizabeth raise her eyebrows slightly. It appeared Gregg's mother would have liked to ask that same question. Caroline laid her knife and fork down, taking a deep breath.

"You've all obviously guessed I'm quite a bit older than Gregg. I think that is between us. I'm not

ashamed of my age." She turned to Gregg. "You go ahead and tell them, it's up to you."
Gregg grinned.

"Caroline is forty seven, and acts like she's my own age."

There was a moment of silence at the table, as Gregg's words sank in. Then Henry burst out laughing.

"Close your mouth mother, it's unbecoming."
Anne snapped her lips together and Caroline couldn't help but smile. Elizabeth didn't look too pleased either, but she remained silent.

"Well come on, dinner will get cold."
Henry announced.

After the meal, Gregg led Caroline to a sitting room. His parents came too, but his grandmother huffed her way in another direction.

"Oh dear, mother is rather upset."
Elizabeth said to them. Gregg settled Caroline on a sofa near the fire and perched on the arm.

"Grandmother gets upset at whatever I do."
He said, accepting a whisky from his father.

"Caroline will have one of those too."
Henry raised his brows and smiled. He poured her a measure, and as he handed her the glass, she saw a familiar flash of blue in his eyes. Though nowhere near as diamond bright or penetrating as his son's. At least she knew where his looks came from.

Elizabeth sat quite stiffly in an armchair, and Caroline had a chance to study her. She was fair and blue eyed too. But her chin was small and off centre. She was tall and thin, but her legs were out of proportion to her torso. Caroline decided Gregg got all of his looks and charm from his father.

“I’m sorry if I’ve caused a stir.”
She said, mostly directing her words to Elizabeth. Gregg’s mother jumped slightly, just managing to avoid spilling the sherry she sipped from a tiny crystal glass.

“Oh, please, don’t apologise. As long as Gregg is happy…”
She left the sentence unfinished, and Caroline suspected Gregg’s happiness was not paramount at all.

Caroline was very grateful when Gregg announced to his parents that he was taking her back to his suite. Henry beamed and kissed her cheek, Elizabeth politely saying goodnight.

“Glad that’s over.”
Caroline said as she slumped onto the bed.

“And I’ve got to get through tomorrow and the next and the…”
Gregg stemmed her complaining with a hard kiss.

“You had the upper hand.”
He told her, when he pulled back. She gasped in surprise.

“What?”
Gregg smiled, beginning the pleasurable task of removing her clothes.

“Grandmother took herself off, and mother was all flustered. That means they didn’t know what to say or do. Father was as usual, welcoming, and that always winds mother up. I think he does it to balance her haughtiness.”
Caroline giggled at his words, then sighed when his tongue found her throat and began to slide down her body, coming to rest at her very wet centre. His grandmother and parents completely forgotten, when he

plunged the tip into the lushness of her garden of Eden, sucking on her forbidden fruits.

Caroline awoke to a silent room, after another night of mind blowing sex. She slipped from the bed and padded to the window. She had no idea what had woken her. Looking out she saw snow falling, huge flakes swirling in a strong breeze. It was an awesome sight, but not one to entertain her.

She turned her back to the window, leaning against the sill. She could see Gregg in the bed. He was sound asleep. She tiptoed over and watched him. His long floppy hair was ruffed and tousled, where she had run her fingers through it. His porcelain skin almost glowed in the dark, his features softened by sleep. He was simply perfectly beautiful. Gently, she slipped back under the covers and snuggled. Without waking, Gregg pulled her to him and she closed her eyes and fell back into peaceful sleep.

Caroline was woken on Christmas morning by a very aroused Gregg. She wrapped her legs about him and enjoyed her first present of the day.

"Merry Christmas."

He murmured when they finished.

"I haven't got you anything. I haven't had the chance."

Caroline said, a little sadly.

"You just gave me what I want Caroline."

She laughed, the sound like tinkling glass. Gregg raised himself up on an elbow.

"You're breathtaking when you laugh."

She lowered her lashes bashfully.

"I mean it."

He said, tilting her chin up with a finger.

"And it's champagne for breakfast."
He said, hopping from the bed.

Later in the morning, Gregg and Caroline walked arm in arm into the sitting room with the big tree. His parents and grandmother were already there.

"Ah present time."
Henry beamed, rubbing his hands together. Gregg had already given Caroline her gift, and it nestled between her breasts. It was a gold locket, and inside she found two tiny photos, one of Leo, the other Liam. Caroline had been speechless, more so wondering how he had acquired the pictures.

"I spotted the two photos you have on your key ring back at Trewen. I, borrowed them and Hal had them copied."
He'd told her. The gift was far too precious for her to be cross with him.

Caroline sat comfortably as the family exchanged gifts. It was completely different to how it happened at her own home. Leo and Liam would laze in bed until nearly lunchtime. Frank, he crept into her thoughts, would be impatient, but she would insist they wait. Eventually when the boys were up, they would plod in and dive for the presents under the tree. It was always boisterous and noisy, and Caroline loved it. Here, it was very formal and quiet. Each of the three unwrapping a gift at a time and politely thanking the giver.

Caroline was relieved when the ceremony was over. She had pasted a smile on her lips whilst waiting, but her mind had been elsewhere, in a cabin in the woods with her sons actually.

"We're done."

Gregg whispered, bringing her back to the moment.

"Come on. Let's go outside and enjoy the new snow."
Caroline beamed, thrilled at his idea.

Hours later, Caroline sat with Gregg in his huge bath, warming up. They had both got soaked playing in the snow like children.

"We don't have much time. Dinner will be served shortly."
Gregg told her. Caroline would have willingly sat curled up in his suite with a turkey sandwich, rather than the formal Christmas dinner she was expecting.

"But we have enough time for this."
She said alluringly, stretching a foot out between his legs, tickling his cock. Gregg laughed and pulled her on top of him. She squealed as water sloshed over the sides. She straddled him and took him deep inside her. The water waved as they moved as one, faster and faster, their orgasms sending it spilling over the edge in a mini flood.

"Oh dear, I think we have made a bit of a mess on the floor."
Caroline panted. Gregg laughed, stepping out into a large puddle.

"I'll just lay towels over it. It will be cleared up when we are having dinner."
Caroline shook her head a fraction. She still wasn't used to having someone run around after her, but it was rather nice.

The dining room was beautiful. A pure white gold embossed cloth, with a rich red runner covered the table. Candles burned in holders decorated with holly, and the china, glass and cutlery gleamed. A tree stood in the corner, glistening with white lights and gold baubles, and soft Christmas carols could be heard in the background. A perfect setting for Christmas dinner.

Gregg held a chair out for Caroline, his father doing the same for his mother and grandmother. Handsworth poured champagne and the meal began. Caroline thought it was going to be formal, with very little conversation. But she was wrong. Elizabeth seemed to have warmed to her, why she couldn't fathom, but she was grateful. The woman asked about her family and Caroline happily told her. Even Anne appeared less hostile.

What seemed like many courses later, the last of the plates were removed and a platter of cheeses, fruit and biscuits were placed before them. Caroline didn't think she could eat anything more. Handsworth offered coffee around and the small group sat back, relaxing.

"Excuse me for a moment. I have a little surprise for Caroline."

Anne said standing up. Gregg raised his brows and Caroline shrugged. The old lady disappeared for a short while, then returned with a young girl carrying a tray. Anne came forward and took a wine glass from the tray, holding it by the stem.

"Here you are Caroline. I had this made especially for you."

She placed the glass in front of Caroline. It was steaming a little.

"Mulled wine. I found the recipe in an old book of mine. Some of the ingredients are from my very own garden."

Caroline sat frozen, the warm wine untouched in front of her. Anne was leaning towards her a little.

"Go ahead, try it."
Caroline didn't know what to do. She didn't want to offend the old lady, but at the same time, she was terrified. Ingredients from her own garden, what on earth was in it? Especially as she had only given a glass to her, not the rest of the family.

"Grandmother, what have you done?"
Gregg asked, his voice stern. Anne looked up.

"What do you mean Gregory. I'm trying to be friendly, as Henry asked."

"Well then you won't mind telling us what ingredients from your garden, you have put in the drink."
He told her. Elizabeth had her hand over her mouth, her eyes looking worried.

"Mother, answer him please."
She said. Anne huffed as she picked up the glass of wine, lifted it to her own lips and drank half of it.

"There. Do you really think I would harm her. I don't mean my poisonous garden, I meant the little one, with fruits and herbs."

Caroline sighed with relief. Gregg stood up and came around the table to her side. Anne was still standing next to her holding the glass. Gregg threw an arm around his grandmother.

"Let me try it."
The old lady gave him the glass and he sipped.

"That is delicious. Why didn't you just bring in a jug for us all?"
Anne pursed her lips and turned her head away.

"It was meant to be a special treat for Caroline."

"Well, is there any more?"

"Of course."

"Then we'll all have some, a treat for everyone."

Anne instructed the girl to fetch the jug. She shrugged off Gregg's arm and stomped back to her place at the table, mumbling under her breath, "Poison as if." Caroline wanted to giggle, but held it in. Elizabeth had relaxed, but Henry looked like he wanted to burst into laughter too. Gregg bent forward and kissed her cheek, whispering in her ear.

"I'm so sorry. She's…difficult."

The girl returned with the jug and Caroline had to admit, the mulled wine was very good, finishing the meal off perfectly.

After the drama of dinner, the rest of Christmas day was very relaxing. Gregg took Caroline up to the suite and into yet another room. It was designed like an office, with a top of the range laptop. He settled by her side whilst she Skyped her brother and parents, wishing them merry Christmas, and promising to visit during the coming year. Gregg kept out of sight of the webcam, and Caroline managed to evade questions about where she was.

They spent the evening in Gregg's sitting room, watching Christmas movies, drinking wine and eating chocolates. Caroline thought she must have gained several pounds in one day, by the time they settled in bed for the night. But after another bout of sensual lovemaking, Caroline thought the exercise would burn most of the calories off.

Boxing day brought with it the beginning of the thaw. Gregg gave Caroline tea in bed, and as she sat up to drink, she could see the sky outside was dull and overcast.

"The temperature is up today. The snow is melting."
Caroline was a little sad about that. The snow was so bright, it raised everyone's spirits in winter.

"There will be guests at the estate today."
He said. Caroline gave a quizzical frown.

"My parents and grandmother have friends over, for the traditional Boxing Day shoot."
Caroline had never been to a shoot before, had no idea what to expect.

They joined the family in one of the larger sitting rooms. Elizabeth and Henry were greeting their friends, as a steady stream of people arrived. Handsworth was directing other members of staff to serve hot drinks and glasses of mulled wine. Anne was smiling, an unusual sight to Caroline.

"Do you think that's Anne's recipe?"
She whispered to Gregg, accepting a glass offered to her by a young man. Gregg snickered, taking his own drink.

"You know. I think she did that on purpose, just to spook you. Why else would she only offer the wine to you? Honestly she can be quite a dragon when she chooses. And look at her now, butter wouldn't melt."

Anne was obviously in her element with people of her own social standing. Caroline thought she should be cross, but found herself enjoying the moment. Yes she had feared Anne was attempting to poison her, but then she'd also thought Gregg was a vampire, or some other unworldly being. She still wondered about him, his pale skin and mind reading ability, but she knew he wouldn't hurt her, so it didn't matter anymore. And Anne, well she had been brought up with this life, she was getting old, and wouldn't change. She had however, sort of accepted Caroline, and that's as much as she could expect.

Once all the guests were there, Anne took over. She led the group into the grounds and organised everyone into position. Gregg had his arm thrown around Caroline's shoulder as they approached his grandmother.

"This is so new to me."

Caroline said, making the old woman jump. Anne swung around, her shotgun over her arm.

"Oh don't startle her Caroline, she might try and shoot you."

He said teasing his grandmother. Anne gave him her haughtiest look.

"If I wanted to shoot her I wouldn't have to try. As you know, I am an excellent shot, I never miss."

With that she yelled, "Pull." And swung her gun high into the air. The crack rang out and something fell from the sky.

"Clay pigeons."

He told Caroline, leading her over to his father. You should have a go.

Henry greeted them and handed Caroline his gun. Between him and Gregg, they instructed her on how to hold it and shoot it. Gregg helped her, directing her aim as he called out "Pull." She missed, but laughed with glee.

"If grandmother had her way, we would still be shooting pheasants."

Gregg said, as they watched Anne shoot down a whole set of clay pigeons. Caroline was glad they weren't.

"When my grandfather was alive, they would have beaters to drive out the birds. Everyone just took it for granted. Then when my father took over the estate, I was very little, I begged him not to kill the birds. I hate any animals being used for sport or their skins. Ever since then, the shoot has been clay pigeon only. Grandmother objected of course, but she didn't have any say. I got my own way and of course, all of this will be mine one day."

Caroline knew that, but hearing him say it still gave her quite a shock. She shoved it to the back of her mind, she had no idea where this relationship was heading, if anywhere, so she just wouldn't think about it. The here and now was all that was important.

CHAPTER 23

The week unrolled in a haze of melting snow and activity for Caroline. As the thaw progressed, patches of green grass could be seen dotting the landscape. As wonderful as the snow had been, it did restrict outdoor activities. Now they could trek further afield on the horses, and walk across fields and through the gardens.

Each day was full and exciting, the estate was so huge. Her first tour had been short, but over the days, Gregg showed her everything he would one day inherit.

"Have you ever thought about opening it to the public?"

She asked one day as they trotted along a bridle path.

"We don't need to. Unlike many of the families with stately homes, we have plenty of money to maintain the estate. We are, simply, filthy rich."

He laughed. Caroline couldn't imagine that kind of wealth.

"The men in our family have always been very astute managing our finances. Where some families squandered their families' wealth, ours has invested well. I told you I have tried many things, but the one thing I did stick to, encouraged by my father, was learning about how to retain our money."

Caroline didn't know how to reply. She had taught her own sons the value of money, coached them in independence. She had always been careful with her own finances, being a single parent, even though the divorce settlement had been generous. But to have the kind of wealth Gregg spoke of and to be responsible for it, was huge, beyond her imaginings.

When the weather changed to rain as New Year's Eve approached, they occupied themselves with indoor entertainment, barely seeing the other members of the family. Some of the time they simply watched television, or curled up together reading. But they also swam and indulged themselves in the jacuzzi.

"Show me the gym equipment please."

Caroline requested. She was beginning to feel sluggish. She wasn't into fitness, had only ever really followed an exercise programme on one of the breakfast shows, readying herself for the wedding. The wedding, she thought. It was a lifetime ago, or so it seemed. Barely a month had passed, but what a month. Frank was out of her life, that she was sure. Gregg was all she could think of. Not only the way he made love to her, but everything about him. He was larger than life, leaving Frank a mere shadow of a past she no longer yearned for.

By the time New Year's Eve came around, Caroline was feeling more alive. Gregg had gently eased her into a programme of exercise and she had explored every piece of equipment in the gym. Of 329 course, many of their sessions had been interrupted by wondrous out of this world sex, on the bench, on the floor, in the shower and the pool. But she had managed some training in between.

Now she sat in Gregg's sitting room, Handsworth standing before them. He was holding a long dress bag in one hand, balancing a stack of boxes in the other.

"Your delivery has arrived sir."

"Thank you Handsworth. Can you take them to the dressing room."

The butler disappeared and Caroline looked questioningly at Gregg.

"Your gown for tonight."

Caroline gasped. She hadn't thought about what she would wear to the ball. Gregg had informed her during the week that the family held an enormous New Year's Eve ball. The guest list was long, at least a hundred and fifty people. She gave herself a little shake, she should have expected this.

Gregg was waiting in the sitting room for her when she emerged from the dressing room. He looked stunning in a black dinner suit, white shirt and bow tie. His blonde hair was groomed to perfection, his pale skin glowing against his diamond blue eyes. When he saw her, his eyes flashed.

"You are sensational."

The gown was silk and sleek, hugging her curves. It was pale gold, covered in sparkling sequins. High stiletto shoes matched the gown, and a tiny gold clutch bag completed the outfit. Her makeup was perfect, light but enhancing.

"Come here."

He whispered. Caroline approached. Gregg placed a light kiss on her lips.

"Turn around."

He murmured. She did. Gregg's fingers brushed her neck under her hair. She felt him unclasp the locket and replace it with something else. He gently eased her to the mirror. Draped around her neck was a gold filigree necklace studded with emeralds. It glowed against her red blonde hair. Smiling he handed her matching earrings and bracelet.

"Now you are ready."

He said, kissing her bare shoulder.

The ball was held in the great hall. An enormous tree reaching near to the ceiling cast bright lights across the room. There were many guests already milling about, drinking talking and dancing, as Gregg led her into the room. They found his parents, and soon, Caroline was being introduced to people whose names she would never remember.

Caroline was having a wonderful time, Gregg barely leaving her side. One such time, he went to fetch them more champagne, having missed one of the waiters. Caroline watched the guests for a moment enthralled at the beautiful gowns on show.

"Hello Caroline."

Anne came behind her, a young attractive woman by her side. Caroline smiled.

"I'd like to introduce you to Victoria. She's Gregg's fiancée."

Shock at Anne's words took the breath from her. She clasped a hand to her throat, feeling dizzy. From what seemed to be a great distance, she heard the tinkle of the woman's laugh.

"Oh Granny, nothing has been finalised and you know it."
Caroline managed to draw in a breath, the world coming back to her. To hear Anne reply.

"But darling, you and Gregg have known each other all of your lives. Finalised or not, we all know it's just a matter of time. Once he settles down."
She directed the last words straight at Caroline. Her intention clear, you are just a dalliance. Caroline glared at Gregg's grandmother, then she lifted her chin, swung around and headed in the direction she had seen Gregg go. He was coming towards her, champagne flutes in both hands. He saw her expression, placed the glasses on the tray of a passing waiter and hurried to her side.

"Caroline?"

"I've just met your fiancée."
She said, her voice breaking.

"What?"
He gasped in surprise, his expression changing to anger as he looked beyond her to his grandmother.

"I see."
He growled. He took Caroline's arm and gently pulled her back to his grandmother. He looked Anne and Victoria straight in the eyes.

"Caroline. I am not engaged to Victoria, now and never will be."
Victoria placed a hand on his arm.

"But Gregg…"

"Do not touch me. If you and my grandmother concocted this little act between you, I can tell you it failed."
He drew Caroline close to him.

"I promise you Caroline, I had no part in this. Yes I have known Victoria since we were children, but I have never had any desire to know her in any other way."

Both Anne and Victoria gasped. Caroline saw a sparkle of tears in Victoria's eyes. She obviously felt very differently.

"Our families, we…"
She gabbled.

"No!"
Gregg's voice came loud and clear. A few other guests nearby looked around, but Gregg continued.

"You grandmother have no right to arrange my life, and you Victoria, have no right to make assumptions, just because our families are connected. Come on Caroline."

He swung them around and headed for the door. Elizabeth saw the anger on her son's face, but Gregg bypassed her without explanation. Gregg, stormed out of the great hall, his hand clasped around Caroline's. He didn't speak until they reached his sitting room. There he dragged a hand through his hair and flung his bow tie to the floor.

"That woman is incorrigible. How dare she."
He ranted. Caroline sank into a chair.

"Gregg, please, it's fine."

"No Caroline, it is not. I've had to live with her interfering for too long."

"But maybe she's right."
Gregg frowned.

"What on earth do you mean. Of course she's not right. I am not marrying Victoria."

"I don't mean that. What I'm trying to say is this…has been a wonderful adventure." She held up a hand to stop him interrupting. "But, I don't belong here, fit in. Our lives are so very different. It's time I went home, in the morning."

Gregg kneeled down in front of her, clasping her hands to his chest.

"No Caroline, I'll make this right."

Caroline stroked his silky blonde hair and felt tears trickle down her cheeks.

"I have to Gregg. I have a family, my agency. This has been a fantasy, wonderful and amazing. But it has to end, I have to go back to my world."

Gregg pulled her into his arms and kissed her. She didn't resist, couldn't resist. He held her, as the tears flowed freely. She would have one more night with him.

"Is there anything I can do to change your mind."

He murmured, reigning kisses down her throat, nipping at her bare shoulders. She shook her head.

"Just let this last night be the best."

He scooped her up in his arms and took her to the bedroom. Slowly he removed her clothes, stroking and massaging her body. He took off his suit and stood before her, magnificent, young and strong. His eyes burned into her as he lowered himself over her. He didn't rush, his every touch precise to give her maximum pleasure. This time when they came it was different. Still intense and powerful, but lasting, both clinging to the other, memorising this moment.

Caroline couldn't sleep for the first time since she had been with Gregg. She suspected he didn't sleep well either. When she thought he was dozing, she slipped from the bed and went into the bathroom. There, she sobbed uncontrollably. She didn't want to leave him, that she knew without a doubt. But she had to. Their lives had become intertwined in a way that couldn't go on. His background, wealth, everything, so far removed from her own, created a chasm so wide, it could not be bridged.

With her tears finally under control, she padded back to the bedroom. Instead of getting under the covers, she sat looking out of the window. It was late, quiet, the party having finished hours ago.

"You'll get cold."

Gregg's deep voice penetrated the night. He threw back the covers and came to her side. He took her hands and pulled her up. He led her through to the sitting room, grabbing a throw from the back of the sofa. He sat down, pulling her onto his lap and wrapped the throw around her. He cradled her in his arms, stroking her hair, trying to give comfort where none could be given.

Caroline dozed in and out of sleep all the while held in Gregg's arms. She had no idea if he slept or not. But as light filtered into the room, she looked up into his eyes. He was looking at her.

"Can I do anything to change your mind?"

She shook her head.

"Just don't make this more difficult, please?"

She beseeched.

"Will you go back to Frank?"

He asked, his voice low and miserable. Caroline sat up taking his face in her hands.

"God, no. Oh no, Gregg. Never. I'm not going home because of him. Not even because of your

grandmother. I promise. I told you, I'm over Frank. But you have to understand. We live different lives. I have to get back to mine, yours is here." She swept a hand around the room. "And everywhere."
Gregg kissed her. She felt her body ignite, but this time, the first time, she wouldn't let it consume her.

"I have to get dressed."

Gregg let her go reluctantly. He left her alone to bathe and dress and didn't argue when she refused breakfast.

"I've called for a car."
He told her as he stood motionless in the sitting room, his voice devoid of emotion. She had insisted on travelling alone. He'd tried to object, but she stopped his words with a finger to his lips.

"It's better this way. You're young. You will soon find a new adventure."
Gregg only gave her his piercing blue stare.

Caroline leaned back in the seat of the car. Gregg stood forlornly watching as it rolled away from the house. He raised a hand and gave a single wave. She waved back, then closed her eyes, not wanting to watch him standing still until the car disappeared from view. She opened them only when she heard the small sound of the gates closing behind them.

The roads were mostly clear of traffic as the big car ate up the miles. Caroline sighed, holding back a fresh flood of tears. What was she doing? She almost instructed the driver to turn back, but bit back the words before they could escape her lips. She delved into her handbag for tissues, her fingers connecting with her phone. She hadn't used it since the day she had stepped into the car with Hal. So long ago, she thought. But she had kept the battery charged. She opened her contacts and found Derby's number. She tapped the screen.

"Hi Caroline, are you home?"

Derby asked chirpily.

"On my way now."

She said, flatly.

"Caroline, what's wrong?"

Derby asked, sensing her friend's mood.

"Can I come straight to yours. The boys will be in bed still after last night and I don't want to be alone."

"Of course you can sweetie."

Derby replied. She didn't need to question Caroline over the phone, she would tell her as soon as she saw her.

CHAPTER 24.

Caroline gave the driver Derby's address and then sat back with her eyes closed. She couldn't sleep though. Gregg's beautiful, glowing face invaded her thoughts. She couldn't get the picture of his body, tall, wiry but so strong, out of her mind. She could hear his deep voice, his sexy laugh, see his alluring diamond blue eyes. Tears fell from her eyes and she let them. She missed him so much already.

After what seemed like hours, the driver slowed the car and eased it into Derby's driveway. The front door opened and Derby hurried down the steps. She had the door open before the driver even got out of his seat. She grabbed Caroline's hand and dragged her into a hug. The driver gave a little cough.

"Your luggage madam."

He said, lifting two large leather suitcases from the boot. Caroline blinked in surprise. She had her overnight bag with her, the one she had barely used.

"Um…"

She stammered.

"Master Taylor-York had it packed and loaded. Would you like me to take it in?"

"Oh, uh…no thank you. Just leave it there." She pointed to the ground. The driver did as she asked, nodded goodbye and drove away.

Derby stood watching the big black car leave her home, her eyes wide.

"Taylor-York. My God Caroline."

"You…you know the name?"

"Of course, they're…well known." Caroline was about to lift a suitcase when Geoff came out.

"I'll get those, you go with Derby."

Derby linked her arm through Caroline's and led her into the house. She turned her into the lounge where Melody was happily playing amongst a pile of toys. The toddler saw Caroline and dived for her. She scooped her up and nuzzled her neck, the little girl squealing. Caroline couldn't hold back the tears. Melody screwed her face up and Derby took her daughter.

"I'll take her to Geoff. You get settled. Hot chocolate I think."

Caroline pulled off her boots and coat and curled up on the sofa. Memories of the last time she had sat there sobbing, flooded her mind. But this time was so different. She didn't even really know why she was crying. Still Gregg's face kept swimming in her tears.

Derby came in with a tray of hot chocolate and homemade cookies. Caroline smiled wanly. Any other time, the chocolate would give her comfort. Then she didn't think anything could.

"So, spill."

Was all Derby had to say and Caroline did. She began with her first meeting with Gregg. She told Derby everything, her fears and imaginings, the first time they had sex and everything that had happened from then on. Derby sat in silence waiting for Caroline to finish.

"So my adventure comes to an end and…I…don't know how to handle it."

She stammered, her voice breaking on a fresh flood of tears. Derby wrapped her arms around her friend and let her cry. When the sobs began to subside, Derby whispered.

"So why are you hurting so much Caroline?"

Caroline sat back, wiping her face with her hand. She looked at Derby, mulled over the question.

"I don't know. Um…I mean, I've only known him a few weeks. I can't be in love with him."

Derby pressed her lips together and raised her brows.

"Why not, I did. Caroline, there is no time restrictions on the heart. We cannot tell ourselves that love has come too soon. We can only know how we feel. So, it may not be everlasting love. That takes time to recognise. But to say it's not love, no. You are in love with him."

"But he's only thirty. He can't love me. He'll find a nice girl his own age, Victoria or someone like her. A girl his family approve of."

Derby shrugged.

"So you've made up your mind."

"I had to. I have the agency and the boys. I'll be alright. Tomorrow, I will go back to work, and everything will go back to normal. I'll remember Gregg and the fun we had, then lock it in a box at the back of my mind. Life goes on, mine will."

Derby didn't try and change Caroline's mind. She knew her friend would work it out one way or another in her own way. Instead she made her welcome, cooked her dinner and settled her in the guest room for the night. In the morning, she drove her home, and walked with her into the house by the marina. There she left her after making her promise to call if she needed her.

Caroline took the pile of mail and dropped it on the table, she had no desire to open any of it. She had opened one of the suitcases that morning, and found just a selection of the clothes Gregg had provided her with. Before putting on jeans and jumper, she held the garments to her face, believing she could smell his scent on them.

The suitcases now stood in her hallway. She couldn't even be bothered to unpack them. She looked about her lounge, at her little tree and didn't want to be in the house. Quickly she grabbed her bag and headed for the office. Adele would be back. They would attack the stack of submissions and the new year would begin.

Adele was in her own office when Caroline walked in. She smiled brightly.

"Hi, have a good Christmas?"

Caroline smiled back. Adele knew the wedding hadn't taken place, but none of the details. She wouldn't ask and Caroline wasn't in the mood to offer.

"Yes, it was very nice thank you."

She flicked the kettle on and held out a mug to Adele. The girl nodded. Caroline made tea for them both and took hers into her own office. She looked about her.

Caroline booted up her laptop and sat back waiting. She closed her eyes and saw Gregg sitting in the chair opposite. She opened them quickly, half expecting him to be there, but she was alone. So alone it hurt. She took a deep breath, a sip of tea and resolved to put the last month behind her. She would bury herself in her work, take her mind completely off Gregg.

As expected, her inbox had hundreds of submissions. She wasn't due back until today, but of course writers chose to ignore that. She was about to check the box and delete the whole lot, when the third one from the top caught her eye. She grinned. The subject heading read, *Submission/Lost In Lust Part 2/Robert Patterson.* She clicked on the email, her eyes lighting up.

Dear Miss, Madam, Caroline.

I am Robert, I am thirty years old and I am me. That is all there is to say. My novel, *Lost In Lust Part 2* will speak for me. Read it and decide.

Yours.

Robert Patterson.

She opened the synopsis. A sketch, detailed and beautiful met her eyes. The man, all Gregg, the woman, herself. She didn't bother with the chapters, knowing what they contained. Caroline clicked on reply and typed.

Dear Mr Patterson.

Please be at my office within the next two hours. I think we should meet."

She hit send and within seconds her computer bleeped an incoming message. He was coming. Would be there in under an hour, Caroline guessed the helicopter would be flying.

Bubbling with excitement, Caroline bounced from her chair into Adele's office. The girl looked up startled at the change in her boss.

"Adele, how would you like to take over all of my clients, well, all except one?"

Adele's fingers were suspended over her keypad, shock in her eyes.

"Um…I…what do you mean?"

Caroline dragged her keys from her pocket and held them out to Adele.

"I want you to run the agency. Maybe even take it over soon."

Adele sat frozen. She had no idea what had happened, or why Caroline was behaving the way she was. Caroline looked at the clock, time was ticking by.

"Ok Adele. Look. Something's come up, a very important something. I won't be able to run the agency for a while, maybe not at all."

Fear spread across Adele's face and Caroline scolded herself.

"Oh no, Adele. Nothing is wrong with me. I'm fine. I can't explain now, I'm in a hurry. Look please just say yes. Here are my keys, the ones you haven't got. Go home today, then tomorrow, come in and…take over for me."

Still Adele didn't seem able to speak.

"Please do it. You know the business is good, you know what to do. You're more of a literary agent than an assistant. It will be good for both of us. And I won't keep you waiting long. I'll know in just a few days if I'll be back."

Finally Caroline's words sank in and Adele blinked.

"Oh, well, ok then."

She grinned, standing. Caroline threw her arms around her and hugged her. She put the keys in Adele's palm and closed her hand over them.

"You're an angel. Now go, have a another day of rest, then come back, a literary agent."

Adele thanked her, picked up her coat and bag and bounced out of the office.

Caroline stood at the window overlooking the boats. She had her arms crossed and was chewing her lip, doubt niggling at her mind. Was she doing the right thing? Would he really come? It seemed like she waited forever, then a big black car glided to a stop below. She drew in a breath. Hal stepped out and opened the back door. Gregg was wearing the same suit he'd worn for their first meeting as he looked up at her window.

Caroline was already pressing the outer door lock before he reached it. She had the office door open as he bounded up the stairs, too impatient for the lift. She was in his arms the moment he reached her, kissing her, filling her.

Gregg walked her backwards into the office, his mouth devouring hers. She tangled her hands in his hair, never wanting to let go again. Finally, they both came up for air, his diamond blue eyes boring into hers.

"I'm sorry, so sorry."

He murmured, nuzzling her neck.

"What for? I left."

"But I should have made you stay. Should have told you Caroline, shown you."

"Told me what."

Gregg bent until he was level with her. His eyes glowed, their diamond rings sparkling.

"That I love you. I adore you."

Caroline's heart skipped a beat.

"You can't, you don't know me."

She gasped, whilst her heart felt like it would burst. Gregg touched his forehead to hers.

"But I do. Time is irrelevant. I do Caroline. I love you with my entire soul."

Derby's words came back to her and she knew Gregg was right. She also knew she had waited for him her whole life. Both Charles and Frank had told her a million times they loved her, she had believed them then. Now, Gregg's declaration, meant so much more. It was real, true, totally believable. She took a deep breath.

"I love you too Gregg. I don't think I really knew until I left. I couldn't breathe, can't live, without you."

Gregg lifted her from her feet and held her, his lips pressed against hers. She clung to him.

"We'll go to Trewen, now."

Caroline nodded in agreement even though questions were going through her mind.

"What do I tell my boys?"

Gregg laughed and swung her around.

"When we get there, you call them. I'll send Hal to pick them up. They can meet me. It will be alright Caroline I promise."

She had doubts, about their love, her sons' reactions, but she wasn't going to let any of it get in the way. Not anymore.

"Ok. We'll go. I'll call them. Derby too."

Gregg's smile lit up his face.

"Invite them all. We can celebrate."

Caroline locked up the office, and with just her handbag, let Gregg lead her to the car. She looked over her shoulder, could see her house. She would have to come back at some time, even if only to sell it, but she wouldn't think of that right then. Gregg opened the car door and helped her in. Once she was comfortable he lifted her chin with his finger.

"I can't tell you what will happen to us Caroline. I can only say, that I do honestly believe we were destined to meet, to be together. I won't hurt you. I made that promise when we first met and I will keep it. If you want to keep your house then that is your choice. I will never demand more than you want to give. Your family is important to you, and I will do everything in my power to ensure they are a part of our life, because we will have a life, together. This is your adventure, your life adventure, and I will always be a part of it, for as long as you wish."

Caroline gazed into his loving face, awed as usual that he could read her thoughts. His diamond eyes flashed and she knew, he only spoke words of truth.

She snuggled into the circle of his arms, as the car sped through the city and onto open moorland. Her first trip to Trewen House had been filled with nervous excitement. This time, Gregg was by her side, loving her and protecting her. She felt no fear now. She was ready for whatever the future threw at her. She was ready for her next adventure, with this young man who could and would, give her everything.

ABOUT THE AUTHOR

Stephanie M Turner has been writing since she could put pen to paper. She has a Bachelor of Education degree, and is a qualified Primary School teacher. She is married with four children, and is also a grandmother.

Other titles by Stephanie M Turner

Fifteen Going On Grown Up

Out Of The Grey

Caramel Cupcakes

www.ingramcontent.com/pod-product-compliance
Lightning Source LLC
Chambersburg PA
CBHW061317170626
46817CB00001B/219

* 9 7 8 0 9 9 2 9 8 8 1 1 1 *